The Kepos Problem

Kepos Chronicles Book 1

Erica Rue

ISBN: 1-945994-20-7

ISBN-13: 978-1-945994-20-3

This is a work of fiction. Any similarity to real persons or events is coincidental and not intended by the author.

Editing by Jessica Hatch of Hatch Editorial Services

Cover Design by Sanja Gombar
fantasybookcoverdesign.com

Published by Tannhauser Press
tannhauserpress.com

Visit ericarue.com for more information.

For my mother, Jane.

For my teacher and mentor, Dorothy.

The Kepos Problem

"Science is a way of thinking much more than it is a body of knowledge."

- Carl Sagan

1. DIONE

Dione Quinn sat alone in the lobby, her bags and equipment strewn around her like a barricade. She checked her manumed every few minutes for a new message. He would remember. She wanted to read on her manumed, but its screen was too small. Without a holo interface, she'd have to use her tablet, but that was packed away. She contemplated taking it out, but a small crowd around one of the giant news screens caught her attention. She synced her manumed with the broadcast.

The Venatorians. At first she thought the broadcast was rehashing the attack from a week ago. The attack that had drawn her father from home in the middle of the night to attend a crisis summit. Listening a while longer, she realized that this was a different attack.

That hadn't stopped Kal's parents from pulling him from the trip. The Venatorians rarely came inside the Bubble, the area of Alliance-protected space, but apparently they'd made two exceptions in the past week to attack the Dappled Rim.

Dione wasn't worried. The Rim was nowhere close to where they were going, and she had been looking forward to this trip for months. She had qualified near the top of her class to get first pick of the Post-16 Internships. She had opted to spend the break from school on Professor Oberon's expedition to Barusia to study hyperadaptive evolution in plants. He would never take them into a dangerous area.

She was so engrossed in the broadcast that she didn't realize she had zoned out until someone put a hand on her shoulder, startling her.

"Hey, Di! How many hours early did you get here?"

"Lithia, you're not late!" Dione got up to greet her best friend, Lithia Min. Lithia's mother and Grandpa Min were there with her.

"For once. Grandpa made sure of that," Lithia said. Lithia was tall and lean, with straight black hair, though she looked more like her father than her mother.

"Is your uncle here?" Dr. Min asked. She knew Dione well enough to guess that her father was probably busy with some Alliance meeting, and that her uncle would have been the one to see her off.

"No, he's off-planet right now, but he sent me a vid message this morning. My dad had to leave last week after the Ven attack." Dione didn't even know where on the planet he was right now. She checked her manumed again, but still no message. He'd forgotten she was leaving today.

Dr. Min gave her a motherly smile and pulled her into a hug. Dione was grateful, but she felt that Dr. Min worried about her too much. Even though her dad was always busy, she was never truly alone. All she had to do was call her uncle, if he was in town.

As she extracted herself from the hug, Dione heard her manumed go off at the exact same time as Lithia's. She checked the small screen to find a message from Professor Oberon: *Time to board. Get a car to the Calypso. Belen's already with me. Bay 3208.*

"We'd better go," Dione said. She picked up her bags one by one.

She turned and saw Grandpa Min giving Lithia a kiss on the cheek. He lived with Lithia and her parents, and was always good for a story. He remembered a time before the Alliance, when the quadrants all had their own laws and procedures. It always sounded chaotic to Dione, but Lithia loved his stories.

Dione and Lithia made their way to the kiosk to call a car to Professor Oberon's ship, but someone was already there, registering their exact same destination. That didn't make any sense. The only other student assigned to this trip was Kal, and he had dropped out.

Dione didn't know what to say, but Lithia recognized him.

"Zane?" she said.

He turned and gave her a faint smile. "Hi, Lithia."

Dione, though extremely confused, managed to say hello and introduce herself. Now that she had the student's name, she figured out why she recognized his face. Zane had just taken an introductory biology class with Professor Oberon. Dione had been the professor's student teaching assistant for that class. Zane didn't talk much, and he had never come in for her tutoring hours either, so she didn't know him at all. Why was someone from Intro Bio coming on this trip? He didn't even meet the prerequisites.

"I know who you are," he said.

Dione just nodded. What was she supposed to say to that?

"So you're going on the Barusia trip?" Lithia said.

"Yeah, there was a last-minute opening. I was just planning to work during the break, but Oberon offered me the spot."

"Nice," Lithia said. The car pulled up, so the three piled their bags into the back and then hopped in. Zane sat in the row in front of them and looked down at his manumed.

Why Zane? Dione didn't get it. As far as she could tell, Zane had no interest in biology. Why not find a different internship?

Where had he even ranked? She didn't remember seeing his name. How did Lithia know him?

***

Professor Oberon's ship, the *Calypso*, was the size of a giant house, but tiny compared to the massive freighters looming in the distance. The cargo bay was open, but there was a ramp on the side leading to the upper level. Dione could hear voices coming from inside, and as she climbed the ramp, she realized they were not happy voices. Belen was arguing with the professor. Well, Elian Oberon wasn't technically a professor at the university anymore, but StellAcademy had been lucky to get him, and the title stuck.

"We're not going anywhere near the attacks. We'll be fine," the professor was saying. He waved Dione and the others in, but didn't break off from his conversation with Bel.

"But the attacks in general are growing more frequent!" Bel protested. "Something's changing. The Vens are getting bolder. They were patrolling common travel routes *inside* the Bubble." She threw her arms up in frustration, revealing an intricate floral tattoo on the back of her hand. Bel was petite, but strong, and her braid of thick, dark hair ran halfway down her back.

"Have you looked to see how the data fit into the larger pattern?" the professor asked.

"Yes."

"And is it a significant spike?"

"No, not yet, but more information means more deaths," she said.

"I'm not forcing you to come along. I understand your concerns. I'm not discounting them. I just think that statistically we are not likely to come across any Vens, even near the edge of the Bubble. I think you're basing your concerns more on how you feel than what the data support."

Bel frowned. "I guess you're right. I just can't shake the feeling that these attacks are the start of something bad."

"Intuition can be a deceptive thing," the professor said. He turned to face Dione and the others as though they had not witnessed this disagreement. "Welcome aboard the *Calypso*. Make yourselves at home. We'll have a brief orientation during the recharging period after our first jump. You've already been tested on safety protocols, but I like to do a few hands-on scenarios." To Belen he added, "Why don't you show the others around? I'll finish loading the supplies."

"Hey, Bel," Dione said, still breathing hard as she set everything down in the common area. "You already settled in?"

"Yeah, I can show you to your cabins, if you want. I'm already unpacked."

"Lead the way," Lithia said.

Dione liked Belen. Bel was working on an independent study with the professor on insect behaviors. Dione didn't know all the details, but it sounded fascinating.

"Here, let me help," Bel said, grabbing one of Zane's bags, even though he had the least luggage.

Not very subtle, Dione thought. They'd probably be coupled up before they even reached Barusia.

The common area took up nearly half the upper deck. In the center was a corridor, and on the opposite side were several cabins. They already had names on them. Zane Delapont was first, then Belen Sangha, and Lithia Min. The last cabin had her own name, Dione Quinn, on a shiny label fresh off the fabricator. She dumped her stuff inside, and was happy to see that her room was closest to the ship's small lab. It would be perfect for running her plant growth experiments.

A minute later, everyone was back out in the corridor.

"In the back are a few empty cabins, the lab, and the infirmary," Bel said.

Lithia looked down the corridor. "Looks more like a first aid closet."

"Fair point, but once we get to Barusia, they've got facilities there. Let's go this way," Bel said, leading them up the hall away from their cabins. "I assume you'll want to see the cockpit."

"It's a Nebula model. They all look the same, really," Lithia said. Despite this, Dione could tell her friend still wanted to see it. After all, she would be the one flying them, once they had taken off. To get out of the crowded spaceport, she would need a full license, but on the way to Barusia, Lithia would be able to practice. Lithia had considered applying for something more flight specific, but those internships were all military, and as Lithia had put it, she didn't want some stuck-up uniform bossing her around. After a decade of friendship, Dione knew that firsthand.

Dione did not follow. She was eager to get her experiment set up. "I'll catch up," she said, but they were already halfway down the corridor. She grabbed a box from her cabin and headed straight to the lab. Might as well get the experiment set up now so she could take thorough initial measurements.

Inside the box were several different kinds of plants. She secured each one to the lab table, admiring their lush green leaves. This experiment, examining the effects of space jumps on plant growth, had been done several times already, but she wanted to try it out on a mantis plant. It was in a different genus than the most commonly tested species. She had created her own set of control data for the mantis plant before leaving home, but for the others, she was using the accepted control data, just to see if she could replicate the results.

Dione liked to do this, test her methodology on well-replicated experiments to see if she was following the procedures correctly. She also liked to throw in an additional sample out of curiosity.

She was about to head up to the cockpit, but Oberon called over her manumed. "Dione, can you help me in the cargo bay? The others are securing the top level."

"Sure, be right there." Dione knew exactly where the ladder to the cargo bay was. She had studied the ship's schematics like there was going to be a quiz.

Dione opened the hatch on the wall and climbed down. A tall man with dark skin was hauling in a giant cargo crate. Dione was surprised that the professor, whom she'd always perceived as a little dorky, could lift such heavy cargo. His curly hair was close cut, and he was barely breathing hard. She was glad Lithia wasn't here to ogle him. It always made her uncomfortable.

The professor positioned his crate on top of another against the wall. The two locked in place. A number of uniform interlocking crates lined the walls, while some of the larger or more oddly shaped boxes and bags were secured closer to the interior. A clear path was left between the supplies to allow easy access to the engine room.

"Hi, Professor," Dione said, grinning.

"Dione, good morning," the professor said, returning her smile. "We're almost ready to go. I've got a few more crates to bring in, but I wanted to see if you would double-check the emergency beacon. I doubt we'll need it, but it doesn't hurt to be thorough."

Dione took the responsibility seriously. She went through the attached checklist and found everything was in order. She reported back to the professor, but he had no more tasks for her.

"The main level's common area has the biggest screens if you want to watch from there," the professor said. "Lithia will be observing me as I take us up and plot the first jump. After that, she'll be doing the navigation. Supervised, of course."

Dione's manumed buzzed. It was a message from her father: *Proud of you. Have fun.*

He had remembered after all.

She smiled and followed Bel and Zane to the common area. Dione had been off-world before with her father and uncle, but she still got butterflies when the ship roared to life beneath her. This was it. She had been dreaming of this trip ever since she learned of its existence in her very first biology class. Now it was actually happening. She watched the planet recede beneath them, surprised at how quickly they were moving. She felt gravity loosen its hold on her for just a moment before the ship's artificial gravity set in.

The blue-green orb grew smaller beneath them for several minutes before the professor notified them that they were ready to jump.

Dione closed her eyes and felt a tingling sensation work its way up her arms and into her chest. For a moment, everything felt numb, but in seconds, warmth flooded her body. She was one jump closer to Barusia.

2. DIONE

It was only the third day of their ten day journey. Professor Oberon had given them the morning to work on their projects, but he had claimed the afternoon for routine ship maintenance. Dione didn't mind, though. Even chores seemed more exciting in space. Dione had intended to learn more about the *Calypso's* systems before they left, but something else always drew her attention away. Today, there were no distractions.

"We're going to keep it simple," Professor Oberon said. "All critical systems were thoroughly checked before departure and are off limits. You're going to calibrate the external cameras."

Lithia groaned. "Maybe I should double-check the next jump to make sure it's plotted correctly."

"Excellent idea. I think I'll take care of that. Zane will show you all how to do the calibrations, and then you can pair up," the professor said.

The smile disappeared from Dione's face. "You're not going to show us yourself?" she asked.

"No, Zane has probably done this sort of calibration more times than I have. I can't think of a better teacher." Professor Oberon smiled and left.

Dione sized up Zane. The professor clearly trusted him, but why? She had never witnessed him do or say anything particularly wonderful in class.

No, she was being unfair. The professor had invited him along for a reason, and if he really was a calibration expert, then she would put aside her bias and give him a chance.

"All right, Zane," Dione said. "Where do we start?"

Zane opened up a panel underneath one of the viewing screens in the common area.

"We'll have to do each camera individually. I'll start here, show you how it's done, and then we can break off into pairs," he said.

Dione took thorough notes on her manumed during the process and asked enough questions that she could tell she was getting on Zane's nerves. By the end of the fifteen-minute procedure, she felt confident she could replicate it by herself.

"Let's pair up," he said.

"I think I can do it on my own," Dione said, scrolling through her notes.

Zane frowned. "That's great for you, but we're working in pairs like Oberon said." What had she done to deserve that response? She was just trying to be helpful. If they worked individually, they could complete the work more quickly. Dione opened her mouth to protest, but Lithia spoke first.

"Full disclosure, I zoned out in the middle of what you were doing," Lithia said. "I'll need help."

"Then Lithia, you're with me. We'll start down in the cargo bay. Bel, you can work with Dione up here."

Zane and Lithia headed down the corridor to the cargo bay access ladder, and Bel led the way to the next access panel. What was Zane's problem? Dione might not like him very much, but she didn't think she'd been rude to him. Bel might know, but Dione didn't know how to ask her. Bel was obviously close to Zane, and Dione didn't know how much Bel would be willing to tell her.

Dione was halfway through the first calibration when she spoke up. "What's going on with you and Zane? Are you a couple?"

"No," Bel hesitated. "It's complicated." Bel resumed the work where Dione had left off.

Clearly Bel didn't want to talk about it, which meant Dione wasn't going to get any information about Zane. The two continued working in uncomfortable silence for a while until Bel asked about the next step. After that, they talked about more innocuous subjects to pass the time, like Bel's research project.

An hour later, Lithia showed up.

"Hey, Bel. Ready to switch?" she said. "I'll take over with Dione now that I've gotten the hang of it."

Bel stood up and stretched. "Sure, thanks," she said, disappearing down the corridor.

Once Dione was sure Bel was out of earshot, she said, "What, did you get sick of Zane?"

"No, I just figured if I joined you, you'd do all the work." Lithia grinned. "You should give Zane a chance, Di. He's not that bad."

"He just shut me down when I was trying to be helpful!"

"Well, you might have thought you were being helpful, but you sounded like a know-it-all. He doesn't know you well enough to tell the difference."

Dione sighed. "What did you two even talk about?"

Lithia shrugged. "Nothing much. Holos, food, the usual. He's not especially chatty, in case you hadn't noticed."

"You seemed to know him when we met him at the space port. Did you spend any time with him at StellAcademy."

"A little."

Dione leaned back a moment. Lithia wasn't telling her something. "How did you meet Zane? Did you have a class with him?"

"I met him through Bel," Lithia said, picking up the tool needed for the next step.

Dione raised her eyebrows. That was suspicious. "So you're helping now?" she asked.

"You look a little tired." Lithia winked.

"What are you not telling me?" Dione asked.

Lithia sighed. "Look, I don't want to cause problems, but don't take Zane's comment earlier personally. He's just not a fan of the Alliance."

"What does that—" Dione stopped mid-sentence. "Is this about my father? Because he works for the Alliance?"

"Your dad practically is the Alliance."

Dione's face grew hot. "No, he's not. He has orders to follow, just like everyone else. The Alliance isn't perfect, but they're just trying to help."

"I know, Di. I've met your dad. He's not a bad person. Neither is Zane. He's had some rough experiences, but he's actually pretty cool. He just needs to get to know you, that's all." Lithia turned back to the open panel. Before Dione could press her, Lithia asked for directions on the next step. And the next one. And the one after that. She had to be doing this on purpose. Finally, Dione gave in.

"I'll take over," she said. "Why don't you check in with the professor and see how your jump-plotting turned out."

"Thanks!" Lithia placed the tool in Dione's outstretched hand and headed off to the cockpit.

The work went more quickly now that she was alone, and by the time Bel and Zane returned, she'd already finished. She handed her packed-up toolkit to Zane and smiled her sincerest smile. "Thanks for the lesson, Zane. Sorry if I was out of line earlier."

Dione returned to her cabin and sprawled out as much as possible on her small bed. This whole situation was ridiculous. Zane disliked her for no good reason, yet *she* had to be the one to smooth things over? If it meant keeping the peace, she would give it a try.

3. DIONE

Dione's experiment was going perfectly. So far, all of her data matched the accepted norms. She unfastened each specimen from its bindings and moved it to the table where she could inspect it at eye level. She made a few annotations about the appearance of each, noting the color and other general observations before she got into more specific measurements. All of the plants were ready, but when she looked around, she realized that her measuring tool, the one she'd brought from home for added consistency, was still in her cabin.

She paused and looked at all the plants on the table. She'd only be gone two minutes, and the *Calypso* was stationary, currently recharging. In fact, they had just jumped, so there was no danger of a jump interrupting her recordings. It would be fine.

Dione hurried to her cabin and grabbed the digital measuring tool, but when she stepped outside, Lithia was already there.

"You have to come see this."

"I'm kind of in the middle of something."

"Your plants will be there in five minutes. Come on."

Dione looked back toward the lab, but followed Lithia to the common area where a large monitor displayed the view outside. In the distance, Dione could see a brilliant red nebula, no doubt enhanced by the external cameras for the human eye.

"Isn't it beautiful?" Lithia said.

"Yeah, it is," Dione replied. Lithia got this way about space sometimes.

"I modified our jump schedule just a little so we could see it."

"Nerd."

"Nah, that's all you. Just thought as long as we were out here, we might as well see the sights."

"I've never been this close to a nebula before," Dione said. It truly was spectacular.

"I wanted to jump inside it, but Oberon said it wouldn't look like much up close. So here we are."

That was true. From inside a nebula, there would not be enough light to illuminate the gas and dust. At a distance, however, the light would be more concentrated and the nebula would be visible.

The two girls stood in silence, staring at the screen for another few minutes before Dione looked away.

"I've got to finish up with my plants. I'll be back in a bit."

Dione walked back down the corridor and entered the lab.

Inside was an absolute mess of dirt and broken stems. No plants were left standing. On the ground, Zane was trying to scoop dirt back into a pot. He looked up when she entered.

"Dione, I'm so sorry. Oberon asked me to bring these boxes here on my way, but I tripped, and…" He broke off, looking at the mess around him.

Dione blinked hard. "*Professor* Oberon." She had been planning this for months, and one moment of carelessness had destroyed it all.

"I think this one might be okay," he said, holding up a plant with only a few broken stems.

She felt a knot tighten in her stomach. It was just a replication experiment. She was about to do her own original research on Barusia. It was fine.

Then she saw the mantis plant snapped clean in two, and the rational part of her brain stopped working. She took the plant from Zane's hands and threw it in the trash. She picked up the next one and did the same.

"Isn't there some way to salvage them?" Zane said.

"No." At least not any way she cared to try.

"I'm sorry."

"It's fine." An unconvincing lie. He was just staring at her, and she wanted him to stop. "What are you even doing in here?"

"I've been working on a translation program, and I was going to use the interface in here to work on it."

"That doesn't sound like a biology research project."

"It's not, but—"

"Then why are you even on this trip?" Dione was tired of playing nice. "You don't even like Professor Oberon's class. Having you on this trip is a waste when someone else with a real project could have come."

"I didn't mean to mess up your experiment." Zane's voice was cold. "It was an accident."

Dione was picking up the last specimen, her mantis plant. She held it up. "Just leave me alone while I clean this up. It's the least you could do."

Zane left without argument or further apology.

Good. She could clean this mess up in peace now. Dione was usually pretty mellow, but to have Zane screw up her experiment had set her off. She'd been spending too much time with Lithia, the queen of overreactions. Now Dione would have to avoid Zane for the remainder of the trip. At least keeping to herself would get easier when they arrived at Barusia.

Dione tossed the mantis plant into the trash. In the corner she saw the boxes Zane had brought in. Why had he been working on a translation program instead of his research project? She shook her head and began to clean up loose dirt and leaves.

4. DIONE

Dione tapped her fingers on the table and gazed at the screen on the bulkhead. It was cycling through the video. The viewports that would have lined a space cruiser were absent on this small science vessel, and she had only the extremely well-calibrated external cameras. She thought she had seen something—a blur of color—but it was probably nothing. She wasn't surprised. After a week in space, jumping tens of thousands of light years in seconds, the initial excitement had worn off. She felt a little crazy. Just a few more jumps to go. As she drummed her fingers, the residual crumbs from their most recent meal danced to her beat.

Lithia slid into the seat across from her. She was wearing the same uniform as Dione: fitted navy leggings, a white, tucked-in tank top, and an unzipped navy jacket, displaying her cleavage. The StellAcademy logo, a capital A turned into a shooting star, shone in brilliant gold on the left side. Lithia, summoned by her drumming fingers, couldn't help getting involved.

"Still mad?" Lithia asked.

"I was never mad," Dione said. "It's not like it was groundbreaking research. I know that. It's just frustrating." It had been days since the plant apocalypse, and she'd been pretty successful at avoiding Zane.

"Is that why you won't talk to Zane?"

"Well, I'm not sure what exactly he's doing on this trip with us. He's only here because of a fluke. He doesn't even have a research experiment planned out."

Lithia raised an eyebrow. "Are you sure about that?"

"He didn't bring along any materials or samples."

"Maybe he doesn't need them. I didn't exactly come along for the research opportunities either," Lithia said.

"I know you're logging hours for a pilot's license, but you're interested in the research, too. I thought you were doing something with serpentines." At least that's the experiment Dione had helped her write up and propose.

"That's what I submitted with my application, but I feel like serpentines are overdone. Now I'm thinking something with amphibians."

Dione shook her head. "You always change your mind at the last second. Just do serpentines. What about amphibious serpentines? There are a few species in the marshes I'll be working in."

"I'll think it over. You still doing menu choices of carnivorous plants?"

"If by menu choices you mean how they adapt their scents to lure different prey based on their current nutrient deficiencies and needs, then yeah, menu choices."

Lithia grinned. "I bet Oberon's impressed."

"*Professor* Oberon." Dione hoped so. "He's going to meet with me in a few minutes to look over the changes to my proposal. I can help you brainstorm later if you want."

"Maybe you could help Zane, if he really doesn't have a project," Lithia said.

"I don't think he wants my help after earlier," Dione said. Zane had apologized, but that didn't stop her from getting angry. Messing up an experiment she had planned carefully and thoroughly was one of the few things that could really set her off.

Lithia leaned forward. "Look, I understand why you don't like him. You feel like he didn't earn his place here, but Belen did. And she vouched for him, so I think he at least deserves a chance. It's not his fault that Kal's parents pulled him from the trip. We've got two months to spend on Barusia working on these projects, and it would be nice if we at least started out on good terms. So root around the plant samples you brought, find the olive branch you packed, and go offer it to him." Lithia smiled at her own joke.

Dione hated that Lithia was right, especially since she was usually the one telling Lithia to apologize. After her meeting with the professor, she would go make amends. She didn't want Belen mad at her, and she probably shouldn't have said those things to Zane, but he still had no business being here. She didn't even think he liked biology, let alone hyperadaptive terraforming-driven evolution.

Lithia leaned in close and whispered. "When we get there, I've got a surprise to show you. As long as you promise you won't tell Oberon."

"*Professor* Oberon. And if your surprise is the holo interface for your manumed you sneaked into your bag, I have bad news. Your mom unpacked it, last minute. Told me to tell you once you figured out it was missing."

"What? How could she—? What am I supposed to do for the next two months? What kind of cruel sadist bans holos?" Dione smiled as Lithia examined her face for signs of deception. "You're lying. She wouldn't."

"You can always go check," Dione laughed. Poor Lithia might actually have to work on her research project, because Dr. Min really did take her holo interface.

In Lithia's absence, Dione was imagining how the conversation with Zane would go when the professor joined her.

"What do you have for me today?" he said by way of greeting.

"It's similar to my initial proposal, but I want to expand the number of species. I want to work in Highwater Marsh and Anders Bog looking at a pitcher plant and a flytrap in two different areas. Highwater and Anders have different nutrient contents, and I want to see if that affects the type of prey these plants prefer, and if so, how they modify their scent to attract certain prey."

"All right, how does the salinity compare? Are you controlling for that?"

Dione nodded. "I'm not sure. Highwater has a higher salinity, but I'm still working on ideas for controlling that variable."

"You might read Kyra Jonsin's paper about dragonfrog larvae. She had to address some of those same issues in her study. It might give you some ideas."

"Okay, thanks. I was trying to decide on the best species, and I was thinking that the best ones would..." Dione trailed off. The professor was staring at the view screen. "Professor Oberon? Is everything okay?"

He turned back to her and relaxed. "I'm sorry, Dione. I thought I saw something, but it couldn't be."

"Me, too. Earlier I saw a flash of green, but then it was gone."

His lips tightened. "A flash of green? You're sure?"

"Yeah, but it was just a camera malfunction," Dione said. "I think Lithia must have messed something up when we did the calibrations."

"When?"

"Maybe twenty minutes ago. It was nothing."

"I hope so." He pulled up the ship's data on his tablet and started swiping through icons: their location, energy consumption, time to next jump, until he stopped on sensor and camera feeds. He selected this last one and reviewed the footage from two minutes ago. She watched this time as the same flash of green blurred across the screen.

"That's what I saw," she confirmed.

"You said twenty minutes ago?"

"I think. Right before our meeting."

Professor Oberon muttered under his breath. "Then there isn't much time. But why are they here?"

Dione could feel her forehead crease. "Time for what? What's going on?"

The professor didn't answer, but his expression grew serious. He was back on his manumed calling Lithia, Zane, and Belen to the cockpit.

Lithia's voice came from the speaker on his wrist. "On my way."

"I'm already there," Zane said.

"I'll be there in a few minutes. I'm just going to put away my bug collection," Bel said.

"Leave them, Bel. Venatorians are going to make an attack. We don't have much time," the professor replied.

"Shit."

"Venatorians? Inside the Bubble? That's ridiculous!" Dione was running to keep up with the professor as he jogged toward the cockpit.

"The Bubble is only as strong as we make it, and we are extremely close to its border. One jump, and we could be outside. I've been doing this trip for almost a decade, and I've only heard of one report in this area, outside the Bubble. It's so sparsely populated out here that an attack would be of little interest to them. The Dappled Rim has these kinds of issues because it's more densely populated." Then, almost to himself, he said, "What could be luring them here?"

Dione could see the scientist in him taking over, questioning everything, but soon his urgency returned and his pace quickened.

They arrived before Bel, but Zane and Lithia were already there.

"What's the ruckus?" Lithia asked.

"Venatorians are going to attack. In this ship, we are an easy target, so you can expect that it's a smaller crew, probably only twenty or so, maybe a scout class vessel. Any more, and we wouldn't be an appealing target."

"What does that have to do with anything?" Lithia said.

"They like the challenge of the hunt, and they've scanned our vessel. Dione and I both saw their drones. They know there are only five of us and that our ship is not armed. Lithia, look for a safe jump location. We're not fully charged, so take the limited range into consideration. See if Campos is currently in our jump radius. That would be our best bet."

Lithia turned immediately to the controls to follow orders.

Dione heard running steps. Bel burst in, breathing hard. Her words were hard to make out.

5. DIONE

The ship vibrated with the shock of impact. *The Vens were firing on them.* Dione struggled to process what was happening. It felt surreal. *They were taking enemy fire.* Why would anyone attack their small science vessel? *Vens were here.* She had not prepared for this possibility, which alarmed her even more. She tried to call up an image of a Venatorian, the stuff of her childhood nightmares, but that only set her heart pounding even faster.

As much as Dione might want to, they couldn't signal the Alliance. Any message they sent with their equipment would take days to reach help. It was too risky to send a message to closer colonies with faster comms and alert the Vens to their presence. Even then, the message would take too long to save them. The battle would be short. They were on their own. Dione was on the verge of true panic when the professor's voice pulled her back.

"Lithia, jump us the second you can," the professor said. He was all business.

"No," said Bel, pushing Lithia out of the way. "Look." She was pointing to the reports coming in from the hull's censors.

"What? I don't see anything," Lithia said. Dione saw it. Subtle but there, hidden among the other feedback screaming for attention. A hiccup, rippling out into space from their ship, as if they had just been dropped into a placid pond.

"A tracer signal," Bel said. "We can't even go to Bithon now. They'll follow, and after they kill us, they'll kill everyone there. And going to clean space will just mean a goose chase. We can't lose them until we disable the tracer, and unless we fight, we'll never get the chance. Professor, we have to fight." She stood grim, her back straight. The professor stared at her, thinking, calculating.

"Why do you think we stand a better chance here?" he asked.

"Once they attach in order to board, they'll stop firing on us. There are five of us, and they won't send a boarding party that outnumbers us. It wouldn't be a challenge for them. Plus, we have no external weapons. The only chance we have to damage their ship, thereby allowing us to jump away and destroy their tracer, is from *inside* their ship. At the colony, they'd send everyone in, and that's no scout ship. That's a Marauder class vessel with at least fifty Vens, and it can easily handle a colony of two hundred. They might call in other ships if they find a larger colony. I don't think the Bubble means anything to them anymore."

Dione trembled at those odds. "But won't five on five be worse?" she asked.

"Here we have a choke point. And if we fail, it's just the five of us," Bel said.

How the hell was Bel so calm? And how did she know so much about Vens? Dione shivered at Bel's matter-of-fact tone.

Another vibration rocked the hull, and the pit of her stomach dropped out of existence. Every second they waited to act, the worse off they were. Lithia opened her mouth to protest, but Dione caught her eye and shook her head. Lithia ignored her.

"But the colony could help," Lithia said.

"We won't condemn a colony to death because you're too afraid to die alone." Bel's response stung like a slap in the face, and Lithia reddened with anger.

The professor spoke up before the argument could get started. He turned to Lithia and said, "Evade them as long as you can, but keep the ship functional and plot a jump, preferably to an uninhabited planet with hospitable conditions. Repairs are hard to make in space."

"Want me to launch the emergency beacon?" Lithia asked.

"No, we'll need that later. Zane, stay with Lithia. Like Bel said, we need to appear weak without actually losing critical systems. Can you work on that aspect?"

"Got it," Zane said.

Dione barely had time to wonder what he was talking about before the professor gave the next set of orders.

"Dione and Bel, go to storage and pick up the weapons we do have. The stun rifle will be useless. Get the machetes and the stun-gas grenades and meet me by the airlock."

He had barely finished speaking when another tremor rocked the ship. Dione was about to ask what on earth she was supposed to do with a machete against a Ven when the overhead and underfoot lighting flickered and went out, hurling them into pitch darkness. An instant later, emergency lighting glowed in a narrow strip on the floor and ceiling.

"Don't worry, the lights were me," Zane said. "The breaches are minor right now, only affecting the outer hull."

Only. Dione shook her head. The hull had armor plating to protect against errant space debris, and though it wasn't even close to military grade, the fact that the Vens had already poked a few holes in it did not reassure her.

Dione, Bel, and the professor left the cockpit together in silence. Before he descended to the lower deck, Professor Oberon put a hand on Dione's shoulder and handed her a small chip key. "Here's the key. Airlock in ten. Sooner if you can." With that, he climbed down the ladder toward the cargo bay and engine room. Either he wanted to take inventory or he was going to the engine interface. Maybe he had brought along some type of Ven-killing weapon, which was stowed away among the cargo.

They didn't waste any time in getting to restricted storage, back near the professor's personal cabin. Weapons, along with a few infirmary supplies, were restricted. This was a school-affiliated trip, after all, and the recollection amused Dione. *Can't trust us with machetes on the ship, unless it's to fend off a few Vens.* They picked out the handful of stun grenades they had brought with them and a machete each. Dione grabbed an extra blade for the professor.

"You seem to know a lot about Vens," she said to Bel.

"I do. We're lucky we have machetes and not guns. Venatorian plating is tougher than body armor. They are vulnerable at their joints, but they've got layers of connective tissue that are tough to get through."

"And they don't use manufactured weapons?"

"Nothing ranged. Usually, only what nature gave them. It's a source of pride."

"How do you know so much about them? Some of this stuff I haven't read in the stories or reports."

"I used to live in a colony on the Dappled Rim with my parents. Until the Vens came. I've been reading every Ven report made available to the public since then."

Dione didn't know what to say. Another strike tilted the ship, giving the artificial gravity a workout. She wanted to ask how Bel survived, but settled on, "I'm sorry. I had no idea."

Bel shrugged dismissively. "Well, the Alliance is good at spreading the narrative it prefers. Too many deaths on the edge of the Bubble, and colonization and the influx of resources comes to a halt. Bad for business."

Dione tried to read Bel's expression, but her back was turned. Bel was so quiet, and they had only started getting to know each other on this trip. This had pretty much amounted to learning what her project was and what vids she liked. She had no idea what Bel's life looked like, but it was nothing like hers.

Dione felt guilt bubbling in her stomach. Her father was high up in the Alliance. She knew there were anti-Alliance protesters, but she didn't expect Bel and Zane to be among them. She had always trusted her father's explanations of criminals who championed loose regulations, and dissidents who cared more for themselves than galactic interests. There were worlds of ideas that her textbooks didn't begin to touch, and the luxury of her ignorance was expiring.

They reached the airlock, but the professor was still not there. Another vibration shuddered through the hull, different from the others. A metallic scraping echoed inside the ship, and Dione shivered. Alarms followed shortly after.

"Zane, was that that you?" asked Dione over the comms. He was still in the cockpit with Lithia.

"No." She didn't find his lack of explanation helpful.

Dione must have looked like a puppy in a thunderstorm because Bel was reassuring her. "They're not going to breach compartments with life support. They're going for our engines, our jump drive, anything that will trap us and force us into hand-to-hand combat."

Lithia's voice echoed from their manumeds until the two broadcasts synced into one voice. "That wasn't a hit. They've extended hostile docking clamps. Good news. They're moving to board."

Dione wasn't sure why Lithia sounded so pleased. She could see the viridian hull growing larger through the airlock's tiny viewport, and it filled her with sheer terror.

"Why do you sound happy?" Dione asked.

"Because we're still fully functional," Lithia replied.

At that moment, the professor jumped into their conversation. "I'm going to be taking the charging matrix offline. The jump drive will still work, but we'll only get one jump. If this works, we'll have plenty of time to fix it up later."

"Where are you?" Dione said.

"This is taking longer than I hoped. Are you both at the airlock?"

"We're here," Dione said.

"You may need to hold them off on your own. I'll be there as soon as I can."

"Dione, are you up for this?" Bel asked, frowning.

Dione took several seconds to answer. Her gut reaction was a wild, uncontrolled no. But that's not what Bel was really asking. She wanted to know that when the time came, Dione would have her back. That she wouldn't freeze into a motionless mess that needed rescuing. She wouldn't allow herself that kind of weakness. Despite her propensity for letting herself down, Dione would not disappoint a friend. She would not leave slack for another to pick up. She took a deep breath. All of the panic that had taken over her subsided into a steady pulsing of fear. The panic would get her killed, but the fear? It just might keep her and Bel alive.

"Yes."

6. DIONE

Dione stood there as Bel opened the airlock control panel.

"I'm going to override the door controls. It should buy us a little more time for Oberon to get here," Bel said.

A few hours ago, she had felt like the smartest person on board. Dione now realized that she might actually be much lower in that hierarchy than she originally thought. In fact, she felt utterly useless. She brought nothing to the table. Lithia could fly the ship, Bel knew more about Vens than most Alliance officials, and even Zane, accident extraordinaire, had somehow managed to fool the Vens into boarding a perfectly fit ship. Dione could identify over fifty species of carnivorous plants by their Latin names, but knowing that it had been captured by *Dionaea muscipula* did the trapped fly no good.

"Dione, snap out of it," Bel said. "I've got a plan, but I need you to tell me more about these gas grenades. What are they designed for?"

The gas grenades were for a side project of hers. She wanted to get a closer look at some of the indigenous animals that had interbred with the species introduced by terraformers. "They're for incapacitating mammals, like a medium-sized dog or a pig."

"Why not use the stun rifle?"

"It was for setting up remote traps," Dione said. She wasn't much of a hunter, though she'd trained with stun rifles before.

"How many kilos' worth of animal does each grenade knock out?"

"About twenty to thirty-five kilos. Too small, it might kill them, any larger, it won't knock them out. The average Ven is a hundred kilos, according to the Koriev reports." That was at least one fact she did know.

"It's probably more. The only ones they get to study are the smaller, weaker ones. Do the effects accumulate?"

Dione nodded. "Yes, and its minimum alveolar concentration isn't that high, but if we factor in the cabin pressure—"

"Save me the explanation. Will it work?" Bel said.

"The confined space could be an advantage. I don't know how much gas is in each, but they were designed for open-air use. We only have three grenades, though. And it's all or nothing. If the gas doesn't pass a certain concentration in the lungs, it won't cross the threshold in the bloodstream, and there's no effect. Once it crosses that threshold, the effects are progressive, leading to unconsciousness." A moment of panic hit her. "Wait, they do have lungs right?" She had not spent much time studying Ven physiology. *Will this even work?*

"What they have are very similar to lungs," Bel said. Dione hoped they were similar in enough ways.

"Well, the effects still won't be equal. It may not knock all of them out. Or any of them."

"Then I guess we're hoping our ugly green friends are all below the fiftieth percentile for height and weight, and that those things pack enough of a punch."

"Bel, we don't have gas masks. How much do you weigh? I'm willing to bet that three grenades knock us both out cold." Dione's mind raced. No gas masks, but…

"Pressure suits! They would protect—"

"They're in the cargo bay. There's no time," Bel said.

"It won't take long, I can—"

Bel grabbed her wrist and looked her in the eye. "Don't you dare leave me here alone with them." Bel, despite her steady voice, was pale with fear. "It's a risk we have to take. The alternative is taking on the entire boarding party. How good are you with a machete?"

Dione was actually pretty good with a machete, though as a tool, not a combat weapon. Before she could share that detail, a walkway extended from the green invading ship like a slow-motion stinger. The walkway found its target and attached.

She saw four Vens, easily half a meter taller than her, walking toward the airlock. Each Ven's face had been decorated with a simple geometric design smeared in white war paint. She wondered about the designs: a spiral, a bisected triangle, a spiked circle, and three nested rectangles. Dione focused in on the one with a simple spiral on his cheek. He was a lot like a gorilla, but with the hard cobalt plates of an armadillo protecting his body. One plate covered his entire head and face and came down like a hood to about chest level, slightly overlapping with the pectoral plate. His large legs were cocooned in thick blue plating, and his toes were tipped with claws. The upper appendages were plated and clawed as well. On his head were two eyes, with rectangular pupils that stared right at them. He growled. The three behind him echoed back his call, exposing their teeth. One bite would send a person into an adrenaline-fueled frenzy. A brief two-minute pressurization and unlocking sequence was the only thing between Dione and death.

"Something's wrong," Bel said.

"What?" Dione asked.

"These Vens don't look right. They're blue. They should be mottled green. They're not as big as I remember."

For all the details she'd noticed, Dione couldn't believe this observation had gotten past her. "You're right. In all the images I've ever seen, they've been green."

Why would these Vens look different? she thought. "They may look smaller because you're bigger yourself," she said to Bel. "Gender differences in many organisms are reflected in color and patterning."

"No, the plating on the females has a scalloped edge. You can see, that one closest to us is female." Sure enough, the plating billowed along the edge.

Dione knew that. She had read that. *Think.*

"Maybe it's from radiation? Like some kind of sunburn?" Bel said. She seemed distracted, like this wasn't what she had expected.

"No," Dione said. "Radiation wouldn't produce that kind of uniform pigment change."

The Vens were right up against the airlock viewport looking in, almost curious. Almost. Or was that uncertainty? Humans could universally recognize certain expressions of emotion across linguistic and cultural divides, but apparently that knack for reading faces did not apply to alien species. Dione didn't know what to make of that look the biggest one was giving her. And that's when she noticed it.

"Bel, it's a hormonal effect. Look, that one in the back with the spiral design is starting to turn green. They're juveniles! That's why they're so small."

"If you're right, this is bad. I've never found any reports like this. Either this doesn't happen very often, or there are never any survivors."

"Let's bet on the former," Dione said, feeling good from proposing what she considered a good hypothesis. If they were juveniles, their odds were even better. Probably.

A chime went off. *Thirty seconds to go.*

"All right, Dione, get the grenades ready. When they try to open the door, it'll get stuck. Throw the grenades in, I'll close it back up, and it just might work."

Another chime sounded. Dione had the grenades ready. She would have to be fast.

The doors began to open, letting the bitter scent of the Vens trickle in. The smell was so strong she could taste it, as if a swarm of lady bugs had flown into her mouth. At a hand's width apart, the doors froze, locked in place by Bel.

"Now!"

Dione threw the first grenade, and pink gas rose in plumes around the Vens. She had the second and third primed, but the Ven with the green on its hood thrust its claws through the gap, up to its first brachial joint. She fell back and dropped both grenades on the floor in between her and Bel. A second clawed arm was pulling at the other side of the door, trying to open it. Dione coughed in the pink smoke and saw the door give a little.

"Get the grenades! I'm trying to hold them out," Bel said, coughing.

The gap widened slightly, and the door slid back a few centimeters. There was more than enough gas to knock out both of the girls. If Dione didn't reposition the canisters soon, they'd be unconscious, but the Vens would be wide awake and headed for the cockpit.

Dione reached for one and slid it through the opening at the bottom of the door. The last was blocked by a clawed foot. She stood, holding the smoke canister away from her, as if it would make a difference. In this confined space, she wondered if the weight estimates were off, because she was starting to feel dizzy.

She was already sinking to the floor when the professor charged in, shouting, "Dione, get back!" He grabbed the extra machete from the floor and sliced down on the outstretched arm of the biggest Ven, catching it right under a section of plating.

The Ven moaned and wrenched back his arm, leaving the gap at the bottom of the door unguarded. Dione shoved the third and final canister through and signaled to Bel, who managed to close the door another few centimeters. They all stepped back from the thin line of pink smoke, and Dione felt better. Bel, on the other hand, looked worse. She was smaller than Dione and was feeling the effects more strongly. The viewport was clouded, but as the gas began to dissipate through the hole, she saw four bodies on the floor.

The professor opened the door and approached the nearest body. Without a second thought, he slid his machete underneath its hood plating into its neural center.

"Dione, help me. We don't know how long the effects will last."

Dione picked up her own machete, but she had no desire to kill these creatures. She had never even killed an animal with her own two hands. She slipped her own machete into the hood gap of the large one with the tinges of green until she hit something elastic, like a tough membrane. She gradually increased the amount of force she applied until the membrane snapped, and her weapon glided freely up into his brain.

She pulled the blade out quickly and wiped it on the Ven's blue-plated abdomen, leaving a small pile of foul-smelling liquid that reminded her of pus. She had killed him. She looked up at the professor who had already dispatched the other three in the time it took her to kill one. He was talking to Bel, who was leaning against a bulkhead. Dione focused in on their conversation, pushing the sickening sensation of the snapping membrane from her mind.

"I'll take Dione. You can stay here and make sure no others make an attack," he said.

"I want to come. Please," Bel said. Somehow, despite the difficulty Bel was having keeping her eyes open, Dione sensed the urgency in her voice.

"You need some time, and I need you to stay here and watch our backs. We won't take long."

"What are you talking about?" Dione said.

He held up a glossy metal cylinder by its handle.

"Is that…"

"The charging matrix, yes," he replied. He must have registered the look of horror on her face because he added, "Don't worry, there's a backup." Dione didn't think there was a backup, at least she didn't remember one from the ship specs. Maybe she had missed it. Or forgotten it.

"I've configured it to explode with a ten-minute timer, so we have to be fast. If we can get to their primary energy hub, it should completely knock out their ship without blowing it up. We are attached after all."

"And if it damages their hull and vents them into space?" It could damage their life support systems and the backups. Or not. After all, it was a makeshift bomb. She wasn't even sure it would explode properly. The charging matrix was the only thing on board powerful enough to make a dent.

"I can live with that," he said. Dione should feel that way, but it was foreign to her, wishing actual, irreversible death on another sentient being. He smiled as if to reassure her, but Dione could see the sweat on his brow.

"If you're up to it, I could really use your help. You weren't much affected by the gas, but Bel is still a bit hazy. I can't force you, though."

Dione did not want to be a hero. She didn't want to board the Ven ship with nothing but a machete and a wannabe bomb. She wanted to survive. She just needed to figure out what would give her and her friends the best chance at survival. The professor wouldn't have asked unless he really did need her help, and their escape depended on his bomb working. There was no choice after all.

"If you're coming, we need to go now. I don't know how long until they send another boarding party." *Another boarding party.* Nowhere would be safe if the professor failed.

"All right. Let's go," Dione decided. When she had put in her request for this internship, she had been nervous. They would be working and staying in a remote location on a remote planet, running into all sorts of new creatures. That's what this internship was about, taking risks and making discoveries. Still, this was not what she'd had in mind. She did not want to die, but if she wanted to survive, she would have to join the professor.

Dione began dragging the green-tinted Ven from the airlock. The one she had jammed her machete into. She struggled with his weight, but then the professor was by her side, taking over his right leg and pulling. His body scratched against the floor, making the hairs on the back of Dione's neck stand on end.

"There's no time to move the others, we need to go now," he said.

She stepped into the airlock with a gulp. She was trapped inside with three stinking corpses and a homemade bomb.

7. DIONE

Two minutes was a long time when an opaque green door hid the reality of what was waiting for them. Those two minutes allowed every possibility to creep into Dione's mind. The Vens must have known they were coming. They were probably standing on the other side of that door in force, right now, ready to avenge their fallen. It had no viewport, though, so the scene behind the scaly green door was a mystery.

As they navigated around the blue bodies, she filled the professor in on her hypothesis about the color.

"Juveniles? Really? Then this could be their first hunt, a rite of passage. But I'm a biologist, not a xenoanthropologist," the professor said.

"I just hope that the Vens on board don't have much of a maternal instinct, assuming I'm right."

The professor frowned and spoke softly to himself. "I wonder if they have been monitoring the progress of the boarding party."

Dione heard every word, but didn't respond. She felt woefully unprepared for what was to come, and this was a new feeling for her. At StellAcademy, she had always been prepared for everything, down to the sneakiest pop quiz. There was no right answer here.

No path of trial and error to explore on her way to success. There were no second chances. She should gather as much information as she could now in the minute she had left.

"Do you know where to go, once we're inside?" she asked. She didn't like the look on his face, like he was trying to solve for a variable without an equation.

"I know the generic layout, and I've sent a map to your manumed, based on data we've collected about the Vens. The Vens like geometric patterns and shapes. The ship's walkways are a series of concentric shapes, probably ovals by the look of the exterior. There will be inward paths at regular intervals. If we head down and toward the center, we should find the energy hub. This door will take us to the outermost corridor."

Professor Oberon has a plan. If anyone could get them through this, it was the professor. Dione tried to coax any memories of the Ven articles she had read to the surface of her thoughts, but it was like trying to catch minnows with her bare hands. A small chime indicated thirty seconds were left.

"It's important that even if we can't get to the primary energy hub, whatever we hit packs a punch. We don't get a second shot."

"Understood."

Dione was shaking, and the professor's voice was softer when he continued. "I'm telling you this because you can't hesitate. Don't think of them as juveniles and mothers. Think of them as predators. Because that's what they are, and to them, we are prey."

She lifted her machete. It felt heavier than it had just a few minutes ago. She was out of shape, it seemed. Her first adventure had been over the holiday to a research lab at the equator. She had helped build a bamboo shelter and hacked her way to a beautiful waterfall oasis. It had been a vacation, though, with the comforts of home a short ride away, should she tire of the jungle. But she didn't. Instead, she had made a notebook's worth of observations on leaf mice and scarlet talcons.

The door gasped open, and that sour Ven smell was so heavy it settled on her taste buds. They were lucky that no defensive pack was there to greet them because she gagged, overcome by the stench. She felt small underneath the high ceilings that allowed the monstrous Vens to roam about their ship. The professor, tallest among their crew, could reach up and touch the ceilings on the *Calypso*, but not here.

Dione did her best to only breathe through her mouth as she followed the professor through grim corridors. The ship hummed. In fact, it pulsed with vibrations. She knew the Vens relied on the vibrations produced by their throaty growls, and wondered what type of message the vibrations were broadcasting through the ship. Would her footsteps and heartbeats be strong enough for the Vens to detect? Or would they get relegated to background noise, like the kind she easily ignored on their own vessel? She strained to pick up any errant sounds, but only managed to work herself up with phantom footsteps.

The professor halted and held a finger up to his lips. Her eyes widened as she heard real footsteps, and they were getting closer. This was it. Dione lifted her machete, but the professor pointed her toward the wall.

A hatch, probably cleaning access to the ventilation system. They climbed inside, quiet as the void, and didn't move. Her own heart thumped in her ears, and she was certain she would give herself away. The footsteps grew louder, and she could hear them them growling. Talking?

After the Vens had passed, she thought that maybe they didn't know they were on board. She doubted they ever expected to be boarded themselves. Had it ever been done? She looked around their hiding spot. The vents were actually large enough for her to crawl through, but she didn't think the professor would fit, so she kept that idea to herself. The professor reopened the hatch, and they continued making turns inward toward the energy hub at the center of the ship.

Dione kept turning around, certain that they would be flanked. How else would they have gotten this far unchallenged, unless they were heading into a trap? The professor slowed and held up his hand again to stop her. She heard the low hum of a Ven conversation—discordant, different tones all at once. More than that, she felt it, like standing too close to the speakers at a concert. Many Vens were talking at once. Maybe it was an argument. Either way, it sent chills down through her body.

When she peeked around the corner, she realized why they had met such little opposition. Everyone was here. Fifteen Vens at least, maybe twenty, large and green, were watching a monstrous screen with four different readouts. Only one was changing. The other three were static.

Maybe something was wrong with their ship? She didn't have time for further conjecture, because just then, she locked eyes with one of the Vens. A female. Her wailing knocked Dione off-balance as the others turned. Dione had already pulled back, but it was too late.

The professor grabbed her shoulders and shoved the rigged matrix into her hands. "Take this. Complete this connection," he said, pointing to two wires, "and then you'll have about ten minutes to get back." He pushed her into the nearest hatch before she could say anything, not that she would have known what to say.

He charged past the Ven-filled room, and Dione heard, rather than saw, his pursuers rushing back down the corridor. Dione didn't waste any time, hoping she would be able to meet him at the airlock soon. The matrix was a glossy metal cylinder, heavy but compact. The professor had pried it open to reveal the inner workings and turn it into a weapon.

She looked again at the narrow tunnels and pulled up the schematics the professor had given her. She had a notification from him. The message was short and misspelled, but it couldn't be right: *St bom n go.*

Set bomb and go? She couldn't do that. She would find him, or he would escape. But for now, she had to set the explosive. She slithered into the air duct and followed it past the room with the giant screens toward the energy hub, or so she hoped.

After just a few minutes, the cold of the vents chilled her. Her fingers tingled with dulled sensation and her eyes watered. The matrix grew heavy in her grip. It was just large enough to be unwieldy. She couldn't stay up here much longer. She peered out of a vent into a large, circular room. At the center of the room was a dome, casting an orange glow over the entire space. Three Vens were patrolling, scrutinizing every shadow, every errant vibration.

The energy hub was loud, but there was no way she was going to plant a bomb unseen in that room, and an explosion from up here in the ducts wouldn't be enough to set off a chain reaction. There had to be another location. Weapons? That wouldn't stop a boarding party. Engines? Jump drive? That might do it. If she placed it just right…

She wasn't sure she could make it back from the engines in ten minutes and she wasn't ready to sacrifice herself just yet. Her heart was racing. *Think.* It was only a matter of time before they sent a second boarding party, if they hadn't already. They were all going to die if she didn't do something now. Dione felt panic welling up, blocking her brain from focusing on the problem at hand. She just needed to get her feet on the ground, so to speak.

On the ground! That was it. The stabilizers. She had passed them on her way here. They provided a counterbalance to the rotational force of the energy hub. Without them, the vessel would spiral out of control. They wouldn't be able to aim even if they could get a shot off. Repairs would be difficult to make, and they couldn't jump in an uncontrolled spin, so they couldn't pursue their craft until they fixed it. She would just have to make sure that the *Calypso* was no longer attached when the bomb went off.

Dione crawled back the way she came, retreating toward her new plan. She was about to pass over the room where she had left the professor when she heard a heart-stopping scream. Blood drained from her face in cold fear. Professor Oberon. She had to check, to see if she could help him.

She pulled herself as quietly as possible through the ducts into the room. The nearest exit hatch felt like a mile away. Her hands grew numb and clumsy in the frigid air and her eyes stung, but finally she got a view of the room. It was clearly the control center.

Fifteen or so Vens remained in the room, eyes glued to the changing readout. On the floor, she could see the soles of the professor's boots. He wasn't moving. She couldn't tell from this angle, but she tried to discern any movement of his chest. There was none. She did, however, see blood. So much blood. How could he be alive after losing that much blood?

He couldn't be dead. She needed him to be alive, but what good would that do? Even if he was somehow still alive, he was dead anyway. The room was packed with Vens. There was nothing she could do to rescue him.

Tears warmed her cheeks, and Dione bit back the bile rising in her throat. Professor Oberon was doomed, and she was terrified. Her fingers tightened around the handle of the bomb as she backed away. That was the reminder she needed. She could cry later. The stabilizers were just around the corner. She would see this through.

No one was guarding them. They were irrelevant, not a target like the energy hub. They were two large metal boxes that whooshed with the effort of keeping the ship steady. Dione was determined to enjoy blowing them up.

She placed the bomb in a dark place, right between the two, held her breath, and connected the wires. *Let the countdown begin.* The timer she set on her manumed showed the seconds slipping by.

Dione was speed-walking through the outer corridors, which had all been empty when she arrived. The vents were so cold her toes were still numb, and she couldn't afford to waste time crawling. She was so preoccupied with the impending explosion that she nearly missed the first Ven patrolling her escape route, but was able to duck back into the frigid vents. Her nose dripped uncomfortably, but she didn't dare move until the Ven had passed. She just might make it back without having to use her machete.

Fear kept her in the vents, but soon her body began to shake with the cold. She left the vents again, relieved to be nearly at the airlock. As soon as she rounded the corner to the outermost oval, she saw him, a monstrous Ven, blocking her only exit.

She looked at her manumed. She had six and a half minutes to figure out a way back onto her ship. No, she had forgotten about the locking mechanism. Make that four and a half.

8. DIONE

Dione retreated down the nearest path, away from the corridor that led to the *Calypso*. She found herself in a small storage room. She was sweating, even though the cold of the Ven ship permeated her leggings and jacket. She unzipped her collar a little and used it to wipe the perspiration from her forehead. The Ven ship was still attached, and that would be a problem. She messaged Zane: *Detach clamps in 6 min*

She could attack, but she didn't like her chances. One machete against a fully grown Ven? Horrible odds. She looked around the storage room. Plenty of places to hide, but hiding wasn't an option. Only one alternative came to mind.

Dione removed her jacket and positioned it so that it just barely appeared from behind a storage container. She pressed herself against the wall near another storage container that resembled a bookshelf. If the Ven looked the wrong way, game over.

A few tools were lying out, so she picked up the one that looked like it might go farthest, maybe some kind of wrench. She hesitated a moment before throwing it.

Was this really the best plan she could come up with? Would it work? The questions became irrelevant as she saw time ticking away on her manumed. There was no time to think. She had to act. Now.

She threw the wrench at the Ven's face, but it landed harmlessly at his feet. Nevertheless, it did the trick. He caught sight of her jacket decoy and ran straight toward the room where she was hiding. He breezed past her hiding spot, concealed by a narrow crate. The second his back was turned, she darted out of the room. The machete in its sheath banged painfully against her back.

The giant Ven wheeled on his feet, impossibly agile, impossibly fast, and lost no time in his pursuit. This was a horrible idea. He would catch her in no time. Even though he was built for power, not speed, his stride was long. The distance to the airlock was short, and the gap was closing with every burning step. He would grab her before she could close the door. Dione felt him move closer. Too close. She could imagine his outstretched hand straining for her hair. She jetted down the corridor, begging for one last burst of speed from her worn-out legs, just enough to make it to the airlock, but it was not enough.

As Dione crossed the threshold into the airlock that joined the two ships, she felt a desperate hand swipe at her back, claws tearing fabric and skin. He had just missed the reinforced strap that held her machete. Something warm glued her tank top to her back, but the pain seared hot on her left shoulder blade. The unexpected pain made her clumsy, and for a moment, she forgot what she had to do.

That moment should have been fatal, but luck was on her side. She turned and closed the airlock door, initiating the pressurization and unlocking sequence. No, that had not been luck. The Ven had been standing there, glaring at her, growling in a low, ominous tone. He could have easily moved in for the kill in her moments of hesitation, but he had not. Some invisible protection had stopped him at the threshold.

Her back screamed in agony, but there was nothing she could do. She shrugged her shoulder, wincing at the pain, but was relieved to have full mobility. The cuts must be fairly shallow.

The time on her manumed was just over two minutes. That had been close. She was about to take a mental breath when she thought of the professor. Is that how she would always remember him, motionless and surrounded by Vens?

A message flashed across her manumed from Lithia: *Status?*

It was time to unmute. "I'm back," Dione said over the manumed. "I'm the one in the airlock." Dione let the silent tears roll down her cheeks. She let them well up in her eyes, blurring the world around her. She wanted to ask Lithia about the jump, but her voice would betray her.

She walked over to the viewport to check on Bel, stepping back through the Ven corpses. She didn't see her. Dione's chest tightened as she realized that the last Ven, the one that she had dragged from the walkway, was not where she had left him. Dione forced the flow of tears to ebb, though her voice was still shaky.

"Bel?" she asked, even though no one could hear her.

It was Zane who answered, though he couldn't have possibly heard her question. "Dione, Bel needs help. One of the Vens—it wasn't dead."

Dione took a deep breath, clearing what shakiness she could from her voice. "What? How is that possible?"

"I don't know. But she's holding him off as best she can."

"The pressurization and unlocking sequence still has another minute," Dione said. "That's about the same time the bomb goes off. I had to put it by their stabilizers, so we need to be detached as soon as I get back inside. The centrifugal force of their engine should spin them out of control without their stabilizers functioning, but we're still attached, so ours will try to compensate for them until we detach."

"Understood," Zane said. Dione normally hated his brisk responses, but this time she was grateful to be left alone. *Get it together. Deep breaths.*

The seconds flowed like cold honey, but with about forty-five to go, Bel limped into view. Blood was pouring from her nose and forehead. The Ven actually looked worse. His right arm hung uselessly by his side and his right leg dragged behind him. Bel was biding time, trying to stay far enough ahead to dodge an attack. Even injured and half-paralyzed, the Ven was a deadly opponent.

"Bel!" Dione shouted and banged against the door. Bel glanced at the viewport and shuffled in her direction. She was saying something, but Dione couldn't understand. Her manumed must have been broken.

The Ven was catching up. Dione watched helplessly as Bel stumbled, and her injured leg couldn't compensate. She tumbled to the floor.

"Look out!" Dione said, banging on the door. The thirty-second chime sounded. Dione hit the door control, but nothing happened. Still locked. She would not get there in time. It was too late for Bel.

The Ven, now right behind Bel, pulled her hair, and smashed her face into the viewport, leaving a smear of blood across the glass. Bel crumpled to the floor. Dione could see the rise and fall of her chest, but Bel did not stir.

"No!" Dione said. She was useless, trapped. Her manumed timer was still ticking down. The Ven stared, his rectangular pupils fixed on her. He knew. Somehow he knew that she had been the one to try and kill him. He wanted revenge.

The Ven grabbed Bel by the shoulder, using his good arm, though she noticed twitches of movement from the arm that dangled at his side. Could such a serious injury already be healing? If so, the reports and profiles had severely underestimated the species' regenerative capabilities. If she didn't act fast, she would lose her only advantage, his injuries.

She rushed into the room. The Ven was out of sight, but she knew what he wanted. She was supposed to follow. To reclaim her friend. To fall into his trap out of sheer emotional stupidity. This Ven was certainly well-versed in the habits of his quarry. Dione swallowed the urge to rush headlong after him.

"Zane, is the cockpit sealed?"

"Yes, how's Bel?"

"She's in bad shape. The Ven took her. He's still loose on the ship."

"On my way."

"No. Zane, you need to get their walkway to disengage in the next ten seconds."

"I'll still need more time."

"You don't have it," Dione said. "Lithia, have you found a place for us to go?"

"Yeah, but I can't reach the professor. I want to run it by him," Lithia said.

"Wherever it is, it's fine."

"Is that what he said? Is he with you?"

"No, he's not." The countdown on her wrist hit zero.

9. DIONE

An alarm went off on her manumed, and Dione braced herself. They were still connected, and the ship would start spinning any second now. Nothing happened.

The Vens must have disarmed the bomb. All of it had been for nothing. The professor was dead, Bel was injured, a Ven was loose on the *Calypso*, and Dione had failed to disable the Ven ship.

"I'm ready to force-remove their docking clamps," Zane said.

"Wait, I have to go back," she protested. "Something happened to the bomb, or I made a mistake when arming it. It didn't—" But then the ship rocked and knocked her to the deck. An external camera showed a spout of flame venting into space from the Ven ship. It had actually worked! Before she could rejoice at her small victory, she remembered that the professor was still dead, and still on that ship.

"Never mind, disengage now," she said. Their ship and the Vens' were rocking like a seesaw, but their stabilizers wouldn't be able to hold both ships for long. The artificial gravity was losing its grip on her. On the next downward swing, she caught some air. The next time, she was thrown against the wall.

Before they launched into a full spin, Zane released the clamps, and they shot off into space. Without the *Calypso* as an anchor, the Ven ship began spiraling more rapidly. It fired off a few shots, but they didn't even come close. Dione opened a group channel on her manumed.

"Lithia, jump," Dione said.

"I can't, the jump drive needs to be reinitialized. I think the Ven did something," Lithia said.

"No, it was the professor. He completely removed the charging matrix," Dione said.

"Now it makes sense. He said we'd only get one jump. I'll need to go down there and reinitialize it manually."

"No, the Ven could be waiting for you outside the cockpit. This could be his way of luring you out. You're unarmed. I'll do it."

"What about Bel?" Zane asked.

"The Ven took her."

"It's too dangerous. You can't leave her to the Ven. I'm coming down there," Zane said.

"We can't afford for the cockpit to be compromised." Dione stared at the red blood gleaming on the floor. Bel. She clenched her fists. No one else was getting involved. "He's badly injured, and I think I have a good chance." What was she saying? A chance against a Ven? She was the reason he wasn't dead in the first place. He had been hers to dispatch. She hadn't been able to kill him when he was unconscious, so why did she think she could now?

Her stomach turned. She would at least try. She didn't think she could actually do it, but she had no choice.

"I'm leaving my manumed link open to both of you," Dione said.

Dione cautiously followed the trail of Bel's blood down the corridor to the ladder. Dione kept reminding herself that it was a head wound, and those bled a lot. It was probably not as bad as it seemed. She felt reassured every time she passed a smear of thick brown and white Ven blood, or whatever the goop was. The Ven had made no attempt to hide his tracks, and she had one guess as to why it was leading her here. It wanted access to the engines, just like she did. Moments later, she caught sight of Bel, slumped against the wall outside the ladder hatch. Her face was covered in blood.

Dione froze, fighting every instinct to rush to Bel's aid. A trap. It had to be. She backed herself against the wall and raised her machete, ready. She examined her surroundings, but there were no good hiding spots. Satisfied it was safe, she approached Bel and felt a few tears trickle down her cheeks once she felt a pulse.

"I've got Bel," she said into her manumed. "She's alive, but unconscious. I think the Ven is in the cargo bay. He's heading toward the engines, too."

In order to reach the engine room, she would have to climb down a ladder and cross the mess of crates and boxes the professor had packed. This area was larger than the rest of the ship, and the Ven would have the space to stretch to his full height. She would be the most vulnerable while climbing down the ladder, but she didn't have a choice. She braced herself to be ready for anything. Dione kept her weapon drawn in one hand and headed down. Each successive rung set her heart pounding against her chest in a painful burst.

When she reached the bottom of the ladder, she raised up her machete and peered around. The tension in her shoulders left her shaking. Was he trying to frighten her into submission? She could smell him, like milk left out in the sun, but she still couldn't see him.

"He's here. I can smell him," Dione said to Lithia and Zane. He was not ready to attack yet. He was waiting for something. Or maybe his injuries were worse than she thought, and that's why he had left Bel.

Numerous crates and containers created the perfect place to hide, and made the trek across the cargo bay feel like a marathon. This suspense was exactly what Lithia loved in a virtual reality holo, but Dione hated it. Now that the stakes were real, Dione was certain her heart was beating so fast that her blood didn't actually have time to deliver oxygen to her muscles. That's why she felt so weak. She almost wished the Ven would just attack already and relieve the tension building inside her.

On a nearby crate, she recognized Professor Oberon's handwriting on a label. He always believed in her and the Vens had taken that support away. She inhaled sharply with the thought and felt her rage push back her sorrow. By the time she reached the engine room door at the end of the cargo bay, she was furious. She glanced in both directions, saw nothing, and punched in digit after digit. Her finger had barely hit the last key when a flurry of blue came bounding from the shadows. The Ven moved fast, and Dione wondered if his leg was already healing.

He knocked her to the ground and rushed the door, but growled in frustration when it did not budge.

"Like I didn't see that move coming a mile away."

From the floor, she was able to stab upward with the machete into his left leg, in between the plates that covered his whole body, bringing him to his knees, or whatever his mid-leg joints were called.

He swiped with his good arm but missed, losing what was left of his balance on his good knee. A strange whistling sound was coming from beneath his hood-shaped carapace as he lay prostrate before her. Was he panting?

Dione stood over the Ven for a second time that day, machete in hand. She knew what she had to do, but that message wasn't making it to the muscles in her arm. The command was stuck in some twilight zone that demanded to know what right she had to take another life. He was in no shape to fight back. What were her options?

They could contain him, find a way to lock him up until they could hand him over to the Alliance patrols. But no, they didn't have a place to put him. And there was no reasoning with him. The Vens were not known for their diplomacy. There was no way to sedate him. She knew what Bel would do. What the professor would do.

This thing had slammed Bel's head against the door, and his friends had killed the professor. Did he really deserve her consideration and her mercy? He posed too great a risk. There was only one option. He looked at her with his large eyes as she tensed, preparing her killing jab. This time she would be certain.

With a groan, he kicked her knee with his newly injured leg, and she toppled to the ground next to him, losing her grip on the machete. He rolled on top of her, rattling and rasping, putting all his weight into the arm against her throat. She tried to call for help, but she couldn't even choke out the words. Maybe Lithia and Zane could hear her gasping on the manumed. Thick white fluid oozed from his wounds onto her clothes, but she was desperate for any air, even if it came with that Ven stench. White light was hovering at the corners of her vision when she heard something. The Ven must have heard it, too, because he lifted his weight for just a moment, just long enough for Dione to grab the machete. She would not hesitate again.

She swung the blade around so that she was nearly hugging the creature and jammed the honed edge straight into the gap between the plates on his back, but this time, she struck something hard. These plates were fused.

"Hey!" It was Zane's voice. She could hear him, running through the cargo bay.

She thrust again, but the Ven smacked her head against the floor leaving her dazed as he got up to meet his new opponent. Dione grabbed the machete and got up, supporting herself on the nearest containers. Her vision was not cooperating and she felt light-headed, like she might pass out and vomit at the same time.

She couldn't believe Zane had come. He was so…

A scream pierced her thoughts before she could complete them. The Ven had bitten Zane, and when he stumbled, the Ven just watched.

Then Zane did something she did not expect. He roared. Not in pain, or fear, but in anger. Dione called Lithia, still leaning against the crates.

"The Ven just bit Zane," she said.

"Shit. Is he?"

"Going berserk? Yeah. The effect was immediate."

"Do something! This is end game."

Zane had just been hit with a dose of adrenaline and crazy, and there was no promise that he wouldn't attack her the second she got close. But if the Ven had done that, he meant to force a confrontation. Though Zane would be stronger and faster now, he would also be far more reckless.

Dione approached slowly, not wanting to attract any attention, but the Ven was aware of her. Zane was, too, but he was far more interested in the Ven. The Ven was limping, but his old wound from fighting Bel seemed to be giving him less trouble. He could move his injured arm, but not with much strength or speed.

Zane lunged, and the Ven dodged. He lunged again, and the Ven used Zane's own momentum against him, grabbing him with his good arm and tossing him into a large metal container. Zane recovered quickly, but the Ven did not. His movement was taking a toll, and he seemed to realize his mistake in dosing Zane.

Dione watched, waiting for her opening. When Zane prepared another charge, she made her own attack. Zane was again thrown off to the side, but the monstrous creature could not recover quickly enough to dodge her. She forced the machete upward into vital sensitive areas, twisting violently, shoving with all her force until only the hilt remained visible. The Ven collapsed. She had done it.

The next moment, she locked eyes with Zane, pleading, "Zane, it's me." He offered no sign of recognition and tensed, as if preparing to jump. That was all the answer she needed. She sprinted back toward the door to engine room, knocking over a few crates to slow her pursuer. He tripped over the last one, giving her just enough time to slip into the engine room and lock the door.

"Lithia, what do I do?" Dione said, louder than she intended. The panic in her voice was evident.

"There should be a flashing panel. Go to it and follow its commands to reinitialize. There shouldn't be any hiccups."

She walked over to the panel. "Except for Zane banging on the door." A loud thump sounded, right on cue.

A minute later, she was done.

"All right, the coordinates are in. Just hit the manual activation," Lithia said.

"Here we go," Dione replied.

She braced herself for the jump. The tickling sensation began in her extremities and worked its way to her core, followed by tingling, followed by a warm numbness. As the warmth dissipated, she realized she had no idea where they were.

"You need to see this, Di," Lithia said. "You're not gonna believe it."

Dione felt uneasy. Where had Lithia taken them? "Sure, how long does the Ven poison take to wear off? Because Zane is still outside, and I'm worried that the Ven isn't really dead."

"I'll get the stun rifle."

10. DIONE

The cargo bay was not a pretty picture. A few crates and containers that had broken through their restraints littered the paths. Drops and smears of blood were everywhere, and Ven stench had permeated the entire area, despite its size.

When Lithia opened the door, she had Zane slung awkwardly over her shoulder. Dione offered to help, but Lithia wouldn't let her.

"That's a nasty scratch on your back. And you're limping. You look like hell," Lithia said. Then with a smile, "But at least I didn't have to shoot you."

Underneath the bad joke, Dione could see how uneasy Lithia was. "Most of the blood isn't mine, I don't think," Dione said. "How is Bel?"

"She was waking up when I got there."

That was good news at least. When they passed the reeking corpse of the Ven, Dione hesitated.

"You okay?" Lithia asked.

"Almost." Dione bent over the Ven, and without removing the blade that protruded from its back, began sawing through any and all possible neural connections that remained. This Ven would not be coming back to life. She wouldn't make that mistake again. Still, the sound of ripping flesh and vessels and the feel of elastic membranes giving way filled her with nausea. After she was done, she vomited behind a nearby crate.

"I see you've called dibs on clean-up down here, then," Lithia said. She laughed, but Dione saw right through it. Lithia's forehead was creased with thought. And if Lithia, the brave one, was worried, she would probably need to throw up again.

Getting Zane up the ladder would have proved a massive task, but Dione still had the sense to rig up a pulley system. It did involve retrieving the machete from the Ven in order to cut the rope, but Lithia handled that. With Lithia pulling from above and Dione guiding his ascent from below, they were able to heave him up to the main floor. Thankfully, this was where all of the common areas were, including the infirmary.

Bel was standing now, though she looked pretty shaken up, like she, too, might vomit.

Still, the first words out of her mouth were clear and focused. "Is it dead?"

"Yes. I made sure this time," Dione said. "Bel, I'm so sorry—"

Bel cut her off. "Don't apologize. Just learn for next time. I should have known."

"We'll get this tracer deactivated. There won't be a next time."

"That's what I thought, but here I am again. Where's Oberon?"

Dione looked away. "He didn't make it," she replied.

Lithia had already figured it out, and Bel didn't seem surprised. An uncomfortable silence settled over the girls.

Bel wiped her cheek and winced as she wiped away a scab that had begun coagulating there. The wound on her cheek started bleeding again, and Dione gasped when she took a closer look.

"What?" Lithia said.

"Bel, your cut. It's in a spiral. It's the same shape the Ven in the cargo bay had painted on his face."

Bel looked more disgusted than surprised. "It marked me for its house. That way, when the Vens catch us and board us, they will know who gets to kill me."

"How do you know—" Lithia began to ask.

"Now's not the time," Dione said. "Bel, the Ven bit Zane, he went berserk, and Lithia stunned him."

"Took two hits," Lithia said.

"He'll probably be clear when he wakes up, but let's restrain him just in case. We need to monitor him, because Ven bites have been known to kill, but usually only in the very young and very old," Bel said.

"We need to disable the tracer," Dione added.

"Then find us a place to land. I'll take care of Zane," Bel said. She didn't look like she was in good enough shape to take care of herself, let alone Zane, but once Lithia set Zane down on the small couch in the infirmary, there was little choice. They had delayed long enough.

***

Back in the cockpit, there were a number of displays and holograms up. The largest exhibited a beautiful world, azure and emerald, marbled with swirling white clouds. What could the problem possibly be?

"Is this the planet?" Dione asked.

"Yes."

"Then what's the issue? These readings show it as habitable. Oxygen's a little high, but not dangerous."

"There's no problem yet. I'm running a few surface scans now. It's this that I'm worried about." Lithia swiped her hand through the hologram and a new model took its place. It was a space station. "We need to disable the tracer ASAP, and we have a decision to make about where to do it," Lithia said.

"I thought you said this planet was uninhabited?" Panic gripped Dione. How many people were now at risk because of them? "Have you hailed them?"

"The station is not responding. It's abandoned. Just look at its energy output. No one's been on board for decades."

Lithia was right. The station was clearly not in use. This whole situation was bizarre. No one poured this kind of money into a station only to abandon it.

"Who built it?" Dione wondered out loud. "Why did they abandon it?"

"I don't know," Lithia said, "but we can either make the repairs up here on the station or land on the planet. I vote the planet. This ghost station gives me the creeps."

Dione disagreed. "We don't know what it's like on the planet, and the station is closer. The station makes more sense. We can get to work on the tracer right away."

"I still don't like it. What if there was a plague?" Lithia said.

"The ship will automatically search for any contagions. Wear a suit if you're worried. I would love to figure out why it was abandoned. Just look at the design of this place. It's classic pre-Alliance architecture. That means it's at least sixty years old. Probably closer to a hundred."

"Is that why it's so ugly?" Lithia asked. It was true. It didn't have the sleek gleam that modern ships and stations had, but it was sturdy.

"I kind of like it," Dione said. "It's like something out of an old vid. The Alliance added a lot of regulations banning this type of wheel structure. It's supposed to have a minimum of six spokes, but it's only got four. I doubt it has all the safety features required by modern facilities." The Alliance liked redundant safety features.

"So you're acknowledging it's a death trap," Lithia said.

"Everything's a death trap in space."

Their manumeds buzzed, interrupting their argument. It was Bel. "The med scanner is broken."

"How did that happen?" Dione said.

"The restraints were old. They must have broken when you blew the stabilizers and our ship was rocking. The scanner and some other stuff got banged up or knocked over."

"Is there anything else you can use?" Dione asked.

"I don't think so. Zane's breathing is getting ragged. Lithia, do you think it was because you had to stun him twice?"

"I don't know. One shot should have worked, though I can't say I've ever used a stun rifle on a person before. They're supposed to be able to take out jungle cats. Glad we packed one, though."

"I don't know if it's the Ven saliva or the effects of the rifle, but I can't monitor his vitals."

"Bel, there's a space station here, orbiting the planet Lithia jumped us to. It's abandoned, but it might still have medical equipment," Dione said.

"It's worth a try," Bel said. "You'll have to explain what a station's doing here later."

She ended the call. Lithia rolled her eyes in frustration, but apparently it wasn't worth the fight.

"Sending a wake-up call now," Lithia said.

"A what?" Dione said.

"Just letting the station know we're on our way," Lithia explained. "It should start heating things up a bit. Absence protocols are usually set to lower temperatures than we would find comfortable." She set a course for the station.

How did Lithia find this place? Why hadn't the station been taken over by smugglers? Smugglers would leave some sort of trail, even if they were a small operation, and there was no sign of life at all coming from that station.

"Lithia, how'd you find this planet?"

"I need to concentrate on flying." Lithia was deflecting.

That was a lie. Lithia could dock this ship in her sleep. Dione persisted. "Where are we?" She scanned all of the readouts. A string of numbers spelled out their coordinates, and Dione puzzled over them. They were off.

She went cold as the void when the realization dawned on her.

"Why are we outside of the Bubble?"

Lithia didn't reply.

"Answer me, Lithia. Why are we outside of the Bubble?"

"Because the only place left to go was out. The only other habitable planet in range was Bithon. It's a farming colony, and I wasn't about to risk them with the tracer. I tried to ask Oberon, ask you, but you told me it was fine."

"But all of those coordinates are classified! There is no way the professor had illegal coordinates programmed into the database."

Lithia winced. "It's a long story," she said.

"What if this planet is inhabited?"

"It's not. The chances of that were small, and I'm not getting any readings to indicate otherwise."

Dione was having trouble breathing. "You jumped us outside of the Bubble. The Alliance will never come outside that protected space. It's in the treaty. They'll never answer our emergency beacon once we send it out." They were all going to die out here without the charging matrix. The Bubble was the only chance they had for rescue.

"We will find a way back. Calm down."

"How could you do this?" Dione clenched her fists. They were trapped outside the Bubble with no jump drive. No way back in.

"Well, maybe if Oberon were still around, he'd be able to tell us how he planned to get us home," Lithia said.

"Are you blaming me?"

Lithia said nothing. Dione's eyes watered, and she blinked back tears. The guilt welled up inside her. No matter how logical her decision had been, Lithia's scorn was well-placed. She should have done something to save him.

Lithia backed down, but hot anger still flushed her face. She said something else, but Dione didn't hear her. She was thinking about the beacon again. That's when she realized it. Their beacon was equipped with a jump drive of its own that would be able to carry it on a series of preprogrammed jumps back to wherever one needed to send a message. It was the fastest way to send an emergency signal.

"That's why the professor blew up the charging matrix. There's one in the beacon," Dione said.

Lithia had been speaking, but now she stopped. "It can't... its size..." She kept pausing. "It would take forever to charge, at least a week. It doesn't have the same specifications."

"After we disable the tracer, we can use the charging matrix to get back inside the Bubble to a colony, reinstall it into the beacon, then send for help. The Vens were inside the Bubble when they attacked, so the Alliance will have to send someone."

"I hope you're right," Lithia said. She seemed calmer now that there was hope for the jump drive.

Dione needed to take a few deep breaths and process everything that was happening. She leaned back in her chair, and immediately regretted it. She gasped at the pain. The scratch on her back from her narrow escape at the airlock stung under the pressure.

"What is it?"

Dione turned to reveal her back. "I'm going to get this cleaned up and see if Bel needs help," Dione said, getting up to leave.

"Okay," Lithia said dispassionately. She turned away from Dione to watch the monitors.

She was glad to have an excuse to leave. Lithia was slipping into one of her moods and would be better off left alone.

11. DIONE

When Dione exited the *Calypso* and boarded the ghost station, she felt as if a weight had been lifted from her shoulders. Then she realized that the station had lighter gravity, just by a little. Bel had cleaned and bandaged her wounds, and fortunately, they were shallow. They already felt better.

All of the lights had come on when they docked. The station's absence protocols, which took care of regular maintenance and cleaning, had done a good job. There wasn't much dust lying around. The air tasted stale, though the oxygen here was slightly higher as well, just like the planet.

Bel swept past her. She was dragging Zane down the ramp on a blanket, though even that effort looked like it would be too much.

"Do you need help?" Dione asked.

"No, I'll find the med bay. You and Lithia need to get that tracer out of the hull."

"How?"

"I don't know. Look it up. The Vens send out seeker drones to pick up any signals. The drones jump back to the ship and relay any info. It's a shot in the dark, but enough shots and eventually they'll hit something. The longer the tracer is working, the bigger a target we are," Bel said.

The green blur Dione and the professor had seen on the *Calypso*, before the attack, must have been one of these drones. Dione didn't know how Bel kept everything together, but she was impressed.

Dione watched her enter the station itself, and the lights turned on ahead of her as soon as she entered. The station was waking up. Bel was heading into that space station alone, and there was no doubt in Dione's mind that she would find the med bay and help Zane.

The air smelled artificially clean, but already Dione could hear machinery whirring to life in the presence of humans. No one had been here in decades. The hangar bay had high ceilings and gray walls, and four rows of shuttles. There were a few empty spaces where shuttles were missing, but no signs of active use.

She was sure this station had been built before even her father was born. He had been a kid when the Vens arrived and the Alliance was formed to keep the threat in check. The Alliance drew an imaginary line in space, a boundary it could protect, and everything on the other side was on its own. The Vens hunted outside this boundary. Plenty of people decided to stay outside the Bubble, for better or worse. She wondered if the owners of this station had been angry that it was not included, or if that was even the reason it had been abandoned.

Lithia was already inspecting the hull damage, looking for the tracer. It wasn't hard to find. It was about the size of a volleyball, metallic and smooth, protruding like a tumor from the hull, right at eye level. It was partially stuck in the hull, no doubt clamped on by some stubborn mechanism.

"Any ideas?" Lithia asked. Dione ignored her annoyed tone.

"I'm checking my manumed," she replied. After several minutes of skimming, Dione found a few suggestions. "There's not much here. It says you can shoot them off but that doesn't work if—"

"If you don't have conventional guns, like us," Lithia said.

"Auto-sledge? Do we have anything like that?"

"How about that giant textbook Bel lugged on board?"

Dione laughed. This was how their conversations were supposed to go, but even her smile of relief faded quickly. "I don't think we have anything that can penetrate its exterior."

"Then what are we supposed to do?"

Dione examined it closely. "Could we disrupt its signal or something?"

"Zane probably could, but I have no idea how."

"I think there's just enough of a gap here that we could pry it out. Once it's detached, it will be a lot easier to destroy it."

The girls retrieved some metal support poles from the cargo bay. Dione was careful to avoid the Ven except to make sure he was still there, dead. Once the tracer was taken care of, they would remove the body.

"All right, I'll go from underneath first, then you—" Lithia never finished that sentence, because at the exact moment she positioned the pole at the base of the tracer, it came to life. It closed the already small gap between the hull and what now appeared to be its mouth, which it was using to grind a way through the ship's exterior.

"Shit, Di. What's going on?"

But Dione was already reading. "Apparently some models are burrowers. Metallovores. They eat their way in, slip between the hull layers, and you can never find them again."

"Well that would have been useful to know earlier. Could an electric pulse fry it?"

"If it's strong enough, I guess," Dione said.

Lithia ran into the ship, but Dione didn't bother asking. She knew she was going for the stun rifle. Dione didn't think it would work, but that had been before. Now they only had minutes to stop this thing.

Dione stood by, useless, watching the mechanical tick scrape through the *Calypso's* outer hull. She had to do something. She reached out and did her best to grab its smooth round surface. She leaned back with all of her weight, attempting to pull on it. Her fingers cramped with the effort, but she was convinced it was helping, even if the grinding continued on.

In almost no time, Lithia was back with the stun rifle.

"Look out," she said.

Dione released the tracer and took a few hurried steps back. Lithia pulled the gun up to her shoulder, took aim, and fired her first shot. In the silence that followed, they could still hear that awful grinding noise. Lithia fired two more shots in rapid succession, but there was no effect.

"It's not working," Dione said.

"Then I'm out of ideas," Lithia replied.

For a few helpless moments the girls stood there, shoulders hunched, with no plan. Dione couldn't believe it. They had counted on being able to disable the tracer, but she had never considered that this might be impossible. This was supposed to be the easy part. This entire trip had been one frustration after another, and all of that frustration was now building inside her. She took the machete strapped around her shoulder, and with no particular plans in mind, began to strike at the tracer with swing after frenzied swing. The clang of metal on metal echoed through the hangar.

"Dione, stop," Lithia said. But Dione could barely hear her. All she could think is that maybe, if she hit it enough times, it would break. Her calculated attempts never worked, like when she had tried to kill the Ven the first time. She had only applied the force that was necessary, and she had come up woefully short. Then a Ven had been loose on the ship, nearly killing them all. So if their plan wouldn't work, she would just have to beat the metallovore into submission.

Then, in between the metallic echoes of her swings, another echo joined in, woefully off beat with her own rhythm. It was moving faster. Out of the corner of her eye, she saw a dark-haired figure racing toward them.

Bel. She was carrying something. Curiosity overpowered her frenzy, and Dione stopped. She found that she was out of breath. Maybe Bel had another idea. Dione looked back at the tracer and noticed a few small indentations.

"I found a defibrillator in the med bay. Its charge should be powerful enough."

Dione dropped the machete and got down to help Bel. Bel positioned one charge on the front, while Dione place the other on the back. They were just about ready to give it a try, when alarms began blaring from the *Calypso*.

"It's almost broken through the hull," Lithia said.

"Clear!" shouted Bel. She initiated the shock. Immediately the scraping stopped. Over half of the tracer's bulbous body was now inside the hole it had dug, but Lithia wasted no time in putting their improvised pry bars back to use. Dione grabbed the other, and together, they shook it free.

"Is it still transmitting?" Dione asked.

"No, it's completely dead," Bel said. "I just hope we got it in time."

"How'd you know to come?" Dione asked.

Bel held up her wrist. "I borrowed Zane's manumed."

Lithia, who was spread out on the ground, began to laugh.

"Have you lost it?" Dione said.

Through her laughter, Lithia said, "You're the smartest person I know, and you were attacking this thing with a machete like the muscle in an action holo. And you never play the muscle."

Dione cracked a smile. What had they gotten themselves into? She glanced at Bel, but there was no laughter there. In fact, she looked sick. Her face looked too flushed, and beads of sweat had formed on her brow.

"Bel, you okay?"

Bel's only reply was to collapse on the floor.

12. DIONE

Bel was heavier than she looked. By the time that Dione and Lithia had carried her into the ghost station's med bay, Zane was already waking up. His hands were pressed against his temples as if he had the worst headache of his life. When he saw Bel's unconscious body, he got up swiftly. Dione offered a hand for support, but he stabilized himself using his bed. He squinted in Bel's direction, clearly in pain.

"What happened? She all right?" he asked.

"She stopped the tracer, but then collapsed. We're not sure what's wrong," Dione said.

They put her in the bed with the built-in scanner, and waited for the results. Dione saw the worry on Zane's face, but it was Lithia who comforted him.

"It's probably a concussion. She just needs some rest."

Minutes later, the results were in. Bel had a minor concussion and a broken rib, but that wasn't the part that troubled Dione.

"It's detected a parasitic infection along with a slight fever."

"What? How is that possible?" Zane said.

"Take a look at this," Dione said. She was pointing to a deep scratch on Bel's leg. Of the three parallel scratches, two were quite deep. Bel hadn't mentioned it when she was cleaning Dione's back wound. There was something strange about it. Dione dimmed the lights. In the darkness, it glowed a gentle green.

"That can't be good," Lithia said.

"It will make the infection easier to track," Dione said. She turned the lights back on and noticed the pinkness around the edges, Bel's natural immune response kicking in. Maybe that, paired with rest, would be enough.

"The Ven gave it to her?" Zane said.

"Probably," Lithia said. "We can see if there's any mention of something like this—"

"Got it," Dione said, scrolling through the file she had pulled up on her manumed, displaying it for the others to see. There wasn't much in the survivor category, but she did find a reference to Ven fever.

"There have been two known survivors of Ven attacks who exhibited flu-like symptoms. One died before treatment could be administered, and the other was treated with an anti-parasitic that targeted a similar protozoan parasite." She frowned. "He responded to treatment, but died from his other injuries. Doctors believe it's an incidental infection as a result of contaminated wounds, rather than part of the Vens' attack strategy."

"So we can give her something for the infection?" he asked.

When Dione requested more detailed information on the parasite, it was listed as unknown, but its phylum had been identified as protozoa. This could be the same thing. The computer showed her a list of similar parasites, and next to each one was the appropriate medication.

"That one," Dione said, pointing to an enigmatic combination of letters. "Malscopine. It's an anti-parasitic. There's no medicine like this on our ship, but we can check around the med bay."

It did not take long for them to realize that nearly all of the station's medical supplies, or at least the ones that could be easily moved, had already been taken. The med bay had been completely cleaned out.

"Must've been pirates," Lithia said.

"Maybe they had a secondary storage somewhere, like a giant supply cabinet," Dione said. She queried the computer, and found that, while there was no supply on the station, there had been a med transfer to the planet. Somewhere called the Forest Base. And of course, the transfer included the kind of medicine that Bel needed. "I bet it's still there on the surface. I wonder how many of these bases there are, and what they were used for."

Zane wasn't satisfied. "What are the symptoms?"

"Fever, chills, nausea, vomiting, and it can even lead to issues breathing." Dione looked up. "We can't leave curing her up to chance."

"So you think we should go down to the surface?" Zane asked.

Dione cast a glance at Lithia. They were thinking the same thing. "We can't all go," Dione said.

"We shouldn't move Bel, and someone needs to stay with her," Lithia said.

Dione watched realization dawn on Zane's face. From his expression, she could tell that he understood what she meant and was not pleased, but Zane kept his complaints to himself.

"So I take it you want me to stay here," Zane said. "You two are leaving me here and taking the ship?"

"Those other shuttles in the hangar are still usable," Lithia said. "If I can fly one of those down, we can leave the ship here so that the nanotech can make all of the repairs. We'll be back before the repairs are even completed."

"And what if you don't find it? What happens to Bel then?" Zane said. He seemed to be asking himself the questions, rather than directing them at anyone, and Dione didn't miss the heartfelt concern in his voice. There was a pause.

"I don't know," Dione said. And Dione hated not knowing. There was still a part of her in denial that all of this was actually happening. It was a school trip. It was supposed to be safe. But now they were alone, Bel was infected with a deadly parasite, Zane was recovering from a Ven bite, and the professor... She could still hardly believe it. Dead. She felt despair welling up like a wave in her chest, and used all of her strength and rationality to push it back down. No problem was insurmountable as long as you broke it down into steps.

"We just need to come up with a plan," she said.

After some brief discussions, they figured out their next moves. First, they would release the nanotech to repair the physical damage to the ship. At the same time, they would integrate the distress beacon's charging matrix and start charging the *Calypso* for the jump. They agreed to put the Ven in one of the professor's cold storage containers on the *Calypso*, because it was easier than dragging it to an airlock. The cargo bay would probably stink forever, but at least they wouldn't have to walk by that thing all the time.

Finally, Lithia and Zane would run diagnostics on one of the shuttles in the hangar. Dione would look around for any supplies they might need on their trip to the planet, or any information that would tell them what to expect at this Forest Base.

"This could work," Lithia said. "What do you think, Zane?"

"How long do you think you'll be down there?"

"A few hours to land, a few hours to find the Forest Base and meds, and a few hours back. Less than a day."

"Assuming things go to plan," he said.

Lithia raised her eyebrows and nodded in agreement. "I'm going to get the repairs started, but I'd like to get some sleep tonight before flying a century-old shuttle to the surface."

"I'll stay with Bel," Zane said.

"I'll look around and see what I can find out," Dione said. She hoped to discover what this station had been built for. Why had it been abandoned?

13. DIONE

The mystery of this place was intoxicating to Dione. There were hundreds and hundreds of rooms to explore, and yet she would only have the chance to inspect a fraction of the station before her trip to the surface with Lithia. The long time needed to charge the jump drive might give her a few days to explore when they got back.

The station's layout was rather intuitive, once she figured out how it worked. The station itself was designed like a giant wheel with four spokes, gently spinning. Each spoke contained common areas. The circumference of the wheel contained numerous crew quarters and specialized work areas, like labs. Finally, in the center, were the vital areas of the station, including the command center, the energy core, and the med bay. The hangar bay was positioned between two of the spokes, providing easy access to any area of the station.

Based on the picked-over state of the med bay, Dione decided to bypass the common areas for now and check out the crew quarters. She thought she had a better chance of finding supplies people had squirreled away. As she walked down one of the spokes, she took stock of the athletic arenas and the small cafés.

The further she moved from the others, the more anxious she became.

Most of the doors had not been locked. The first room was empty aside from its furnishings, but the next still had some art hanging on the wall and a few toiletries in the bathroom. Most of the rooms were like these first two, but Dione did find one room with quite a few things left behind. On what she presumed was once the dinner table, she found several drawings painstakingly done by hand and several pages of notes. Dione puzzled over the drawing for several minutes, but until she read the notes she couldn't make full sense of what she was looking at.

It looked like a giant dog, with sharp fangs and thick, mottled fur. It reminded her of an over-sized wolf, except its snout seemed rounder, and she could see the wag in its curled tail, even in the two-dimensional drawing. It looked practically domesticated. She had never seen or read about such a creature before, though it certainly reminded her of other canine species.

The first page of the notes described the so-called "maximute," but not in the way that a child who had dreamed up some fantastic beast would. These notes were clearly written by a scientist, talking about the different genetic bases that would go into forming such a creature. But something seemed off about the notes. They weren't... hypothetical. These were informal notes written by someone who had attempted and succeeded, at least in some capacity, to engineer a maximute. The last few pages were field notes, from the writer's personal observations on the planet below, and they even gave the planet's name.

The realization hit her like the vacuum of space, and she returned excitedly to the others. She knew what this place was, and it filled her with more awe than fear.

***

By now, everyone was back in the med bay, and Bel was waking up. Lithia had programmed the nanotech, which was working steadily to repair the *Calypso*. Once Bel was awake, Zane had been able to help Lithia integrate the beacon's charging matrix and get an idea of how long the charge would take.

"Good, Di, you're back," Lithia said. "Looks like the ship will take about a week to charge. Better than we hoped."

Dione was too excited to ease her way into the conversation. "I know what this place was for. Look," she said, holding up the drawings and the notes. "This animal does not exist. At least, it didn't, until whoever drew this created it. This station was an advanced terraforming research station. Who knows what we'll find on that planet."

"What do you mean?" Lithia asked. Zane stopped shuffling blankets. He was paying careful attention, too, though he kept his eyes on Bel. Bel looked annoyed to be trapped in bed.

"The researchers here were terraformers, and considering where this place is, they were pioneers. Who knows what they seeded that planet with."

"You think it's dangerous?" Lithia asked, amusement in her eyes. The two had very different ideas of danger, and Lithia loved to take risks. Of course she wasn't going to take Dione's concerns seriously.

"Yes, but I still think we should go. We have to get those meds. After we return with the anti-parasitics, we could even go back," Dione said. "We're stuck here for a week after all."

Bel spoke up. "A few shiny engineered drawings and you've already forgotten what's out there? Oberon is gone. The research trip is over. Until we are back in the Bubble at a Level Two colony at least, we are in survival mode. The Vens could still find us." She frowned at the drawing in Dione's hand.

"There's really nothing we can do if they show up before we're charged," Lithia said. "And we have plenty of food and water in the cargo bay. But I don't think we should spend more time on the planet than we have to."

"This drawing gives us more information," Dione insisted. "We know what this station was for now, and we know that the planet probably has animal life. We should take the stun rifle with us. We can talk about going back once we have the anti-parasitics."

"No. You shouldn't even go down there at all, but Zane and Lithia outvoted me. I'd rather wait until we're charged and get treatment at a colony, but that will apparently take too much time. The Vens are still out there, and the planet is probably dangerous. Are you so sheltered that you can't recognize how screwed we are? I don't care who your father is, he can't help us out here. I thought you were the smart one." Bel put a hand to her head, as if all those bitter words had hurt her, too.

Dione felt all sense of wonder and joy drain from her body, leaving nothing but a nasty hollow in the pit of her stomach. Their focus had to be on survival. Dione held her lips as steady as she could and said, "You're right. It was a stupid thing to say, but I did find out what this planet is called." She needed to change the subject.

Lithia raised her eyebrows in inquiry.

"Kepos," Dione answered.

14. DIONE

Dione dressed in a fresh white and navy StellAcademy uniform. She thought she would beat Lithia to the shuttle dock on the opposite side of the hangar bay, but Lithia was already there, working on a shuttle. Her friend gave her a wary "Are you okay?" look. It seemed she felt bad enough to call a truce on their own disagreement.

"How does the shuttle look?" Dione asked, making it crystal clear that she didn't want to talk about it.

"Nate's just fine. A few more places to inspect, but he's in good shape."

"Nate?"

"Yeah, N-8, right on the side here. Nate." She pointed to the lettering along the side.

"Please tell me Nate is the best shuttle and you didn't just pick him for cosmetic reasons."

"He's in the best shape of them all, though they're all in great shape." Lithia shook her head in wonder. "The absence protocols on this station must be phenomenal."

"And you can fly these old clunkers?"

"Yeah, just like the ship in *Paths to the Universe*."

"For the record, I'm trusting you because you've got more flight hours than most solar chauffeurs and not because of the hours you logged in a boring and repetitive holo game."

"You're just mad you always crash."

The two girls made the final checks and strapped in. The readouts looked old, but fortunately not too foreign. The entire shuttle was large enough to fit about fifteen people, and seemed to be a transport model. There were a few larger ships in the hangar as well that Lithia thought were for cargo.

Dione pulled out two meal bars from her bag. She had grabbed two basic packs from their cargo bay. She handed one bar to Lithia, and for a moment, it felt like a road trip. When the planet loomed on the view screen, that feeling evaporated. It was insane, really. Stupid. The professor never would have allowed it, especially if he had known what they did about the terraforming experiments. But he wasn't there, and the best chance Bel had was on that planet in a forest patrolled by whatever lived there.

The trip from the station to the upper atmosphere was uneventful. Dione even managed to get some reading done. She pulled up a book on her manumed that the professor had given her. He thought it would be helpful for her project, even though it was on *pseudophyta*, false plants, rather than the true plants that she would be examining. "Keep your mind open to other ideas," he said, "because sometimes that lizard you've been studying is just a very strange bird."

"You know you don't have to read that anymore. Homework is the least of our worries at this point," Lithia said. Dione noticed how careful she was to avoid any explicit mention of the professor.

"I find it calming." Dione just needed to get her mind off of everything that had happened. The professor was gone. He had died to save her. To save them. And it may have all been in vain if the tracer sent back a signal with their last known location. Somehow, reading the last book he had assigned her made her feel better.

After Dione reread the same sentence for the fifth time, she decided that maybe it was time to give up. They were nearing the bumpy part of the trip anyway. She should probably say something now, before the flying got rough. Last night, she had made up her mind to talk to Lithia and clear the air. She didn't like having this giant wedge between them.

Dione's stomach did a flip, but it had nothing to do with Lithia's flying. She'd played through the scenario in her head a few times, planning for different outcomes, just like she always did. Now that she was finally alone with Lithia, and all immediate threats were out of the way, they could afford a disagreement. This was not the best time, but their unfinished conversation from the cockpit had been gnawing at the back of her mind, and Lithia couldn't avoid her now. Dione started with the most obvious question, one she was afraid to know the answer to.

"How did you find out about this place? Aside from the Rim, all planet locations outside the Bubble are classified."

"The Alliance archives," Lithia replied. She kept her eyes fixed on the readouts, paying far more attention to the stable readings than the situation merited.

"But those are restricted. You can't even break into them unless you have an access portal." The moment the words escaped her lips, every muscle in her body tensed. She had been going over the possibilities in her mind until a memory surfaced. A few months ago, Lithia had needed her help. She said she needed the access for a personal project. There was some data from an Alliance research project that wouldn't be made public in time. Dione hadn't seen the harm.

"When I let you use my father's access portal, this is what you were doing? You told me it was for one of your projects."

"It was, just not the one you were thinking of."

"You lied to me," Dione said, raising her voice. She almost couldn't believe it. Lithia lied all the time, of course, but not to her. That was the unwritten rule.

At that moment, they hit the initial entry turbulence. Lithia maneuvered them through before responding. "I didn't have a choice. You never would have helped me if you knew."

"How did you do it? No way you found that information by yourself."

There was a long pause as Lithia checked through the readouts, though Dione suspected it was more for show than necessity. She waited, staring at the side of Lithia's head until she turned and met her eyes.

"Zane."

"Zane? Really?" Dione said. "I didn't know you were friends."

"We weren't. Bel knew him, though. He may not be that into biology, but he knows his way around network safeguards. Maybe if you took a minute to get to know him, you'd realize that he's actually crazy smart."

"Why, then?" Dione was yelling now, her voice bigger than normal in the small confines of the shuttle, and louder after the end of the turbulence. "What was so important about this place that you lied to me and put my father's job at risk?"

That was the biggest piece Dione was missing. Something had driven Lithia to betray her trust, but she couldn't imagine what it could be. She was looking for a reason to understand, but Lithia's silence on the subject was all the proof she needed. Lithia was caught up in something bad, and if she didn't trust Dione with the truth, they would have nothing to talk about.

They were nearly to the surface, but Lithia gave no indication that she would respond. When she finally spoke, her response threw Dione completely off-guard.

"You left Oberon on the Ven ship, didn't you? I never would have left him," Lithia said.

Using the professor as a redirect. That was a low blow, and an effective one Dione hadn't expected. She already hated herself for leaving him, even though she knew it had been the right decision. "If you had gone and stayed, you'd be dead. We'd all be dead. Because you would have charged on in, gotten killed, and you never would have set the explosive."

"At least I would have some honor left. Did you even try to save him?"

Lithia was impossible. Sure, Dione had her flaws, as Bel had made abundantly clear, but at least she could admit that to herself. One day, Lithia's obstinacy would get her into bigger trouble than she could handle.

Before Dione could respond, there was a terrible creaking sound, then a burst of light hit the ship. Lightning with no storm? Before she could process the implications of being shot, her head connected with the console in front of her with a sickening thwack.

When she lifted her head, the readouts went black, and if it weren't for the actual viewing glass present in older models like this, they would be in the dark. They were falling now, and Dione's heart—or worse—was in her throat. It wasn't a free fall, but it was uncontrolled. The crash would kill them.

"I can't do anything! We're going to need to eject," Lithia said.

"Eject? Are you serious?" Dione said.

"I inspected everything, and it checked out." Despite being impressed, Dione was still angry, and the pounding in her head wasn't helping anything.

"So now you're an expert on hundred-year-old emergency equipment?" she said. The world around her was shaking and vibrating, and the pain in her head somehow unsettled her stomach.

"You're welcome to stay here," Lithia replied, fastening the tertiary safety strap and tightening her harness. Dione had banged her head because hers was too loose, and if they were ejecting, she was going to be certain that her harness was snug.

This was actually happening. They were going to eject from the shuttle and parachute down onto an unknown planet. A planet that had been terraformed on the edge of space one hundred years ago for some mysterious purpose. Dione buckled the additional straps and braced herself.

"Ready?" Lithia asked.

Suddenly the Nav display lit up and instantly Lithia was back at the controls, pulling them out of their nosedive. Except it wasn't working. They still felt out of control. "The backup systems aren't giving me enough power. We have enough to land, but it's not going to be pretty."

Dione liked pretty things, and was sorry to hear that this landing was going to be rough. Bile rose up in her throat, and she dutifully choked it back down. Almost there. If she was unconscious, would her stomach still feel the need to void its contents? The thought almost made her hope that she got knocked out in the landing.

She could see the tree tops fast approaching. They were going to crash in the forest. *No, no, we are going to land in the forest. Come on. Be optimistic.* Their craft was moving too fast and the clearing Lithia was aiming for was too small. Dione's understanding of physics told her this was not going to work.

15. BRIAN

Brian wiped the sweat from his brow and ignored his growling stomach. It was already hot, even though the sun had only just showered the horizon in gentle pink and gold. He had been working all night trying to fix this damn Artifact plow, and he had finally gotten it. He thought. Jackson came in, right on time. The anxious farmer had been checking in every hour, slowing him down. But that's what he could expect from an Aratian, wanting miracles in nothing more than the shift of a shadow.

"Sun's up, Brian, and I can't have you here," Jackson said, looking out the window. "Wife's up, too, and you know how she feels."

She probably feels like she wants her damn plow fixed. Brian knew enough not to be rude until after he got paid. "All done, give it a try."

"Took you long enough," the farmer said. "Solar's charged?"

"If that's how you left it, yeah." Brian walked over to his pack and dropped a few tools in.

Jackson powered on the machine, and a smooth hum filled the barn.

"I don't know how you do it, but you've got the knack."

"Which is why I come at a price. I'll take my payment and be on my way." *Your wife can reach her own conclusions about where you kept rushing off to in the middle of the night.* Brian studied Jackson's face, and he saw it there. A flicker of guilt.

"Brian, look, there was a problem getting the full amount."

"I see," Brian said. "So how many do you have?"

"Two."

"Two? That's not enough. We agreed on six." Brian strode over to the plow again, caressing its sturdy metal frame. He popped open a panel on the side. "I know you have it. You just don't want to pay. And I don't work for free." With a few swift movements, the humming died off.

Jackson's face dropped. "Don't be like this. I'll leave you the rest at the exchange site, later this month. Turn it back on."

"Later this month? And if my family starves before then?"

"We didn't poison your irrigation water, boy. You did that all on your own."

"Where is it?" Brian watched Jackson's eyes for another betrayal, and they delivered as he glanced over at the grain storage trunks. "Once I take what's mine, I'll set the plow right, and leave. Original deal upheld."

Brian began opening the trunks until he found what he was looking for, ten packages tied up neatly. He took only his six, put them in his pack, and then returned to the plow. Jackson was still sitting there, furious. Brian fixed the plow a second time and sprinted from the barn, eager to leave before he found more trouble.

He had just reached the tree line of the adjacent forest, the nebulous no man's land between Aratian and Ficaran territory, when he heard it. He looked up to see something falling from the sky, trailed by fire. *Only death falls from the sky.* They were old words, ones he remembered his mother saying long ago. He didn't believe them, but they came automatically.

This wasn't death though. The falling object looked familiar, the same smooth metal exterior. A Flyer. And if it was a Flyer, he knew there was only one choice: find the pilot. Home lay to the southwest, and judging by the trajectory, the crash site would be east, not far, but squarely in Aratian territory. If the Aratians caught him with what he was carrying, they would assume that he was a thief and execute him.

Still, this could be the answer to finding his father. He had to risk it. Brian secured his pack and ran further into the forest where his golden maximute was waiting. He sang the words of greeting, and the giant dog wagged its tail and lowered itself, allowing him to hop on. "Come on, Canto." He had to get there first. Every Aratian had seen that crash, and they did believe the old words. They were probably already on their way.

16. ZANE

Zane tried calling again, but it was no good.

Bel was the one who spoke first. It was always Bel who broke the silence. "Did they crash? Are they dead?"

She was standing behind him, gripping his shoulder with one hand as she looked at the screen in front of them. Dione and Lithia were already gone by the time she woke, and she had insisted on joining Zane in the command center. The old security protocols were surprisingly effective after all this time, but Zane had cracked through in a few key areas.

"There's no way to tell. Their manumeds have cut out. The station takes satellite images every few hours. That's when we'll know."

"Hours?" Bel sat next to him and closed her eyes.

"We have to wait until the imaging device rotates back into position."

"What happened, anyway?"

"There's no way of knowing. It's weird, I'm not getting any sort of communications signals from the planet, at least in the area where the anti-parasitics are," he said. He should have noticed it earlier, though admittedly, Bel's condition had taken up most of his attention. Even an abandoned planet would make some detectable noise, but the area where Dione and Lithia had headed gave off no signals, even though it was the region with the old research bases. He emphasized his point by showing her the screen. "None. But the station did pick up an energy surge low in the atmosphere. That was about the same time that the station stopped receiving any telemetry or communication from the shuttle."

"What would cause that?" Bel asked. She massaged her temples.

"If a surge blew that component, it wouldn't be able to send or receive anything. Malfunction. User error."

"Destruction?" Bel asked. He wished she weren't so blunt sometimes.

"That, too."

"Was the energy surge natural or man-made?"

"Man-made?" Zane said. "Not likely. The planet is uninhabited. The station logs say this place was evacuated."

Zane kept his concern about the strange signal dead zone to himself. No need to worry Bel.

"Was there an electrical storm in their way?" Bel asked.

"No, but there are probably other natural phenomena that could produce that type of surge." But it was unlikely one would cut off comms in the shuttle and their manumeds.

"Mmhmm," She still hadn't opened her eyes back up. She was wincing.

He put a hand on her shoulder to soothe her. "How's your leg?"

She wore loose-fitting sleeping pants that she had brought for nights on Barusia. Not shy, she pulled the waistband of her pants low enough to reveal her bandage, which she carefully peeled away. He did his best to look only at the wound.

The scratch was swelling and its color darkening to a swampy green, surrounded by a red itch that signified the battle her body was fighting. Bel covered the wound back up. Zane thought she stood a chance against the infection, but he still hoped that Lithia and Dione were okay and would be on their way back soon. The logical part of his mind amplified his doubts about her chances of recovery and wore down his optimism.

"You should get some rest. Your leg is clearly hurting you."

"As long as I'm able, I plan to be here. Helping. And when the occasion calls for it, napping."

Zane made no reply. He never won arguments with other people, so he tended to avoid them. They seemed to depend more on emotional appeals rather than logic, and that always bothered him.

"I'm going to see if I can speed up those planetary scans. Why don't you work on the manumeds?" she said.

"All right," he said. "But be careful. Your manumed is broken, so I can't reach you."

Bel waved off his concern, but gave him a smile all the same. He tried to ignore the butterflies that one smile gave him. There was too much to do to be distracted.

Zane decided to start back on the *Calypso*. It was the source of the signal their manumeds used to interact. *Why did they just stop transmitting?* The nanotech was probably just interfering. Still it was strange timing for their comms to go out. Reluctantly, he left Bel to go back to the *Calypso*.

Zane was glad he was up here with her. She knew him well enough to give him space. Dione and Lithia tried to talk to him, but their polite interest in his life and hobbies was more annoying than anything else. He just wanted to be left alone, go unnoticed.

The irony of his current attempt to repair their communication system was not lost on him.

Zane found the right console and got to work. He had grown up on ships, though much bigger than the *Calypso*, learning how to maintain, streamline, and even adjust systems. The adjustment bit had been brought to the attention of one of the officers, who, instead of reprimanding him, had given him information about a scholarship to StellAcademy. Quite different from Dione's admission story, he was sure. Assuming the daughters of Alliance power players even had to apply.

An initial check of the software looked good, but he ran a diagnostic anyway. If it were a hardware problem, he'd be lost, so hopefully the diagnostic would turn something up. Otherwise, the nanotech would have one more repair on its plate.

He would check on Bel while it ran. No matter how tough she tried to play it, she was not in good shape.

The walk back felt longer, his mind focused only on her. He should have insisted she get some rest. She might actually listen to him, unlike the others.

He reached the command center to find his worst fears confirmed. Bel, lying on the floor, eyes closed. He rushed to her.

The green lesion on her leg glowed faintly through the bandage and thin fabric, and he thought he detected a few other luminescent regions under her arm and neck, but it was probably his mind playing tricks.

"Bel," he said. Her eyes opened slowly, as if their lids had been stuck shut.

"I'm here. Just needed to lie down. The floor is nice and cool."

He reached out a hand, hesitated, then touched her forehead. He didn't know what normal was supposed to feel like, even using his own forehead as a comparison, but he didn't need to. He was certain she had a fever.

"You're going to the med bay." It was perhaps one of the firmest statements Zane had ever made. Grateful for the reduced gravity, he scooped Bel into his arms and walked her the short distance to the med bay. He set her back on the medical bed whose scan had sent Dione and Lithia to the planet in search of the right treatment and asked the computer to update him.

"How's the fever?" Bel asked, almost as if she were in a dream.

"Not improving." The medical bed was able to provide a numerical temperature, but Zane didn't see any good in sharing that number. "It's giving you more fever suppressants and requiring you get some rest." He found a blanket in one of the storage compartments and covered her.

"I'm too sleepy to argue." Bel yawned.

"Good," he said, but Bel was snoring before he finished speaking.

Now it was time to tackle the planetary scans.

17. DIONE

Dione white-knuckled her restraints as their craft scraped the canopy and skidded through the clearing. Metal crunched as their momentum lodged them in between two majestic trees.

"We're alive," Lithia said as the dust settled.

Dione hoped so. Her head was burning where she had banged it during their fall. A few fingers to her forehead confirmed what she already suspected. She was bleeding. This head injury couldn't be good for her brain, which was her best asset after all. In a moment of panic she began to recite the digits of pi to herself. It always calmed her down. Dione had gotten to the twenty-third decimal when Lithia interrupted her.

"Did you hear me?"

"Sorry, what?" Dione wiped away the blood that was gathering in her eyebrow. She needed to keep it together. It was just a cut. Head wounds bled more because the capillaries were closer to the surface. *Focus on the facts. They'll keep you grounded.*

"Are you all right?" Lithia handed her a piece of cloth bandage from the first aid kit before wrapping her own headband around Dione's head to hold it in place. "Here, use this," she said. Dione wiped away the blood and was relieved to find only a small cut underneath.

"What in the void just happened?" she asked.

"I can't reach Zane. Something must be interfering with the signal. I think we were hit. I can't find any evidence of a natural source for that much energy."

"But who would attack us? There's no one here."

"Maybe the researchers left behind some automated defense system."

"I guess so," Dione said. This planet made absolutely no sense.

"Check the maps. We need to know how far we are from the Forest Base. I'm going to figure out what happened."

A horrible thought occurred to Dione. "If it's a weapon, won't we trigger it on the way out, too?"

"Now that I know what to look for, I might be able to outmaneuver it," Lithia said.

By her tone, Dione could tell she didn't even believe herself. Lithia was always so reckless. "And if you don't, what happens the next time we get shot down?" She was raising her voice again, knowing full well that Lithia would shout right back. Deescalation was not her strong suit.

"Oh hell, Di, just stop. This isn't about the shuttle, you're just mad at me."

She crossed her arms. "Why can't it be both?"

Lithia sighed. "Just figure out how far we are from the Forest Base. We don't have time for this right now."

"I can check the maps from my manumed. At least we can access the stored data and apps." Dione couldn't turn off her feelings of betrayal. Her anger bled into every word.

"Fine. But I'm going outside. I need to perform a visual inspection, just to make sure that the diagnostics weren't damaged and are feeding me accurate data."

"What do the readouts say?" Dione asked.

"Could be worse. I think I can get him flying again."

"Even with the hull damage? What about the energy weapon that hit us?" This was not Dione's area of expertise.

"I have no control over that. I have no clue what hit us. All I can do is get this shuttle flying again."

That was at least one thing they could agree on. Now was not the time for this argument. Dione would let Lithia worry about fixing the shuttle while she planned their next move. Someone had to worry about what had hit them, and apparently it was her burden to bear.

Dione led the way off the shuttle. After the sterile solitude of space, life surrounded her. The bright warmth of the sun blinded her. A deafening humming overwhelmed her, but she knew that in just a few minutes it would fade to the background as she acclimated, just like she had gotten used to the low buzz of the life support system on their ship. The hum of the bugs was so much richer than the hum of machines, and she wished Bel were here to experience it. Birds were chirping, squawking, and even screeching. She smiled as she inhaled the fresh air. After a week of stale, recycled air, she could taste the pollen with each breath. The day had just dawned, and a light layer of dew coated the grass at her feet.

Lithia had the stun rifle strapped to her body just in case something found them. Dione was absentmindedly strapping her machete across her body and mentally cataloging the plants around them, from large leafy growth to smooth-barked trees covered in coarse spikes. There were both familiar and unfamiliar species around her, but something about the unfamiliar ones seemed strange, even for engineered species. She couldn't quite place it. An impatient sigh from Lithia snapped her back to the task at hand.

Refreshed, Dione got to work, sitting on the edge of the shuttle door as Lithia walked around it. Right before they had been hit, they had lost all contact with their ship and the station. She couldn't be completely sure where they had landed, because the shuttle didn't know, but she used what she knew about their trajectory and velocity to extrapolate their position. Biology might be her favorite subject, but with the right equations, physics was no problem. Even with some of the data missing thanks to the shuttle's power outage, she was still able to get a pretty good idea of where they were. After she established their location, it didn't take long to map out a path that she plotted into her manumed.

"The base is a few hours away on foot, but we'll have enough daylight to get there and back," Dione said, loud enough for Lithia to hear up at the front of the shuttle. "I don't want to get caught in the dark with whatever is out there." She hoped that the maximute was the scariest thing they might find.

After the dull black and gray of space, the green of the forest, unfiltered through a viewing glass, was brilliant. And beautiful. But it was more than the color and the smells. So many living creatures energized the air around them. The gravity was lighter, like the gravity on the station, and the oxygen-rich air made her feel calmer and more alert, even though her head still throbbed. The bleeding had stopped, at least, though she didn't dare remove her bandage. It might tear away the scab with it and leave her bleeding again. Coagulation was a beautiful thing.

"Dione, you need to see this," Lithia called. She was staring at the front of the shuttle. The composite was scorched. Dione knew exactly what that meant.

"Something shot us down," Dione said. "That's an energy weapon scar."

The sun disappeared behind a cloud, casting all the bright greens into pale darkness and sending a chill through Dione. Her tiny hope that it had been an accident, some natural electric discharge, died.

"We need to leave as soon as possible," she said.

"Divide and conquer?" Lithia looked lost in another time.

"I don't think we should split up. We don't know what's out there," Dione said. She would certainly appreciate some alone time in this strange forest, but now that she knew they'd been attacked, it was not the time to divvy up tasks.

Dione heard something. The thump of footsteps? Most animals would run from a scene like this. What would return? Certain predators. Territorial creatures. Curious ones. Humans.

But there were no humans here.

Dione moved close to Lithia and whispered a warning.

All confrontation gone from her voice, Lithia agreed softly, "I feel like we're being watched. Draw your machete."

Dione nodded, ears straining to single out any useful sounds. Lithia raised her rifle, alert. Dione drew her weapon, ready to kill if necessary. She had learned that lesson. Lithia was scanning the clearing. They put their backs to the shuttle, then listened. Mosquitoes or some new type of itch-inducing pest bit the nape of her neck. Dione kept seeing movement and shapes where there were none. It reminded her of nights spent in a dark room, searching the shadows for monsters, listening for the telltale creak of an intruder.

Dione and Lithia snapped their heads at the same time, in the same direction, to the edge of the clearing at the shuttle's stern. Dione didn't flinch, but she did see something move in the undergrowth. While they were facing one side of the clearing, something charged in from the opposite direction.

Every biology class Dione had taken still didn't prepare her for the surprise that greeted her when she turned around.

18. DIONE

"Lower your weapons. You've trespassed into Aratian territory."

A human being, speaking the common galactic tongue, was yelling at her. He held up a gun in his hand. Sweat was his most prominent feature, followed by some nervous foot shuffling. Dione had never been held at gun point, at least not in real life. She had played quite a few holo games with Lithia, but that experience didn't prepare her for this, having a real gun pointed at her. She was pretty sure this one contained bullets.

"Lithia, are you seeing this?"

"I do have eyes, yes," her friend replied.

"He's pointing a gun at us."

"Put your weapons down," the man said.

Dione placed her machete on the ground. Lithia stood defiant, rifle raised.

"Put it down, child."

"I will, as soon as you tell me who you are." Though she was trying to hide it, Dione heard the uncertainty in Lithia's voice.

"You don't ask the questions here, demon." Dione saw something move out of the corner of her eye and turned back to the man. Weapon still pointed, he took a horn from his belt and put it to his lips. Its sound echoed through the trees, scattering birds. That could not be good.

"I'll say it again, child, put the gun down, or —" but the man never finished his sentence. A rock came flying from the opposite end of the clearing, hitting him square in the head. In his moment of confusion, Lithia didn't hesitate. She shot him, and didn't flinch like Dione when he hit the ground with a thud. She aimed in the direction the rock had come from.

"Who's there?" she said.

Out of the foliage stepped a young man, about their age, hands in the air as a show of submission. He wore a gray sleeveless shirt and loose fitting pants. His eyes were dark brown, but bright, and his tan skin was taut over strong arms. His black hair was long, tied back in a short ponytail. He was smiling.

Despite the danger of the situation, Dione thought he seemed trustworthy, or at least not dangerous. He had created a distraction for them. She tried to tell herself that it wasn't just because he was one of the most attractive guys she had ever seen, but even she didn't buy that.

"I'm Brian," he said. "I know you have little reason to trust me, but that tracker scout just called the rest of his party here. I don't know how they got here so quickly, but we need to go. I can help you."

"And why would you do that?" Lithia asked. She still aimed the rifle at him.

"Because if you came down in that Flyer," he said, nodding to their shuttle, "then I could really use your help. I've been looking for a pilot."

"The shuttle, or Flyer, or whatever, is badly damaged. It needs repairs before it will fly again," Lithia said.

"I know where we can find another Flyer," he said. "We have several."

"Then why do you need our help?" Dione asked.

"We don't know the spell, the key, to unlock them," he said. "You do."

Dione nodded to Lithia, who lowered the rifle. He had said 'we.' Clearly there was more than one group of people on this planet. After all, this Brian guy did not seem to be working with the man who had pointed a gun at them. Had the weapons that crashed their shuttle taken down a few other ships? Were the survivors of those crashes here?

"Did your ship crash here?" Dione asked.

Brian raised one eyebrow. "Um. I was born here."

The theory budding in Dione's brain was crushed. Luckily, Lithia changed the subject with her own, more pressing question.

"Who are these trackers, and what do they want with us?"

"There's no time to explain now. Just know that if they catch us, they will kill us, or worse."

"Why are they after us?"

"Because only demons fall from the sky, or so the saying goes."

"Then why are they after you?" Dione said.

"They are Aratians, and I am not," he said. "Please, we have to leave now."

"What's an Aratian?" Lithia said.

"I'll answer all of your questions later, but there's no time now." A horn bellowed in the distance. Dione had no doubt it was in answer to the unconscious man in front of them.

"Di, he knows more about this planet than we do. He saved us. We should go with him, at least for now," Lithia said. Before she could argue, Lithia turned to Brian. "I'm Lithia, and this is Dione." He nodded to Lithia, and when his eyes settled on Dione, warm with welcome, they widened in surprise. He called out a warning, but it was too late.

Dione felt tiny sharp claws scurry up her leg, spiraling around her body, leaving a warm, wet trail. The cuts on her back tingled as the foul-smelling liquid soaked through her jacket. She tore off the jacket, but her tank top was already damp with something awful. The bandage Bel had applied to her wound had thankfully protected it. The furry creature ended up on her head before jumping onto the shuttle and disappearing into the branches of a tree. The effect was immediate. A putrid scent rose from her like heat off of pavement.

After that first whiff, Dione didn't know how she was going to breathe. Lithia took a few more steps back, her nose wrinkled in disgust.

"Tracking squirrel," Brian explained, his lip curled. "Now we really need to go. We'll be easy to follow until we reach the river. Leave that jacket here, though. It may throw them off for a little bit."

Dione didn't move. She could feel the spray soaking into her clothes and her hair. She thought she might vomit, in front of the incredibly attractive Brian, no less. But nothing, not even vomit, could do more damage to her appeal than the tracking squirrel already had. *Those terraformers were messed up, that's for sure.*

Lithia grabbed both packs and a few other supplies from the shuttle while Brian took everything of use, including their assailant's gun. A horn sounded again, closer than before.

"What's with the horn? Don't you have communicators?" Lithia said.

"The communicators were taken away decades ago. Follow me," he said, leading them out of the clearing.

Who had taken them away? Where were they? Dione and Lithia crashed inelegantly behind him. She imagined, uneasily, that their trail would be easy to follow, soul-crushing stench or not.

Dione was in the back, running along with surprising ease, grateful that her speed allowed her to breathe in fresh air. The combination of the lighter gravity and the slightly higher oxygen gave both her and Lithia an edge that allowed them to keep up with the much fitter Brian.

Lithia stopped so suddenly that Dione, who had been staring at the ground, watching for things to trip over, nearly ran into her. As soon as Dione looked up, she saw it. A maximute. Even with the scaled drawing and detailed notes, she had been completely unprepared for how large they would really be. All three of them could have climbed comfortably on its back, and considering it had a harness, it looked like the giant dog was expecting it.

"Dione, it's one of those dogs that you showed us," Lithia said.

Dione simply nodded, because now that she had stopped moving, the pungent cloud had settled back around her, making her reluctant to open her mouth.

Brian approached his maximute and gave it a loving scratch on the neck.

"This is Canto." Even Brian, tall as he was, had to look up to meet its gaze.

"Can I?" Dione asked, reaching out her arm.

"Sure," Brian said.

She stepped forward and gently touched the golden fur on his neck. Canto pulled his ears back and stuck his tongue out.

"He likes you," Brian said, smiling. Lithia also stepped forward to pet Canto.

A creature like this couldn't easily maneuver in the forest, but she imagined it could reach remarkable speeds on an open plain.

She heard Brian speaking to the dog, but she couldn't make out what he was saying. Then, it almost sounded like he was singing to him, and as if he understood, the maximute cantered off into the woods.

"Canto will create a secondary trail to confuse the trackers, then double back and meet us at the river. We're close to the river now, but we can't stop moving," he said.

Lithia handed Dione one of the self-filtering water bottles from her pack, and said, "After we get to the river, you get to carry both packs."

After they all had some water, they continued at a slow jog toward the river. The undergrowth was thick here, and Dione realized that they were no longer on any sort of trail. As soon as Dione heard the rushing of water, she raced past the others, and jumped in the river before anyone could tell her otherwise. The cold water washed away the power of the stench, but all of the scrubbing couldn't completely eliminate the odor. Dione whimpered as she scrubbed her beautiful brown hair in vain. She could almost feel it seeping into her split ends. She knew what she had to do.

She splashed out of the water toward the bank, cool in the shade of the trees, and dug around in her pack until she found it. A knife. Without an ounce of hesitation, she sawed off her contaminated pony tail, one chunk at a time, and tossed it in the river, to be washed downstream. She breathed deeply and smiled. She would be sporting the longer-in-the-front look, but it was nothing a well-placed headband couldn't handle.

Lithia stared at her, shocked probably, that she had done something so impulsive. Brian looked at her and chuckled.

"I like it," he said, "but there is one final touch we need to add that you might not like." And with that, he scooped up a handful of mud and smeared it down her arm. She would've been angry if his touch weren't completely electrifying. If she was going to get covered in mud, then she certainly didn't mind that he was the one doing it. He smeared mud down her arms and legs while Lithia burst out laughing.

"Once you dry out and Canto gets back, we can press on."

"Why did that guy call me 'demon?'" Lithia said.

"Like I said, *only demons fall from the sky*. The Icon supposedly doesn't shoot you down unless you're bad. I don't believe in all that, though," he replied.

"Well, we're not demons. We're humans," Dione said. This Icon sounded like the weapon that shot them down. She made a mental note to ask about it later.

"I'm more upset he called me 'child,'" Lithia said.

"Then be glad you weren't born an Aratian. All unmarried women are called child. Even the old spinsters."

Lithia rolled her eyes. "Of course, they are. Welcome to life outside the Bubble, Di." She looked back to Brian. "But let me guess, your people, they're enlightened, right? They respect all people equally?"

Brian laughed. "I wouldn't say enlightened, but at least better. Equality is a luxury none of us can afford. My people are called the Ficarans. Where do you come from? What do you mean by 'bubble?'"

Before Dione could answer, Lithia said, "How did you end up here?"

Brian looked at her for a long moment. "It depends on who you ask. The Aratians believe that the Farmer created us all, and gave us everything we would need to thrive."

"But you're not Aratian," Dione said. "What do you believe?"

"Ficarans believe that the Architect came to us and revealed the Farmer's lies. She told us that he did not create us."

Dione furrowed her brow. "But is that what you believe?"

"I think that the Farmer was a liar, but the Architect, well, my people almost worship her as another god, even though that's exactly what she didn't want. My father... he didn't think she told us everything, that she wanted us to discover it for ourselves. He thought we came from somewhere else, like the southern island."

Dione turned to Lithia, who was giving her the best "what the hell" look that she had. The Farmer? The Architect? Dione tried one more time for answers. "If the Farmer or the Architect didn't create you, then how did you get here?"

"Good question," Brian said, but he quickly changed the subject. "So are you from the southern island? No one has ever come from the southern island before, but no one has piloted a Flyer either, at least since the Great Divide."

Lithia replied immediately. "Yes. The southern island."

Dione gave her a look, but Lithia ignored her. Brian perked up a bit. "Have you met any Ficarans who reached your shores?" He sounded hopeful.

"I'm afraid not," Lithia said. Brian's smile faded. "We've come to find some medicine for our friend back home who's very sick. There's a building in this forest, not far. Can you take us there?"

"The temple?" he asked.

"I'm not sure. Here's the map," Dione said, showing him on her manumed.

"Yes, that's the temple. I'll take you there, though I doubt you'll find what you're looking for."

"Why not?" Dione said.

"It's been mostly cleared out. There's not much left to go through."

"We have to try," she said. They didn't have any other leads.

Brian seemed hesitant. "I have one condition. Help me start a Flyer."

Dione wondered why he wanted one so badly, but it wasn't that strange to want a fast method of transportation. "What do you need a Flyer for?"

At that moment, Canto bounded through the trees and stopped in front of his master. Brian scratched behind his ear, hummed a command, and the dog lowered himself so that they could mount him.

"We've spent enough time here. We need to move on," he said.

As if on cue, a horn blared in the distance, farther than the first time they had heard it in the clearing. They were certainly not out of the frying pan yet, as Lithia's grandpa liked to say.

The three climbed on top of the large, furry dog, Brian in front, Dione, mostly dry, in the back, and Lithia in the middle. Dione was pretty sure that Lithia was holding on to Brian a little too tightly, but she didn't say anything. The mud-covered girl never got the guy, and she had bigger problems to worry about than vying for some stranger's attention, no matter how unbelievably hot he might be.

19. DIONE

Dione was surprised how fast the maximute could move through the trees. Eventually they reached a point where the growth in the forest was so thick that it was easier for them to walk and give the maximute more freedom to maneuver. Brian sent Canto off to make another false trail. Dione had never seen such a well-trained animal before. He seemed to respond to a variety of musical commands, and even though the tunes were brief, she could tell Brian had a beautiful voice.

Dione was still trying to identify the plants she saw. This place had been terraformed, certainly, but there were some odd choices. Many of these trees were hard to grow outside of their original habitats. Like the *Bolma* tree over there, which usually grew in much cooler climates. *Bolma* sap was an efficient binding agent, and would be a useful natural resource. The *Bolma* she walked past had been grafted with some other hardier tree, but these types of tree grafts were notoriously fragile. The tree was old, not a recent addition. Clearly the terraformers hadn't been here in decades. How had it lasted so long without constant maintenance?

There was something carved into the tree. A symbol. A triangle with a spiral inside that closed off into a circle. A trail marker? She would have to ask Brian.

Dione looked up to realize she had fallen behind. Lithia and Brian were several meters in front of her, laughing. Dione bit her lip. Lithia certainly knew how to make new friends. This always happened. She thought someone was cute, then Lithia met them, and there was no hope for her. Lithia was beautiful. Standing next to her was like putting a duck next to a peacock. There was nothing wrong with the duck until you saw the peacock. And Lithia was a million times better at flirting. If the roles were reversed and Lithia were mud-covered and putting off some residual squirrel stink, Brian still would have been more interested in her.

She was being ridiculous. There were a million other more important things to think about, like avoiding the trackers, or even observing the terraformed world around her.

Dione noticed an odd looking flower and decided to turn her thoughts to that. There was something off about it that she couldn't put her finger on. It was large, nearly the size of a bush, and its leaves were thick and green with red veins. She thought it was pulsing.

"Hey, Lithia, take a look at this," Dione said.

Lithia was not paying attention. She was still flirting with Brian. Until suddenly, she was not. She stumbled and fell, but she wasn't getting back up.

Lithia screamed. When Dione turned, she saw only Brian. She rushed forward to see that Lithia had been pulled into the ground and was holding onto the stun rifle, which was balanced over the opening to the hole. It had been the only thing to save her from being swallowed completely.

"Something's got my leg!" Lithia cried out.

"What is it?"

"It's pulling me down. Help!"

Brian was already grabbing her underneath her arms, but as he pulled, Lithia screamed again.

"My leg! It's pulling harder."

"Brian, hold her up, but don't pull," Dione said.

Dione looked at the stun rifle. There was no way to grab it without disturbing Lithia. Its strap was around her shoulder and she was still using it to stay above ground. If Brian let go, it would be the only thing to save her.

"What did it look like?" she asked.

"I didn't see it," Lithia said.

"I've never heard of a creature like this," Brian said.

Dione looked around. There had to be something. Her machete was useless. The culprit was too far down, whatever it was.

"I'm slipping," Lithia said, true panic edging into her voice.

Dione saw divots in the ground where Brian was being dragged forward by the creature's pull, too. She needed to try something fast.

Dione grabbed the water bottle from her bag and poured it down the hole.

"Anything?"

Lithia shook her head quickly. "Nothing. There's no time for the scientific method, Dione! Shoot it."

"With what? I can't exactly take your rifle."

"The gun the tracker pulled on us."

Dione had forgotten about the pistol Brian took from the man in the clearing. She grabbed it from the holster at his side and took aim.

"I can't get a shot."

"Do something!" Lithia said.

Dione aimed the pistol, but couldn't bring herself to pull the trigger. Lithia was squirming, and she was just as likely to shoot her friend as she was to shoot whatever had her.

"This won't work," she said, returning the gun to its holster. She picked her water bottle back up and tried to think. What else did she have? How could she figure this out? She had already lost the professor, and cosmos be damned if she was going to lose Lithia, too.

Dione cursed and threw the empty water bottle. Seconds later she heard the crunching of metal and saw nothing but a hole where the bottle had been. She had been standing there a few minutes ago, looking at that weird plant. But the plant was gone. Things began to click into place.

"It's that plant. The creepy one."

But this wasn't typical plant behavior. Pulling like this involved muscles. Venus fly traps used rapid growth to quickly change their shape and catch flies, but even rapid growth couldn't be sustained for this long. Probably. Dione remembered the professor's words. *Sometimes the lizard is actually a strange bird.* Could this be a new type of *pseudophyta*?

"Lithia, is it pulling in bursts, or steadily?"

"Steadily." Lithia whimpered. "Dione, it hurts. I think it has teeth or thorns, or something." If it was pulling steadily, it had to be a muscle, not cycles of rapid growth. This was no plant.

She looked at Brian who said nothing. He was completely focused on keeping Lithia out of that hole. If it wasn't like the plants she liked to study, then maybe it was like something else. Dione glimpsed another flower with pulsing red veins. She pulled her machete from its sheath.

"Brian, Lithia, hang on."

Dione sliced underneath the bloom with her blade parallel to the ground. When the bloom fell away, there was nothing left underneath except a hole. It screamed. No, that was Lithia. Lithia screamed.

"What happened?" Dione said.

"It pulled really hard for just a second, but she feels lighter now," Brian said.

Lithia was crying and clenching her jaw.

Dione saw one of the flowers emerge from a hole nearby, prepared to lay its trap.

"Found another. Get ready."

Thwack. Another bloody blossom. Another cry of agony.

"She just passed out," Brian said to Dione's back, "but I think I can pull her out."

"No, wait." Dione watched as Brian pulled and the flowering angler worm pulled back. Brian was at the edge.

This isn't working. Why isn't it working?

This creature didn't need its appendages to perform vital, life-sustaining functions. It was like cutting off fingers or toes. All she was doing was torturing it. Dione needed to find its nerve center and stop the pull signals before they even started. But that nerve center was probably underground. Unless its tentacles were a necessity because it was fixed to the ground and needed large prey to survive.

She glanced around, trying to remember where the flowers had been, looking for the pattern, until she saw it. A young tree that was practically in the center of the flowers she had destroyed. The wolf among sheep. The animal parading itself as a tree.

Dione raised her machete and hacked at the tree, leaving a deep, bleeding wound in its trunk. It was tough, but not as tough as wood. Dione heard Brian grunting to hold on to Lithia who was no longer able to pull up on the rifle.

"Dione, I can't hold her!" Brian yelled across the clearing. "It's pulling me in, too."

"Just a few— " *Thwack!* "—more seconds." *Thwack!*

The tree was still standing but its connection to its tentacles had been severed. Dione heard Brian and Lithia topple backward and rushed to help them. Brian lay on his back, panting. Dione looked at Lithia's bare foot. The grabby tree had gotten away with her boot and left some nasty lacerations, making her ankle swell. She couldn't tell if it was broken. The rest of her leg seemed okay.

Dione wrapped a bandage around Lithia's ankle and splashed a little water from her reserve canteen on Lithia's face, which was enough to wake her.

"Brian," Dione said, as Lithia stirred, "thank you. If you hadn't been here, she'd be gone." Lithia yelped as Dione pulled the bandage tight.

"Don't thank me yet. She's not going to be able to walk," Brian said. "I've seen injuries like this before. She needs to stay off it for a few days at least."

"Is it broken?" Lithia frowned.

"No, but it's a bad sprain," he said.

Overhead, the sky was growing dark rather quickly. Dione could smell a storm building.

"We need to get to shelter. Now," Brian said. "The temple's not far, but I haven't been around here in almost a year. I don't know what else is out here."

"Won't they catch us?" Dione asked.

Brian shook his head. "A storm is coming. A bad one. I don't know what you all have in the south, but if we don't find shelter soon, we risk getting caught in a mudslide. With any luck, the trackers will turn back."

***

Soon, Brian's maximute returned and carried Lithia the rest of the way to the temple.

"We're close now. I'm sending Canto back home. He won't fit through the door anyway, and I don't want him caught in the rain." Brian flipped a colored disc on the harness and sang to him again, a tune they hadn't heard him use yet, and the maximute ran off. Without Canto, Brian and Dione took up residence on either side of Lithia, supporting her as she limped along, in too much pain to speak.

"Why do you sing to him?" Dione asked.

"It's how we communicate. All domesticated animals, and even a few wild ones, respond to these spells, though I've taught Canto quite a few new tricks," he said.

"Spells?" she asked.

"How would you explain it? Every maximute responds to these songs from birth. We don't teach them. Like that one. He knows that means 'home.' He always has. I may not believe in gods, but magic? I see that with my own eyes every day."

It certainly seemed like magic, but Dione knew there was a scientific explanation. Science allowed for miracles, but not magic.

"There has to be some explanation," she said.

Brian smiled. "You sound like my father. I look forward to hearing your explanation, once you figure it out."

Dione liked that about Brian. He kept an open mind.

"There," he said, pointing to a large structure, barely visible through the trees.

"When you said temple, this is not what I imagined," Dione said. She had pictured statues and incense, maybe even chanting. This building was like a stack of crisp circles. Many of its windows were broken, and vines wove their way up one side. Graffiti on the walls had faded, but it looked like the building where she took her cell biology series. The space station computer had called it a research base, the Forest Base, and that was still mostly what it looked like. From the outside, at least.

"It's been abandoned. All of its valuables have been moved to other locations in less contentious areas. This temple is too far from the Vale Temple, the Aratian settlement, for them to use it. The Vale Temple is a much more defensible location."

They entered the building. The place had been eviscerated. The bare white walls of the vestibule were yellowing, and evenly spaced holes betrayed missing artifacts like plaques and shelves. They walked further inside to find that the rooms off the main hallway were also empty.

"I'm surprised they didn't rip the piping out of the walls," Dione said to Lithia.

"To destroy the structure would have been a crime to Aratians and Ficarans alike," Brian said.

"But letting it crumble is fine," Lithia replied. She limped over to a wall so that she could lean against it. Dione was glad to see that she could put pressure on her foot, even if it hurt.

As the three prepared to take a rest, a horn blared outside.

For the first time, Brian looked worried. "They're still coming, and they're looking for shelter. I thought they would have turned back before now. We need to hide. If we go to the sublevels—" He stopped and pulled out his gun. It was the same gun that the man in the clearing had pulled on them, and now he was pointing it straight at them.

"What are you doing?" Dione said, hand resting on the hilt of her machete. Lithia didn't even try to aim the stun rifle.

"Come out," Brian said. "Now."

20. ZANE

Zane stood up in that panic that often accompanies waking up in a strange place. He had fallen asleep on the bed next to Bel, intending on taking a brief nap. Once he could discern Bel's shape on the bed expanding and contracting with breaths, he relaxed. His manumed said that he had been out for a few hours. He had needed it, and he wasn't ashamed to say so. So many people pushed themselves beyond their limits, but Zane thought this was stupid. He needed to do his best work, which meant he needed to be well rested and focused.

After checking Bel's vitals, he was satisfied that she had not gotten worse. Her fever was down a degree. In the light of the infirmary, no eerie glow emanated from her leg wound or anywhere else, but he knew it was still there.

He headed back down the hall to the command center. The new scans would be complete. A notification on his manumed assured him that the *Calypso*'s transmitters were perfectly functional, and that they had not been the reason he lost contact.

Deep down he had known that. It was too much of a coincidence for the shuttle's communications to fail at the same time they got to the planet. Unless the shuttle had been destroyed.

Zane's stomach dropped after he examined the scans. No sign of the shuttle. At all. Even if it had been completely destroyed, there should be debris or evidence of damaged trees. But if the pieces were so small that they couldn't be detected, there might be no physical evidence left.

Still, he had expected to find something. Even a small change. He was really expecting to find the shuttle, damaged, but intact. It was unlikely that a crash would completely pulverize it. Maybe the imaging scans had missed it.

No, *he* had probably missed something. He needed to take a closer look. He called up scans from the previous days, eliminating any that had been taken at night. They had crashed on the planet in the morning, and not much would be visible in the darkness anyway.

The scans themselves centered on a very specific area that was divided into regions, almost like biomes: forest, mountain, vale, plains, and lake. This was the region that the people on this station were studying, probably testing different biome adaptations. Dione would have a better idea about that stuff. After all, Dione and Lithia had gone down to a research base in the forest biome. It seemed that the station's rotation was synced up in such a way that it took images of the planet three times a day, mid-morning, late afternoon, and night.

Zane ignored the last night's photos. Instead, he focused on the most recent images, taken around late afternoon yesterday, before they even arrived. He put the two images up, side by side. He looked over the general stats for each biome it had labeled, focusing in on the forest biome.

He didn't notice anything unusual. The general stats like temperature and precipitation seemed normal, and his visual inspection of the biome, slow and painstaking, revealed nothing.

Zane wracked his brain for another straw to grasp. Maybe looking at a scan from the same time yesterday, the mid-morning scan? That would reveal more, right?

Zane tried to feel hopeful as he called up the previous day's image, again looking for some change that might give him hope. A disappearing bush, a metallic gleam of the shuttle in the sunlight, anything. Looking at the images side by side, Zane found no change, but that was even stranger. Everything was the exact same, down to the birds in the canopy, including the hawk with a small red-feathered snack in its beak.

The images that were supposed to be from today were copies of yesterday's images. Of course there was no evidence of the crash. The current images were missing. Something strange was going on. When he looked into the metadata, he realized that it had only been edited to seem like the new scans. The real image set was nowhere to be found. He looked further into the archives and found that significant portions of the data had been erased. Some of the biomes had no coverage whatsoever, though he hadn't bothered to check before. Every image was gone. The vale biome only had images of one tiny corner. The rest were lost.

A shiver made its way down Zane's shoulders to pool in the pit of his stomach. He didn't know which question should bother him more, why someone had edited the photos or who had edited them. He hoped it was an automated protocol built into the system for some completely sane reason, but things never worked that smoothly. Zane looked over his shoulder, half expecting to see someone watching him from the doorway. He blinked, and realized how dry and sore his eyes were from staring at the screen for so long.

More digging yielded no new information. He decided he would have to catch the interloper in the act. There was just under an hour until the next scan. He would be ready to recover the images and trace the source.

While he waited, Zane grabbed some ready meals from the *Calypso* and took one to Bel. She woke up, looking refreshed. Her fever was down another degree. Maybe she'd be okay after all.

"Did you find them?" she asked, stretching her arms above her head.

"No, someone or something is tampering with the images," he said, explaining what he had discovered and what his plan was.

"Think someone is on the station?"

"I doubt it, but we'll know soon, once the afternoon scans are completed. It's almost time."

"Let's go," she said. She winced when she put pressure on her leg, but walked to the command center on her own.

Zane had the computer copy every image to a secondary location on the *Calypso*. Just seconds after each photo appeared in the database, it was either gone or replaced. Zane traced the origin of the intruder in the system. It was definitely not an automated function, but it also wasn't coming from the station.

The command to modify the image data came from the planet's surface. He was a little relieved that there was no one on the station sabotaging them, but this was replaced by worry when it led him to his next discovery.

"Bel, it's coming from the planet. And some sort of dampening field is emanating from the same place that's changing the images. I think that's why there's no contact from the surface, except for whatever is deleting the images."

"So, they're not dead?" she asked.

"I still don't know. We have to go through the images. But that might explain what hit them, if it was a weapon. Someone is hiding something on the surface of the planet, and the sooner we look at these images, the sooner we'll have answers."

Zane downloaded them onto his manumed, just to be safe, before pulling them up on the larger screen in front of them. Zane's first order of business was to examine the image for evidence of the shuttle crash. It didn't take long for them to find it, because it looked out of place. Several people surrounded it, and though he couldn't see their faces, he knew that they were not Dione and Lithia. There were people there, people on the planet that should not have been there at all.

"Who are these people? Where are Dione and Lithia? What are they doing with the shuttle?" Bel said.

"I have no idea, but the shuttle looks mostly intact. It's very likely they survived the crash, and just can't communicate with us now. Let's look through the other pictures."

Zane called up the pictures of the vale biome and couldn't believe what he saw. He knew there would be a research station there, after all, each biome had one. But the images showed far more than a simple research station. He saw the rows of small buildings laid out in grids and swaths of colorful fabric providing shade over what he assumed was a market. There was field after field, plowed and planted with thriving crops or dotted with grazing livestock.

"There's a whole colony here, Bel," he said. He saw darkness cloud Bel's face.

"Did Lithia know about this? How did she even find this place?" Bel said.

"I know why she was looking into these restricted coordinates," Zane said, "and she wouldn't have come here if she knew. She never would have come here if she thought there was a colony."

He knew what Bel was thinking, and he almost reached out to comfort her before he remembered himself. It's what she was always thinking, even when she slept. The Vens. If they did show up, these people would be even more defenseless than the colonies they had avoided, even if they did have some sort of defensive weapon. If it couldn't destroy a shuttle, it would barely scratch a Ven Marauder class vessel.

"But why didn't we pick them up in the initial readings?"

"The dampening field. They're so rare that I didn't even think to look for one until I stumbled across its source. Now that we know that there are people down there who probably attacked our friends, we need to shut down the dampening field and reestablish contact."

Bel frowned. "But this dampening field doesn't stop satellites from picking up the images. It doesn't make sense."

"I guess they thought that when the readings were unremarkable, no one would bother to actually look."

Bel nodded, but she closed her eyes tight, wincing in pain. He saw her reach for the bandage on her leg and resist the urge to scratch it. He offered her more medicine, but she declined. Zane needed to know where Dione and Lithia were, and now he knew what he had to do. Somehow, from all the way up in the space station, he would need to disable the dampening field remotely, all using hundred year old tech.

Fantastic.

21. DIONE

Something made a high-pitched squeal. Brian stared beyond them, raising his pistol in the direction of the noise. Dione turned. A little girl with plump arms and watering eyes stepped out from behind the corner at the end of the hall. She had dark skin and short curly hair. Her bright orange parachute pants were a stark contrast to the muted gray of Brian's clothes. Finger-sized stains of dirt streaked away from her stomach as if she had wiped her hands clean on her white shirt more than once. Her chin wrinkled, and her bottom lip overextended into a frown.

Lithia was at her side when the first sob escaped like a hiccup. "It's okay. We're not going to hurt you." To Brian, she said, "Put that gun away."

Dione watched him lower the gun. What kind of world was this that he would aim a gun at a child?

The girl, to Dione's surprise, hugged Lithia. "Do you know my cousin? Cora? You look just like her."

"I don't, I'm sorry. My name is Lithia. And this is my friend Dione. What's your name?"

The girl sniffed and took a few breaths before she could speak. "Evy."

"Evy? That's a strong name. How old are you?"

"Ten."

"You're very brave to be out here on your own, Evy. But even brave people get scared sometimes. Are you lost?"

Evy nodded and let out another sob. Lithia let her cry for minute until she had calmed down.

"A-are you Ficarans?" she asked.

"No, I'm not a Ficaran," Lithia said. Evy's eyes widened.

"Then you're Aratian? Do you know my dad? He's First Geneticist Benjamin Bram."

Dione heard Brian gasp, but he said nothing.

"I don't know your father, I'm sorry. But I think we can help you. Are you hungry? Dione, do you still have the snacks you packed?"

Evy looked at Dione and laughed. "What's wrong with your friend? Why is she so dirty?"

Dione became painfully aware of the dirt cracking on her brows when she wrinkled her forehead.

"Anything for the sake of fashion," Dione sighed. She handed a small package to Lithia. "How about a cookie?"

"A cookie?" Brian said, face reddening. "You're giving this Aratian food, when my people are starving? The Aratians won't trade with us anymore, and they produce all the food."

"What are you talking about?" Dione said.

"The Aratians know that my people are starving," Brian explained. "They have plenty of surplus food to trade, but they refuse and then spread lies about us."

Lithia dug around in her bag and produced another cookie. She threw it at Brian, hitting him in the chest. "Here. You sound like you need a cookie, too. No matter the issues between your peoples, you can't expect me to believe that Evy is responsible," she said. "Brian is a Ficaran," she told the girl, "but Dione and I are not."

"My father says it's because the Ficarans are destroying our Artifacts instead of fixing them," Evy said to Brian.

"Well, your father is wrong, and it's killing my people. Sometimes things break and you just can't fix them." Evy looked like she was about to cry again, and Brian softened his tone. "We're not the bad guys. We're just trying to feed our families." He scooped the cookie off the ground, tore open the package, and took a giant bite. From the look on his face, Dione wondered if he had ever had a cookie before.

"Maybe I can tell my father," Evy said. "If he knows it's a mistake, then everything can be fixed."

Brian smiled. "As much as I'd like that, things are never that simple."

While Evy enjoyed the cookie and talked with Lithia, Brian pulled Dione aside. "She's Benjamin Bram's daughter," he said. "Do you know what that means?"

Dione shook her head.

"Benjamin Bram is the First Geneticist of the Aratians. He's the highest advisor to their Regnator, and also happens to be his brother."

"So the Regnator is the ruler, but what does a First Geneticist do, aside from advise?"

"He's in charge of guaranteeing their harvests and livestock, and he runs the Matching."

"The Matching?" Dione asked.

"All Aratian marriages are arranged in order to increase genetic diversity and to reduce the chance of disease. Sometimes the matches are... not desirable, but they believe it's for the greater good. It's one of the primary reasons the Ficarans split off. We believe in the freedom to choose."

"How many people live here, Aratians and Ficarans?" Dione asked.

"I think the Aratians have more than a thousand people. There are over six hundred in the Ficaran settlement, but our numbers keep growing. People want to leave the Vale Temple, especially women. The Aratians treat them like broodmares." Brian's solemn expression crept into a smile. "But if more women want to join our settlement, I won't complain."

Dione thought the Matching made scientific sense, even if she didn't agree with it on principle. Genetic drift would be an issue for the colonists. With such a small population, certain uncommon traits could become unusually frequent. That was fine for something harmless, like colorblindness, but if there was a high frequency of a deadly genetic disease, that could be disastrous.

So these colonists knew about genetics, enough to worry about genetic drift in their population, but they still believed in gods and magic. They had shuttles, but didn't seem to know about the space station. These people were contradictory in every sense of the word. Dione wondered how these gaps in knowledge could arise naturally. Some sort of illness?

"Okay, Evy is important. What are you getting at?" she finally said. She thought she knew, but she wanted to hear him say it.

"She's our ticket out of here. Those trackers won't touch us if we have Bram's girl as our hostage."

The dirt creased her forehead again as she frowned. "What's wrong with you? We're not holding her hostage. She's a little girl."

"She's Aratian nobility. We don't actually have to hurt her. The ransom we'd get would feed my people for a year."

"No. There has to be another way."

"Tell me why it's so bad. We won't hurt her. This is the best luck we could have had."

"Where we're from, you don't threaten children to get what you want. You find another way," Dione said, surprised at the firmness of her tone.

"Then it must be nice, wherever you come from, to have other options," he said, "but when we have no other, I hope you'll be able to do what's necessary."

Dione hoped it wouldn't come to that. She hated how familiar she was becoming with the concept of doing what was necessary.

"We'll hide. Let's check out the lower levels," she said.

If they didn't intend to hurt her, would it be unethical to hold her hostage? Could Dione really put a gun to Evy's head, assuming Lithia even let her? Brian didn't seem like a bad guy, but he also didn't seem to have issues crossing lines. Or maybe it was just that his lines were in different places.

The basement was dark, but Dione had a flashlight. Evy looked at it with suspicion.

"Why do you have a Ficaran light?" she asked.

"A Ficaran light? What do you mean?"

"It's a stick light." Evy pulled a small sphere from her bag. "We use glowglobes." With a vigorous shake, the globe's light brightened, providing a dimmer but wider radius of soft pink light.

Dione stared at it in fascination. What made it glow?

"Can I see that?" she asked.

Evy handed her the ball of light. The glow was emanating from some sludge at the bottom.

"The material allows for some air flow. I've seen the light change color based on what food scraps they put in there," Brian said.

"What's glowing? Some kind of bacteria?"

"Yeah. It was something the Farmer taught them how to do. Can't turn them off, though. You have to wait for the bacteria to settle again. Not great for situations like these."

"But why do you have a stick light?" Evy asked again, impatient.

"They have them where we're from, too. We're from far away."

Lithia and Evy stayed on the first basement level while she and Brian explored the lower levels. Rooms were either locked or left no place for them to hide if someone came looking.

Soon they returned to Lithia, and Dione heard the first raindrops fall on the roof.

"Any luck?" Lithia said.

"Nothing. We don't have time for this. The trackers will be here soon," Brian answered.

Evy's eyes lit up. "Trackers? They're looking for me?"

Dione saw him reach for the gun. "We need to move to Plan B," he said.

"No!" Dione said.

"Plan B?" Lithia asked.

Evy was picking up on the tension. Dione worried about where this situation was headed, yet she felt confident that Brian wouldn't hurt the girl. That would prevent him from using her as leverage.

"We didn't check this level yet," Dione said to buy some time. There was a side corridor with doors that locked, but that was the problem.

"I've tried them all before," Brian said. "There's no way to open them or pick them."

This did not stop Dione and Lithia. Each took a side of the hallway, and tried the doors. Dione finished first, with no luck, and offered to help Lithia check her side. Her limp was slowing her down, but when Dione tried the last door on her side, Lithia shooed Dione away.

"I can do it. I don't need your help," Lithia said. Dione sighed, and backed away, knowing better than to argue with Lithia when she was being this stubborn.

When Lithia tried the last door, the hallway was so silent that everyone heard the gentle click.

"It's open," she said.

"But I tried that door! It was locked," Dione said.

"How did you do that?" Brian said.

"I can't explain it," Lithia said. "It just opened."

They all tried the door handle, but Lithia was the only one who could open it. Dione inspected the door more closely. It was a DNA lock, keyed to open for certain markers. But that didn't explain how Lithia's DNA opened it. A bizarre coincidence? That didn't seem right. She wondered again why Lithia had asked Zane to help her get all those coordinates. What had she been looking for?

The sound of heavy boots thumped on the floor above them. Now was not the time to press the issue.

"Let's go inside, before the trackers get here," Dione said. Evy seemed reluctant.

"But they'll take me home," she said.

"We're on a very important mission, but we'll let you go tomorrow morning and make sure they find you," Lithia said.

"I won't say anything. I promise," Evy said. The little girl's lip quivered.

"We know, but we want your help." Lithia bent down to her level. "We're not from here, and you know so much, you could help answer our questions. I bet you could help us a lot," she said.

"Okay," Evy reluctantly agreed. Dione could see her eyes light up when Lithia asked for her help. It surprised her how quickly

Evy had warmed up to Lithia. This was a good thing, or so Dione hoped.

22. DIONE

For the first time since crashing on this planet, Dione felt safe. The door was thick and soundproof. This place, behind the DNA lock, was more than a room to hide in. It was a fully furnished apartment with power. By some luck, or perhaps design, the solar for this part of the base was still working. A lot of the food, mostly cans and lined packages, was still good, because it had been designed for extended shelf life. Brian seemed most interested in the food.

There were only two doors down the little hallway. The first was a modest bedroom, and the second was the bathroom.

"Shower dibs," Dione called into the living room, not waiting for an answer before locking the bathroom door. Getting rid of this mud was priority number one. She stripped off her stinking clothes, leaving piles of dried river silt all over the floor. The clothes went directly into the trash, even though she knew no one would empty it. She found fragrant soap that left her smelling like lime and coconut, and once she was clean, she wrapped herself in a towel.

She went to the bedroom in search of new clothes, but found it had very little in the way of personal items. The wardrobe was practical and well-worn. She raided the closet and found some leggings and a lightweight top. Her synthetic StellAcademy uniform had been suffocating in the heat compared to the light cotton of these clean clothes. They were a little long, but otherwise fit just fine. Her hair, raggedly cut as it was, looked much better without all that mud.

Dione hesitated with her hand on the door knob. She needed just another minute alone, another moment with her thoughts and no one else's.

She sat down on the bed, and looked around the room. The frames on the wall held photos of exotic landscapes and animals, but no personal photos. Displayed prominently on a shelf, there was a violin that had been 3D-printed to look like a swan, each feather in place. Whoever had lived here clearly loved music, because that was the only personal item she could see in the room. If this was the apartment owner's most prized possession, why hadn't she taken it when she evacuated?

Her thoughts drifted back to her own problems. Real problems. The Aratians thought they were demons and wanted to kill them, probably, though Evy seemed nice enough. The Ficarans, well, Brian said they had shuttles they could use. Why were the shuttles locked, anyway? Even though they hadn't searched the whole base, Dione was certain they would find no anti-parasitics here. And if they found the meds and figured out how to unlock the shuttles, there was still whatever shot them down. The Icon, Brian had called it.

After everything, they were back at square one. Square negative one, because now they didn't know if there were anti-parasitics down here at all. They needed to make a new plan, but in order to do that, Dione needed answers. In order to get answers, she would have to go out there and ask some questions. And Brian was already suspicious.

She started to push herself off the bed, but her right hand came down on something hard, hidden beneath the pillow. She pulled out an ornate book bound in leather with gilded edges. A quick glance through the pages told her it was a journal. She held on to it. Maybe it would reveal something about the person who had lived here or about this planet, which had certainly piqued her curiosity.

When Dione emerged, she saw Lithia elevating her ankle while Brian gingerly cleaned it with some sort of disinfectant.

"That feels so much better," Lithia was saying. "I just may be able to walk again tomorrow."

"Give it a few days," Brian said.

Dione watched while she grabbed his hand and thanked him.

Lithia turned to notice her freshly clean friend standing in the doorway.

"Typical Dione. Been here less than half an hour and you've already got a book in hand," she said, pointing to the journal.

"We can't change who we are," Dione replied.

Brian, still in Lithia's grasp, looked up and smiled when he saw her. "You clean up nice."

"I bet you do, too," Lithia said to him.

"I think Lithia's volunteering to assist," Dione said. Brian laughed and released her hand.

"I'm only here to help," Lithia said, winking. She was clearly interested in Brian, and that meant what it always did. Dione didn't stand a chance with him, but it didn't matter anyway. Why was she even thinking about this? *Stupid human teenage brain.* They had more important things to worry about, and if Lithia wasn't going to worry about them, then she would.

Plus, why did she have a crush on a person who pulled a gun on a kid? That should be enough to make her dislike Brian, but he hadn't done it with bad intentions. In a way, he seemed just as lost as she did. He had offered to help them—admittedly, because he needed a pilot—and now he was a target alongside them. He probably could have escaped on his own, but he'd stuck with them.

"Dione, you okay?" Lithia said. She had zoned out.

Enough of this. Time to refocus.

"Yes, we need to come up with a plan," Dione said, salvaging the moment as best she could.

"Is that what you were thinking about?" Lithia said.

"Kind of. I think I'm just tired."

"Here, try this. It'll help you think," Brian said, handing her a warm mug.

"This better not be some weird Ficaran drug." Dione sniffed it, skeptical. "Wait. Hot chocolate?"

"Found it with the other food. It's Evy-approved, too," Lithia said. Evy sat there, sipping from her own mug. They had asked her to stay because they needed her help, or so they said. This could turn out to be true, if a few things fell into place.

"Evy, how did you end up out here?" Dione said. She edged her way through the room to sit near the girl.

"I was looking for bugs. Titus got spooked, and threw me off." Dione smiled. Bel would love this girl.

"Titus? Do you have a maximute, too?" She couldn't imagine how that would work. Evy was so small.

"No, my *machi*. My dad says I'm too little for a maximute. After Titus ran off, I was too far to make it home, so I stayed here, hoping someone would find me." Dione didn't know what a machi was, but she assumed it was some kind of pony or smaller dog.

"Find any good bugs?" she asked.

Evy wasted no time in putting down her hot chocolate, and pulling a giant beetle out of her satchel. "This is the biggest Cela beetle I ever saw." The beetle was dead, thankfully, but that didn't stop Evy from inspecting it in wonder.

Dione glanced at Brian, and even he had a smile on his face, no matter how grudging.

"What mission are you on? Why do you need me?" Evy said.

"Our friend back home is sick. We heard there might be medicine here in this base, this... temple, to help her, but everything is gone. Do you know if the Aratians have the medicine that used to be here?" Dione said.

"We have lots of medicine. We have the best doctors, too. What's wrong with your friend?"

"She was attacked by a monster, and when it scratched her, it made her sick. Now, her scratch glows green."

"That sounds familiar," Brian said.

Evy stowed her beetle, and launched into what sounded like a story she had heard many times before.

"A long time ago, before the Great Divide, demons fell from the sky. The Farmer took thirty men to defeat the demons. But the demons were fierce, and they fought back. The four men who survived along with the Farmer returned, but one of them was hurt. The demon had grabbed him and poisoned him. The poison made his cuts glow green and he got sick. Unwilling to let such a brave man die, the Farmer examined him, then went to the Forest Temple and came back with medicine. The medicine cured the man, and no more demons fell from the sky. Until today." Evy looked suddenly alarmed. "You're not demons, are you?"

"I know Dione probably looked like a swamp monster when you met her, but do we look like demons?" Lithia asked.

Evy giggled. "No. They were horrible. Bodies with giant green scales, narrow eyes, sharp claws."

Dione and Lithia exchanged a look. Dione's heart was pounding. That description sounded like the Vens, and paired with the glowing "poison," it seemed fairly likely that the Vens had been here before. "Are you sure?" she said.

"That's the same story I've heard," Brian said.

"So why do only demons fall from the sky?" Lithia asked. "Because we fell from the sky, but we're not demons."

Evy thought about it for a good minute. "Then maybe it's just usually demons. Not always."

Dione liked this girl. When confronted with facts that challenged her beliefs, she modified them. Many adults who liked to shout over the vids didn't seem to grasp that concept.

There were still so many questions. What was this Great Divide? She had to prioritize. *Figure out if the Aratians have the meds.*

"Do the Aratians still have some of this medicine?" Dione asked.

"I think so," Evy said. The uncertain confirmation of a ten-year-old was a lot to hinge a plan on, but they didn't have much choice.

Lithia had been mostly quiet, but now she jumped in with a question of her own. "Why did the demons fall?"

It was Brian who answered. "The Icon."

"The Icon?" Dione said. "You mentioned that earlier."

"It's a weapon up in the Mountain Temple that protects us," he said. "Don't you know about the Icon? It protects the southern island, too, right?"

"Who runs it?" Lithia asked, dodging his question. She was quite good at that, Dione noted.

"The Farmer gave it instructions to protect us before he went away," Evy replied. Lithia looked to Brian, but he just shrugged. So, no one ran it? Or the Farmer, whoever he was, set some program to run it. At least she could rule out an actual deity.

"Where in the mountains? Can you take us there?" Lithia said, placing her hand on his arm. Dione pretended not to notice.

Brian leaned in. "No one's been there in a long time. It's unreachable without a Flyer."

It was his turn to ask the questions. "So are you going to tell me how you got the Flyer to work? How many do your people have?"

Lithia lied as easily as she breathed. "Our ancestors left us with the secrets of the Flyers. We have a couple more, but we don't often use them."

"Why not?"

"Conservation of resources. We only use the Flyers if we have to, and this was an emergency."

"Do you think you can take the spell off of our Flyers?"

"Maybe, I don't know. But even if I can, there's the Icon. It attacked our Flyer and made us crash."

"Then you flew too high." Brian was matter-of-fact. It also meant that there was no way to leave the planet as long as it was functional.

"So if you don't go too high, you can still use the Flyers without getting zapped," Lithia said. Dione could see the gears turning. "Evy, do you think you can get some of those meds they used to cure the man from your story? They could save my friend's life."

Evy swung her foot while she thought. "Maybe. Cora might have to help me. They let Cora do everything."

"That's your cousin, right?" Lithia asked. "Can we trust her?"

"Yeah. But what do I do with the medicine?"

"Sell it to Hector in the market," Brian suggested. "I'll handle it from there. How does that sound?"

"Good," Evy said. She looked excited to try out some espionage. Dione had doubts about a ten-year-old pulling this off, but Evy didn't seem like an average ten-year-old.

"And don't bother turning Hector in, because he doesn't realize who he's working with," Brian added.

Evy nodded solemnly. She seemed to take this task very seriously.

"Then all we need is a Flyer," Lithia said to Brian.

"I think Victoria, my leader, will help you, but she'll want something in return. She'll want you to unlock all the Flyers," Brian said.

"Why wouldn't we?" Dione asked.

Brian ignored her question. "And I want the one you use when you're finished, no matter what Victoria says." He clearly had a strong goal in mind for this Flyer. Maybe he'd share that with them soon.

"Done," Lithia said.

Dione nodded. It all seemed too easy, which set off warning bells in her head. She mentally put those bells on mute. At this point, it was their best chance.

23. DIONE

Lithia decided it was her turn to shower, and limped off on her own. Evy was falling asleep in her seat, and Brian explored the kitchen some more. He couldn't possibly be hungry after the pile of food Dione had watched him eat, but it sounded like his settlement was experiencing some sort of famine.

Finally, she had a few moments to herself. Dione looked down at the exquisite journal in her hands, the one she had found under the pillow in the bedroom, and opened it up to the first page.

The Architect kidnapped me and brought me here to destroy the Farmer, but she underestimates him. It's not going to work. He'll never surrender everything just to get me back, because he knows it's not what I would want. So Architect, when you read this, like I know you will, realize that this will never work. You seem to think that if I write this by hand, and I recognize my handwriting, I'll realize that the words inside are true. All of these words certainly are.

That witch injected me with something. It's making my mind hurt. I don't know what sort of sick experiment she's running, but I hope it kills me. Then all her leverage will be gone. All those people who trust her, I'd like them to see me now. I think she gave me some sort of drug, because I'm seeing things.

Things I know can't be true. Like, I see my wedding, but it's not my wedding. I'm marrying some man I don't even know and the Farmer is nowhere in sight

Based on the very little that Dione knew about the Architect, this account seemed off. In fact, it was disturbing.

"Brian," Dione called toward the kitchen, "can you tell me a little about the Architect?"

"Sure," he said around a mouthful of crackers, "like what?"

"What was she like?"

He swallowed thoughtfully. "Everyone says she was really smart, and she knew things that only the Farmer knew. At first everyone tried to worship her as a god, too, but she wouldn't allow it. She called the Farmer a false god. She said she was just a person. She was the architect of the rebellion, though. Without her, the Great Divide never would have been possible. What the Aratians see as heresy and defiance, we see as our freedom. The Architect let us make our own choices."

"So what happened to her?"

"That's the end to a longer story, but I'd be happy to tell you." He smiled at her again, and just that one look sent butterflies through her stomach. She really needed to get control of herself.

"Is that the Great Divide that you keep mentioning?" Dione asked.

"Yes. Have any stories like that on the southern island?"

"No, but just because we don't war out in the open, doesn't mean there's no conflict," Dione said. She was thinking about the Alliance, and what Bel had told her about how they were handling the Vens. The author of the journal certainly didn't share these lofty opinions about the Architect, but was it possible that the Architect was doing the wrong things for the right reasons? Was such a thing even possible? Dione wasn't sure yet, but she planned to read the rest of the journal. Maybe it would provide some answers.

At that point Lithia came out of the shower, and Dione couldn't help noticing Brian noticing Lithia's long legs when she walked, albeit clumsily on her injured ankle, into the bedroom. They both jumped when a very loud snore erupted from Evy, sleeping in the chair.

"I think Evy has the right idea. We should all get some rest," Dione said.

Dione woke up Evy and led the groggy girl to the bedroom, making her a little nest out of blankets and pillows. Dione and Lithia had agreed to share the bed, while Brian volunteered to take the couch. It sounded like he was taking his turn in the shower, before going to sleep.

Lithia was already in bed by the time Dione entered the room. When Dione crawled into bed next to her, it reminded her of when they were little and would have sleepovers at Lithia's house. She missed that. The giggling and the staying up late. Dione wanted to tell Lithia about the journal, but her friend wasn't accessible. The wall was still between them, and she felt like only Lithia could dismantle it and let her in. Dione took a deep breath, sighed, and closed her eyes. In just minutes, the exhaustion of the day crashed over her, and she was asleep.

24. LITHIA

Lithia started awake in an unfamiliar bed, in an unfamiliar room. Her confusion at finding Dione sleeping next to her subsided as she realized where they were. She glanced down at the pile of blankets where Evy had been curled up, only to find them empty. She was probably just in the bathroom or something. Lithia checked the chair in the corner for Evy's bag, knowing she would never leave her bugs behind.

The bag was missing.

Lithia was suddenly wide awake. Was Evy going to betray them? What if she led the Aratian trackers straight toward them? They could find a way in or starve them out. She swung both legs out of the bed, grabbed the stun rifle, and crept down the hallway. Her ankle throbbed under the pressure.

Brian was asleep on the couch. She tiptoed past, imagining he was a lighter sleeper than Dione, and left through the door. She was the only one who could get back in, after all, and that fact made her uneasy. What if they forced her to open the door?

About half-way up the staircase was Evy, moving slowly and quietly. On the floor above where they had entered just hours earlier, she could hear the low voices of men and the hypnotic rhythm of snoring. The trackers were still here. What was Evy doing?

When Evy turned the corner of the staircase, Lithia waved her hands wildly to get her attention. It worked. Evy stopped and squeaked in surprise. The little girl held up a finger to her mouth and dismissed her with an open hand.

Be quiet. Stop. These didn't seem like the commands of a traitor, but everything seemed quiet. Then she realized that the men's whispers had stopped. Boot falls echoed above in the empty chamber.

"Someone's here," said a young male voice. "There she is. Sir, it's Evelyn."

Lithia tried to sink into the wall, but there were no corners to hide her. She had no choice but to put her hope in the darkness.

"How did you miss her? I told you to search every inch of this place," said a gruff voice. The snoring had also stopped. It seemed the two watchmen had woken the rest.

Lithia's heart was pounding in her throat. She couldn't possibly make it back to the apartment now, especially with her ankle, and any attempt would give Dione and Brian away.

"I was hiding from the storm," Evy said. "I'm just really good at hiding."

Was Evy trying to protect them? It just might work. If she could distract them long enough, Lithia had a chance to retreat. If Evy had wanted to harm them, she would have given away Lithia's position by now. For a few moments, she felt hopeful. Then the gruff voice spoke.

"Search again. If you missed the First Geneticist's own goddamn daughter, who knows what else is down there."

The young tracker looked down the stairs, his face dark and unreadable with the light of his partner's glowglobe at his back.

His response was immediate. "Alpha, someone's down there!"

"Don't move," the gruff voice commanded. Both trackers pulled their weapons. The older man carried a gun while the younger held a baton in his left hand.

"Don't hurt her!" cried Evy. Lithia couldn't run. There was no chance to raise her rifle. She knew that if she moved, they would shoot, and she doubted their weapons were non-lethal, like hers. There was no place to hide. She couldn't hope to win in a fight. Already three more trackers were on the stairs. Luckily, she didn't see the man she stunned in the clearing. He would have kept looking for Dione.

"I'm raising my hands above my head. I intend you no harm." Lithia put her arms up. The young tracker and one of the newly awoken came and bound her hands. Another took her rifle and her manumed, and for the first time since the crash, she was glad it didn't work. Unfortunately, it looked more like tech than jewelry.

"Are you alone?" the gruff guard asked.

Lithia remained silent. As much as she'd love to offer up a witty retort, she thought that nothing would piss this man off more than getting no response. She was right. He slapped her across the face.

"You answer when spoken to."

"Stop it," cried Evy. "She helped me. Leave her alone!"

Her words had some effect, though she had a feeling that once Evy's eyes were closed or looking in another direction, he would have a few more questions.

"Pack up, but stay vigilant. There may be others out there."

"Shouldn't we look for them?"

"No, now that we've found Bram's girl and the storm's over, we need to get her home. That was our primary mission. We leave in ten minutes."

"Yes, Alpha."

"I'm sure Bram will want to deal with the kidnapper himself."

Kidnapper? Lithia thought about setting the record straight, but she knew it would do no good. Better to hope Evy's own father would believe her.

***

They were out the door in eight. She shivered in the chill left by the rain. It was still rather dark in the forest, but Lithia could see faint light peeking through the trees. Her ankle ached in protest, and the young tracker held her up. She slipped a few times on the wet leaves, but she didn't fall. She was even in enough pain to be a little grateful as she leaned on him.

After a while, even his support wasn't enough to keep her upright. She shivered in the cold, wishing she had put on her jacket before chasing after Evy. At least the leggings she'd found in the apartment were warm, if a bit short. When her ankle finally gave out beneath her, the tracker tried to hold her up, but she fell too fast. She banged her shoulder on the sharp rocks of the forest floor and her ankle throbbed.

"Hold up, she's down," he called to the front. He looked at her for the first time in the light, good light, and his eyes went wide. "Alpha, you need to see this."

The Alpha came over, carrying Evy in his arms, asleep, and for a moment, it was hard to hate him. He handed the girl off to a subordinate, then got down on a knee to really examine her.

"Who are you?" he asked emphatically.

Lithia remained silent. Instead of anger this time, she saw uncertainty.

"Blindfold her and gag her. She'll go straight to First Geneticist Bram. No one is to breathe a word of this to anyone. That's an order."

Why were they taking her to the First Geneticist? What had that tracker seen when he looked at her? A ghost? There had been a DNA lock on the door she'd opened. Evy had set her heart pounding when she said that Lithia looked like her cousin. Were there others running around with her eyes and nose on the planet? The Min genes were strong. She looked just like her father. Just like her grandma, Miranda Min, from the pictures. Now that she was older, she saw it in her grandpa's eyes every time he looked at her. Her resemblance to Miranda had opened old wounds for her grandpa. Her grandfather felt pain when he looked at Lithia, and that was something that tore her heart to pieces. Grandpa Min had lived with them for as long as she could remember. His pain was her pain. He was the reason she was trying to find her grandmother. Miranda Min had been the love of his life, and she hadn't died young, like Lithia had always believed. Miranda abandoned her grandpa and her father, and Lithia wanted to give Miranda a piece of her mind.

Lithia was afraid of that. Ever since they had discovered people on this planet, she'd had her suspicions. According to her research, it was never colonized, and no colonizer had ever come close to this place. It was outside the Bubble. Hell, she hadn't even found anything about the space station, and that's something that should have been in the archives. The restricted ones that Zane had helped her access.

Someone had erased everything about this planet except its existence, and that puzzled her. Had the corporation that did all the terraforming erased it to hide this place, full of their intellectual property? Why hadn't they destroyed it? Maybe back then there had been hope of returning here. Either way, these people got here somehow, and Lithia had already convinced herself that this was the planet where her grandmother had come to start a new life.

Lithia spent the rest of the trip in darkness, thanks to the blindfold. She now had a tracker on each side, helping her stay upright. Finally, they stopped. This must have been where they left their mounts, because she could hear panting and smell manure. The group paused for what she assumed was a short meal before she was loaded onto some sort of animal, and she thought it might be one of those giant dogs that Brian had put her on, though she couldn't be sure. It felt leaner and not as fuzzy. Maybe it was one of those machi things Evy had mentioned.

Lithia hated admitting it to herself, but she was afraid. What was the penalty for kidnapping? Would she get a chance to explain herself? What would these people do with her if they found out that she wasn't Aratian or Ficaran? Her southern island story would only work for so long.

Dione and Brian were probably awake by now, looking for her. Dione. She would never get to tell Dione the truth. If Lithia had been a crier, she would have lost her composure at this point. Fortunately, she discovered at a young age that she was far too stubborn to give in to tears.

She was going to get out of this. Really, it was the best thing that could have happened, because now she was going to steal Bel's medicine herself.

25. DIONE

Dione woke up slowly, unalarmed that the room, full the night before, was now empty. She was usually the late sleeper of the bunch. Her clothes were wrinkled, but still clean. She grabbed another outfit, just in case there were any more tracking squirrels out there, and put it in her pack. She was running low on food, too, and would need to take a couple of meal bars from the apartment's stock. She was no longer optimistic about the length of her stay on this planet. She just hoped Bel would hold out long enough, and that Zane was keeping his cool. Bel had to be okay. She was the most tenacious person Dione had ever met, and considering Lithia was her best friend, that was saying something.

She left her room to find Brian awake and eating. His hair was down, but he pushed it back when he saw her coming. Before she could ask about Lithia and Evy, Brian offered her a small packet.

"Breakfast?" he said.

"What is it?"

"Delicious. I think it's nutritionally balanced, too."

Dione took the package from his outstretched hand and puzzled over that for a moment. It was a long-term ration. Of course it had all of the nutrients and calories she would need, but even after a few bites, she still didn't see how Brian could find them delicious. Edible, sure, but why the focus on nutrition?

"So, that's unusual?" she said.

"Yeah, I may just eat the rest. I found a literal closet full. There won't be any left for Lithia and Evy."

"Where are they, by the way?" Dione asked, looking around. She saw no sign of their presence, but when she glanced back to Brian, she saw a sudden darkness there.

"They're not still asleep in the bedroom?" he said.

"No, Lithia's always the first up."

Both of them were already out of their seats. Brian opened every closed door in the small apartment, and Dione returned to the bedroom to look for anything that might provide a clue.

Evy's bag was gone. The rifle was missing. How had she missed such obvious signs?

"Evy took her bag and Lithia took the rifle. Her pack is still here," Dione said, holding it up. Brian took it and frowned. Dione looked down at the thick silver band around her wrist and the sleeping display. She couldn't call Lithia. Their manumeds were useless without the *Calypso*, except to view already downloaded material.

"Pack up. I may be able to track them," Brian said.

Dione gathered her things and came out to see Brian stuffing Lithia's bag with meal bars.

"What are you doing?"

"I may never get another chance to come in here. When I said my people are starving, I meant it. Every ration counts, and these are even better than the ones the Aratians produce."

Dione took another look around. He was right. Without Lithia, they weren't going to make it back in here, and that thought scared her. What if the Aratians had taken her? Had Evy sold them out? If so, why hadn't the trackers taken all of them?

This planet had too many questions and not enough time for answers. The journal itself raised more questions, but she had tucked it safely in her pack. She would have to keep reading later.

Dione desperately wanted someone to talk to, but Brian was not in the loop. He thought they needed a Flyer to go to the southern island to save their sick friend. He knew nothing about the space station or Zane. Nothing about the Alliance. Nothing about the home she feared she would never see again.

After just a few steps outside, Brian turned to her and she could tell. Bad news was in his face and posture.

"The trackers took her, I'm sure of it."

"Which way?"

Brian took a deep breath and held up a hand to stop her. "We can't follow. We're outmanned and outgunned. It will only get us killed."

"So we let them kill her? Is that your plan?"

"If they had wanted to kill her, she'd be dead and they would have left her body behind."

"Then what do they want with her?"

"I don't know."

Dione wasn't buying it, and sprinted off into the trees. After a minute, the sprint faded into a jog, and finally a walk. She had no idea which direction was the right one. She sat down at the foot of a tree and pulled her knees up to her chest. She felt utterly lost.

What was she doing? Brian was right. Even if they did find her, they couldn't take her from a bunch of Aratians. Dione had run off without a plan, but that's something Lithia would have done. In fact, that's probably what happened. Lithia must have left the apartment for some reason and gotten caught, because the trackers never found them.

A few tears were rolling down her cheeks, and when Brian walked up, she wiped them away. He sat down next to her and put a comforting hand on her shoulder.

"I don't think they will kill her," he said.

"Really?" Dione was hopeful.

"No, not for a while. I think they're interested in what she knows. That will buy her some time."

"They're not going to torture her, are they?" Dione brushed a hot tear from her cheek.

Brian didn't answer her question. "For some reason, they want her alive. They might spare you, too, but me? I'd be a dead man."

"Why? Why do they want to kill you so badly? Do they really kill every Ficaran on sight?"

Brian hesitated. "No, I have goods that they will consider stolen."

Dione dropped her hands to her lap. "So you're a thief. Great. We probably should have just taken our chances with the Aratians then. It sounds like you're the one they want."

"Make no mistake, even if they don't want you dead, they are not your friends. I haven't lied to you, but I suspect you can't say the same," he said. He stared straight at her, daring her to break eye contact. Dione's face went red.

"And as for the goods I took, it's food, and it was supposed to be payment for some work I did under the table for an Aratian farmer. When the time came to pay me, he changed his mind, forcing my hand. My family needs to eat."

His voice was firm but quiet. He was in control, and Dione was the one losing her grip, fighting against the tears burning in her eyes. *Come back. Settle down. Three point one four one five nine...*

After ten more digits, she was back. Ready to listen.

"So you have a plan? Any Aratian contacts that won't betray you?"

"None that could help with this. But if we go see Victoria, my leader, she will help." Brian put a comforting hand on her shoulder, and it was all she could do not to melt into his body. She so desperately wanted comfort, for someone to tell her it would all be okay, but even he couldn't do that.

He continued, "I think I can finally convince her, especially if you can start one of the Flyers. You could save more than just Lithia that way."

Brian sounded so hopeful. He had saved the two of them more than once, and now he had a plan to do it again. She looked into those bright brown eyes and knew she could trust him. She knew he just wanted the Flyer, but she thought there had to be some other reason he was being so helpful. He had to care about her and Lithia, at least a little bit. Because she cared about him.

26. ZANE

Bel was sitting up, but she might as well have been lying down. Zane had been begging her to eat, but she insisted she wasn't hungry. In reality, he knew she just felt too nauseous to eat anything, but she didn't want to say it.

"I want the med scanner to check you out again. You must be starving. You've barely eaten anything in the past twenty-four hours. And don't think I didn't see you throw away most of your lunch." Zane would not have pegged himself as the grandma of the group, but the role seemed to come naturally to him.

"Fine. But it's not gonna change anything," Bel said.

Zane saw her brace herself on the chair when she got up, even though she tried to pretend that she was fine. She climbed back into the med scanner and waited. The machine didn't take long to give its professional opinion.

"You're dehydrated. The supplies are still here to give you fluids intravenously. The process is automated. What do you think?" If he tried to order her, he didn't think she would appreciate it.

"I guess it can't hurt," she said. She nodded to him, and he initiated the automation. Bel didn't flinch. "So I guess I'm stuck on this bed now. How long do I have to lie here?"

"I don't know. It doesn't say. But we will find a way to get Dione and Lithia back, along with the anti-parasitics. In fact, while you rest, I'm going to try something I've been thinking about."

Zane headed to the *Calypso*, feeling tired, even though he had just taken a nap. He wanted to make sure that the ship repairs were proceeding as scheduled. All of the physical damage to the hull had been fixed, and there were only a few minor repairs left.

He climbed down into the cargo bay to check on the charging matrix in person. It was still under fifty percent. Somehow, he knew that if Dione and Lithia didn't return with the meds, that Bel would be dead before it hit one hundred. Maybe sooner, at this rate.

Where were they? If he didn't figure this out soon and get communication restored, he knew what he would have to do. He would have to fly the *Calypso* down to the planet, defensive weapons or not. He wasn't going to let Bel die, even if she didn't return his feelings. Every time they got close, she put up another wall. He could take a hint, but somewhere, deep inside him, he still had hope.

Confident that if worse came to worst the *Calypso* would be ready to fly down to the surface, he prepared to go back to the command center. On a whim, he stopped by Bel's cabin and grabbed the giant textbook, *The Chemistry of Life*, from her bunk. It was lighter than he imagined it would be, and he hoped she would laugh when he read her bedtime stories from it later. But first, he needed to restore communications, and that meant taking down the dampening field. Someone at the Mountain Base was powering it. He didn't know why, but he assumed it had something to do with all those people down there. The ones that shouldn't exist.

Zane thought that if he sent a barrage of small requests and created a feedback loop, he might be able to overwhelm the computer. After all, if the tech up here was a hundred years old, then maybe the tech down there would be as well.

So he tried it. At first, it seemed like it just might work. Each request generated two more, which generated two more, and so on. Eventually, it would be too much and the systems would not be able to handle it. They would shut down, and along with them would go the dampening field. Simple.

For a while he could see those small requests multiplying. They should have been enough to take the system over capacity. But then he realized that something was clearing away the requests at an impossible rate. He slumped back in his seat. It wasn't going to work.

After hours of brainstorming, this was the best plan that he had come up with. And now, he had nothing. There must be a whole team of people working down there or a really good AI fending off his attack, which made sense. This dampening field required an insane amount of energy to maintain, so why would they leave it vulnerable? What could he do that they wouldn't expect? He was just one kid.

He lugged the textbook to the med bay and sat down next to Bel.

"I picked this up for you, in case you were having trouble sleeping. How about a bedtime story?" Zane opened the book before Bel could protest. "Wait. What is this?"

Inside the textbook were not pages, but a hollow cavity which held a single pencil and pages and pages of drawings. No, they were comics.

"Just something to pass the time," Bel said.

"Can I look at them?" he asked.

She shrugged. "I guess so."

It only took a couple of pages to realize that the comics were about all of them on a journey through space. The professor was the spaceship, and each of them had a superpower. They traveled through the galaxy battling evil. Dione had perfect memory, Lithia had mind control, and Zane could control electricity.

"This is awesome. What's your superpower?" Zane couldn't find it in the pages he had read.

Bel shifted in the bed. "I haven't decided yet," she replied.

In the episode Zane read, they were fighting some bug that Bel had brought on board, very small, in her "insect catalog." In a matter of hours, it grew to an insane size. The group teamed up to defeat it. In the final frame, Bel was contemplating throwing out the bug collection that had gotten them into the mess.

"Our passions kill us," comic-Bel said. "But what better way is there to die?"

By now real-life Bel was asleep again, and Zane had an idea.

"I'm going to sneak a small spider in, dressed up as something it wants, then let that spider weave a web in the background," he told himself. "The web will only divert small amounts of power, growing thread by thread until it will be impossible to clear in time. The only way to stop it will be to shut down the dampening field."

He had tried a brute force attack, but whoever was on guard down there was smart. Hopefully not smart enough to catch this.

"One problem," Bel mumbled, apparently awake.

"What's that?"

"Spiders aren't insects."

***

Zane was back in the control center. When the Mountain Base had accessed the system to erase the images of the planet, it had first downloaded copies. It stored that data somewhere, and that was his way in. He would have to find a way to hide his 'spider' in the image files in the brief time before they were copied. And he would have to create the spider.

He set his ambush, making sure that it would be hidden in the image files the next time they were taken. By morning, if everything had worked, he would be able to eliminate the dampening field, reestablish contact, and save Bel.

He went back to tell her the good news, only to find her coughing uncontrollably. She was gasping, red in the face. She rolled her head to the side, coughing blood that spilled and dripped onto the floor.

Warning lights were flashing on the diagnostic panel, and Zane didn't know what to do. Some of the readouts were familiar, but most were gibberish to him. He thought there were more red lights and text than before, and that couldn't be a good thing. There was nothing to do, except stand by and watch.

Bel wiped the side of her mouth with a piece of gauze Zane gave her, her face pale with fear when she saw the blood. He cleaned the blood from the table, and finally the floor. Bel's eyes were glassy, like she was trying not to cry.

"Zane, I want you to know something."

"You need to rest right now," he said. He was afraid of what she might tell him. He preferred to wonder about her feelings, rather than know she didn't feel the same way.

"I'm getting worse. I just wanted to explain why I never—" She broke off to cough again, covering her mouth with the gauze.

"Don't try to talk right now," Zane said, giving her some water. "It just makes it worse."

He silenced the alarm that went off to let him know something bad was happening, and noticed a flashing icon. It had been grayed out until now, so he pushed it. A compartment on the side of the bed opened, and he pulled out an oxygen mask. He inspected it to make sure it was working, then gave it to Bel, who pulled it up to her face and took a deep breath. He held her hand and told her what he had done, and soon, she was asleep.

He worried as he stood over her, the machines quietly whirring and beeping around them. The med bay could keep patching her up, but not for much longer.

27. DIONE

Dione and Brian didn't talk much that morning as they walked toward the Ficaran settlement, or Field Temple, as Brian called it, which she imagined was another research base. Her legs were sore, her back hurt, and she had a lot on her mind. She kept running through likely scenarios in her head, assigning them probabilities, but what good did that do? The Aratians had her best friend, and they could be doing anything from ripping out her finger nails to throwing her a tea party. Dione had no way of knowing.

"We're not moving fast enough," Dione said. "Bel, my friend, is dying. She doesn't have a lot of time. Lithia could be dying."

"We can't go any faster without a mount, and Canto is back at the settlement."

Brian said that the shuttle would help, but she didn't see how. A shuttle didn't exactly scream stealth rescue, and they weren't equipped with weapons. A doubt crept into the back of her mind. Maybe Brian had no intention of helping her rescue Lithia, and was just using her to get a shuttle for whatever desperate reason he had. Probably to impress girls. He was almost as bad a flirt as Lithia. After all, nothing else would explain how friendly he'd been.

She was about to press for details about his plan when a shrill whistling resounded through the trees. She opened her mouth to speak, but Brian put his fingers to her lips and gave her a meaningful glance. Her heart skipped a beat.

"Follow me, and match my pace. It's important," he said. Was it another tracking party?

They approached a cluster of strange-looking trees. Their thin bark had peeled into curls.

"They're whistler trees. If you move by them too quickly, they make a whistling sound. They're a poor man's alarm. Smugglers like to set up base near them, but not too close."

"Why can't we go around?" Dione asked.

"I want to save time. Whoever went by was mounted," he said. She gave him a puzzled look, so he continued, "You said we were moving too slow, and you were right."

"How do you know it was a mounted person?"

"Just trust me. I know what a rider passing through whistler trees sounds like."

They crept through the grove, careful not to sound the alarm, and Brian followed the tracks up a hill. At the bottom of the hill was a small stream, where a large man was picking mushrooms and paying no attention to his surroundings. He was singing some tune Dione had never heard. Munching grass about halfway up the incline was a giant tapir. Or at least that's what it looked like, with its short trunk and boar-like torso. It did look furrier than a tapir though, and much larger. On its back was a saddle.

"Are we stealing his... mount?" Dione asked. "What is that thing?"

"It's a machi," Brian said, "and it's more of a short-term borrow. We'll send it right back once we're close. He's an Aratian anyway."

She put her hands on her hips. "And that makes it right? How can you tell he's Aratian?"

Brian sighed. "I don't recognize him."

"And you can recognize every Ficaran?"

"All the foragers, yes, and he's not one of ours."

Dione was surprised how okay she was with the idea of stealing this man's machi. It was short-term, after all, and she had a good cause. Lives were at stake. It made her think of the Architect and the journal's author. Did the Architect have a good reason to kidnap her and, if the author was to be believed, drug her?

"I may need your help. Listen up," Brian said, climbing back down the hill. "Different tunes are different commands. This animal has default commands it was born understanding. "This one lets it know you want to climb on." Brian hummed a six-note sequence. "These five notes tell it to go faster." He hummed a simple arpeggio.

"What about slow down?" Dione asked.

Brian grinned that wicked grin of his. "You won't need that one."

Brian whistled the brief tune. Immediately the machi perked up its ears and took a few steps toward him. Brian approached quietly, still unnoticed by the man. Brian hummed the same tune he had whistled, but this time, it happened during a lull in the man's song, and he whirled around to see who was there. He whistled, and his machi came running.

Brian stood motionless for a moment, then sprinted down the hill toward the man. Before he could climb on his machi and ride away, Brian tackled him to the ground.

"Dione, now!"

Dione may not have been a perfect singer, but she could carry a tune. She reproduced the six-note sequence he had taught her, and the machi, trunk rolled under in submission, approached and lowered itself to allow her to climb on. She aimed the beast toward Brian and sang for it to go faster. On her first pass, Dione came by too wide. The man tried to sing something, but Brian punched him in the gut.

Dione cringed at the violence. *There's a reason for all this,* she reminded herself.

She needed to turn, and quickly. She sang the arpeggio again, and she was flying, far faster than she expected. There were not a lot of settings on these creatures. Her unexpected speed sent her hurtling by one more time. Pulling on the reins slowed it down some, but it clearly was conditioned to respond to the music.

"Come on!" Brian said. When she turned once more, she had lost enough speed that Brian was able to swing himself on.

"I need her to get home!" The man seemed shocked that someone was taking his machi, but more than that, he seemed heartbroken. *What have I done?*

"We'll send her back in a few hours. My friend is dying. It's an emergency!" She hoped he understood.

They sped away quickly, but once the man was out of sight, Brian sang a different arpeggio, slowing the machi down. It was an older animal, though still strong. Dione was holding on tight to the reins. Brian was holding onto her, his powerful arms around her waist. He pulled himself close, probably worried by her driving. Even after they slowed down, he loosened his grip, but he never released her.

"So how does that whole song thing work?" she asked.

"What do you mean?"

"You said that a lot of animals are born responding to music like that?"

"Machi respond to certain tunes. Some wild animals, too, but the Aratians have been breeding them to strengthen the response. And Ficarans, to a lesser extent."

"Then it's an inherited trait, not learned. It's not magic."

"Does it matter?"

"Of course, it does! The more you understand about the world, the better choices you can make."

"My father would have loved to meet you," Brian said softly. Dione blushed, and was glad he couldn't see her face.

"Tell me more about the machi."

"Most of them can be trained further, but certain responses are in their blood. The Farmer claimed that he created them that way to help us."

More engineered animals? If that claim was true, then the Farmer must have been one of the terraformers. Did that mean the Architect was a terraformer, too? Dione couldn't imagine what kind of a person you had to be to claim that you made people and animals. Still, the animal part might be true, based on what she had found on the station.

***

There was nothing romantic or glamorous about riding a machi with another person. Even the hugging bit got sweaty and gross after a while, so they dismounted and stretched before trading positions. She was sore from sitting and stiff for fear of moving in the wrong way and bothering Brian. After several hours of uncomfortable riding, it was late afternoon.

"We need to stop for the night, but we'll make it to the Field Temple tomorrow morning," Brian said. "The machi is getting tired, and if we send it back now, that man might make it home for dinner. Well, a late dinner."

"So *now* you're worried about him?"

Brian dismounted. "Don't put this on me. You helped. You're the one in a hurry. I'm just trying to help you." He rubbed his knuckles absentmindedly, and Dione could see the bruises there. Evidence of the fist fight.

"That's because you want something from me. Would you be doing this if you didn't want a Flyer? Why do you want it, anyway? To steal more food from the Aratians, help out your smuggling operation? Or is it to impress the girls back home?"

A cloud passed over Brian's face. "You don't understand."

Dione was taken aback. Why was she being so belligerent? A few moments of reflection gave her the answer. She felt guilty. They had taken that man's machi because she needed it. She had sung the songs to take it.

"Then explain it to me," she said, now speaking in a calm voice.

Brian didn't. He hummed a few measures Dione didn't recognize to the machi, which snorted and trotted off into the forest. "We're in Ficaran territory now. There's a small shelter in another mile or two where we'll rest for the night. In the morning, we'll go to my settlement."

Dione looked up at the sky, imagining the station orbiting beyond. If Bel and Lithia could just hang in there for another day, she would make it.

28. LITHIA

Lithia would have spent the day pacing in her cell and banging on the door, but her ankle still hurt. There were no windows—only a small cot and a bucket in the corner. When a bearded man with dark eyes came to visit her, she assumed that he was Benjamin Bram. After all, that's where those trackers said they were taking her. Aside from the same nose, she didn't see much of Evy in this man.

He didn't say a word to her, so when he pulled out an autoneedle and didn't explain, she balked. One of his men raised his gun, and she stopped struggling. Once she realized he wanted a blood sample, she held out her arm. "Go ahead. No drugs. No demon blood." He stared at her for a moment when she said that, and she stared right back.

When he turned to leave, she couldn't help but add, "Or maybe use it to find me a good husband! I'm already seventeen. My expiration date is fast approaching." The man paused and looked back at her again, but he maintained his silence. She couldn't tell what he was thinking, but the whole idea of the Matching that Brian had mentioned made her sick.

She might be terrified, but she was still alive, and she figured there was probably a good reason for it. She got the feeling that the people in this building didn't hit women, unlike the trackers. Or at least, not in public. The very thought made her angry.

She sat in her cell, trying to come up with the most believable story, but Evy could so easily unravel some of her spun tales. A woman came with a tray of food. The woman sampled the meal, as if to say, "Here, we promise we didn't poison this." It didn't exactly inspire confidence, but Lithia was hungry.

"The tea will help your ankle," she said before retreating back into the hallway.

The tea also made her sleepy, but when she woke up, her ankle did feel better. She was surprised to find that she could easily put weight on it, but she was still sore. No more limp, though. She didn't expect care like that out here, especially for a prisoner.

Lithia spent the rest of the afternoon trying to think up a means of escape, but the door was locked and she had nothing that might work as a pick. Maybe she should have been nicer to Bram. She was starting to get hungry again when a girl, maybe fifteen years old, appeared at the door. The first thing Lithia noticed were her eyes. They were her father's eyes. *Her own eyes.* This girl looked impossibly like her. The fear she had held in her heart about this place was now a certainty.

"Hello, Lithia," the girl said cheerfully.

"How do you know my name?"

"Evy told me."

"So you must be Cora, then," Lithia said. Evy had said she looked like her cousin Cora, and she… well, the resemblance was certainly there. Lithia hoped she didn't look as starry-eyed as this girl, though.

"Yes! I'm here to get you ready for dinner."

"Dinner?"

"My father wants to meet you."

"Your father?"

"Regnator Michael Bram," she said, standing up a little straighter.

"And why does he want to meet me?"

"He didn't say. I'm supposed to get you cleaned up and find you something to wear."

For about ten seconds, Lithia thought she'd be able to ditch this girl and escape, but waiting right outside the detention center were two guards who followed after them. Cora took Lithia to a large cylindrical building that looked much like the Forest Base. This must be another research facility. The base, along with the city, was protected by high cliff walls, towering above in the north and east. To the south was the forest, the path by which she had come, and to the west were farms cascading down the steep hills in tiers. In the distance, she could see the moving dots that were men, animals, and machinery. In the town itself, it looked like some sort of preparations were underway.

"What's going on?" Lithia asked, pointing to a group of people assembling what looked to be a stage in the main square.

"The Matching! It's in a few days. It's when you discover who the Farmer intends for you to match with. It's a great honor to be chosen."

The Matching. It's when women were handed out to the men like candy. Delightful.

"How do you feel about the Matching?" Lithia asked.

Cora blushed. "I'm excited. This year I will be matched for the first time. And I'm certain that it will be to my friend Will."

"Wait. The first time?"

"Yes, some people are lucky enough that the Farmer chooses multiple matches. My father thinks that in the future, I will be selected for a second match."

Lithia wasn't especially romantic—that was Dione's job—but this sounded a bit troubling even to her sensibilities.

"What do you mean a second match?"

"People with superior genetics are often matched more than once, to ensure their genes will survive. As the Farmer's granddaughter, my genes are superior."

Great. Another chapter in the saga of genetic superiority.

"Do you want a second match?"

The girl looked serious. "If selected, it will be my responsibility. We don't know when the Farmer will return, and it's our responsibility to preserve genetic diversity until he comes back."

Lithia detected a hint of hesitation there. Cora didn't want a second match, probably because of this Will guy. She didn't know what the Farmer's return had to do with any of it, but she didn't ask. It probably had something to do with the ridiculous belief that the Farmer was a god. "So I take it you want kids?"

Cora looked at her like she was the crazy one after that comment. "Of course I want children. It's also my responsibility as the future Regnator to produce a strong dynasty."

"You said it was an honor to be chosen. Isn't everyone matched?"

"Most are, yes, but some who carry too many dangerous genes are forbidden."

"And what if they want kids?"

"They can take an active role in teaching and childcare. My favorite teacher was not permitted a match, and she has been like a mother to me."

For that poor teacher's sake, Lithia hoped that those who didn't match at least could have... *liasons*, but based on her short encounter with Aratian culture, it didn't seem likely.

The detention center was not far from the base, and soon Cora was leading Lithia up several flights of stairs to what must have been Cora's room. The apartment was similar to the one she had seen in the Forest Base, but this one was larger, probably originally intended for some project manager back when this place was used for terraforming research. It was also immaculate and smelled wonderful, like citrus and lavender.

While Lithia was washed and perfumed, her thoughts of escape were quashed by the guard she knew stood outside the door. The windows also did not open, though she was too high up for that to be a viable exit anyway. Apparently, she was going to dinner. When Cora presented her with an outfit, Lithia was only mildly irritated. She had expected layers of puffy skirts, but instead was given dark green harem pants and a loose white blouse. The clothes were too baggy for her taste, but at least she'd be able to move around easily. When Cora, dressed in an orange and tan version of the same outfit, stood next to her in the mirror, the similarities were undeniable. Cora seemed to notice it, too.

"Where are you from?" she asked.

"Far away."

That answer seemed to reassure her. A commotion in the hallway drew their attention.

"I don't want to go to dinner!" a voice screamed. Lithia recognized that voice. Evy. "I'm not hungry."

Cora opened the door to reveal Evy, covered in mud, squirming against one of her attendants. After being home for less than a day, she had already escaped again. Lithia grinned. She loved this girl.

Evy's eyes went wide and she stopped struggling when she saw Lithia. "I'm sorry," she said. "I wasn't going to tell the trackers were you were. I just wanted to go home."

Lithia shrugged it off. "It wasn't your fault. You coming to dinner?"

"Are you?"

"It's starting to look that way," she said, glancing toward the guard.

Evy thought for a moment. "Then I guess I'll come, too."

The attendant gave a relieved smile when Evy walked herself into another room down the hall.

Cora looked annoyed. "That's Evy for you. I never ran off into the woods when I was her age."

Lithia bit back her retort. For some reason, Cora seemed friendly toward her, and she imagined that having the Regnator's daughter as an ally could be helpful.

***

This is going to be a long dinner. Based on the number of utensils, she guessed there would be more than one course. Two men were already seated at the long table. The one on the right she recognized as the man who had refused to speak to her when he took a blood sample. Next to him was a dark-skinned woman she assumed was Evy's mother. On her left was an empty seat. At the head of the table sat the man who was clearly in charge.

"That's my father," Cora whispered.

The Regnator had light brown hair and blue eyes, but more wrinkles than she would have expected on his sun-tanned skin. Lithia looked hard for the family resemblance, but she saw very little of him in Cora. On his left side were two seats. Cora sat next to her father and directed Lithia into the other seat. Lithia stared at the empty chair across from her, wondering if Evy was coming after all.

"Welcome, Lithia," the Regnator intoned. "My name is Michael Bram. This is my brother Benjamin, the First Geneticist, and his wife, Amelia. You already met my daughter, and my niece, who has been delayed." Amelia frowned at those last words.

Lithia just stared. Was she supposed to say hello? The stakes were too high to be herself. She had to put on her polite veneer, the one usually reserved for her parents' dinner parties. *Don't use their first names to their face,* she reminded herself. Adults hated that for some reason.

"Thank you for the invitation to dinner, Regnator," she said.

Just as the amuse-bouche, some type of fried dough in a green sauce, was being served, there was a racket in the hallway. Benjamin closed his eyes for a long moment and sighed. Then the screaming started. It was exactly the sort of scream someone might make when the world was ending, or if you tried to dress a child in stripes when they wanted to wear polka dots. *Sounds like Evy decided she wasn't hungry after all.*

An exasperated woman dragged Evy into the room. Lithia looked around at her dinner companions and found that she was the only one smiling.

"Evelyn, sit down," Michael said. There was no anger in his voice, but its authority ended the struggle and Evy took her seat. She glared at him.

He wasn't finished with her. "You need to learn restraint, child. A whole party of trackers was sent to find you yesterday."

Evy frowned at her uncle. "I told you I didn't mean to. I was trying to catch a Cela beetle and it kept flying away. Then Titus got scared and ran off."

"Evy, the time for chasing after bugs has come to an end. You need to attend to your lessons."

Evy pretended not to hear him and stuffed an entire dough ball into her mouth at once. The sauce dribbled down her chin. Lithia bit back a smile. *You go, girl.* Michael gave his brother a look, and he nodded. Evy was going to hear about this later, but apparently the dinner table was not the place to escalate a fight with a ten-year-old.

The first course was some sort of roasted Brussels sprouts, still on the stalk, arranged to stand like a whimsical tree. The plate was garnished with brilliant pink orchids. She looked at the generous display of silverware, picked a knife and fork at random, and looked up, hoping for some clue about how to eat it, when she realized they were all staring at her. She put down the utensils and waited. She had missed something. Well, if they locked her back in that room, it probably wouldn't be because she had bad table manners. Probably.

Michael picked up his utensils and took the first bite. After that, the others followed. Lithia watched them all before making an attempt. She tried to gingerly lay the green trunk on its side, but her grip with the utensils slipped and it fell with a quiet *thunk*. Lithia didn't look up to see their reactions. She proceeded to saw off a green bulb and put it in her mouth. She chewed. She swallowed. She smiled.

It was disgusting. It was not a Brussels sprout. Its soapy bitterness stuck to her tongue, but when the others continued eating, she knew she'd have to choke down a few more.

She ate slowly, and stopped eating when Cora did. She seemed like a better model to follow than Evy, who had abandoned her utensils. Her mother hissed quietly at her to use her fork, but with little success.

As they waited for the next course, Lithia braced herself for the interrogation, but it never came. She ate a tasty game bird complemented with a dark purple tuber in peace. The men discussed what sounded like harvest numbers. It was dry, boring talk. Evy thought it was boring, too, and began to fidget in her chair. Benjamin and his wife exchanged one look, which communicated everything, and Amelia left with Evy, who seemed happy to go, even without dessert.

Cora got to stay for dessert, a crisp white fruit in a lavender honey sauce, but her father dismissed her with a nod once she finished. Lithia was alone with the Regnator and his brother, and she was afraid.

"Lithia," Michael began, "I would like to know who—or what—you are, and how you did it."

"Did what?"

"Fooled our DNA test. Altered your appearance."

"What are you talking about?"

"Tell us how it is that you share such a resemblance and so many genetic markers with my late mother-in-law."

"Your late mother-in-law?" she said. Even as she asked the question, she knew what was coming. She needed him to say it.

"Miranda Min."

There was no more denying it. She had never imagined that this planet would be the one or she never would have come here. There were so many other habitable worlds in the appropriate range that Zane found when she gave him access to the Alliance systems. This one had been marked uninhabited. There was no way this could have been the planet. But here she was, confronted with a truth she was not ready to face. Miranda Min had lived here, and died here, too, and Lithia would never get the chance to confront her.

"When did she die?" Lithia asked. She had always known that finding Miranda alive was unlikely, but she was convinced she would beat the odds. Apparently, Lithia had been mistaken.

He seemed confused by her question. "A long time ago. Tell us your trick."

"It's no trick. I'm Miranda's granddaughter."

"That's not possible," Michael said.

"Why not?"

"Clara, my late wife, was her only child, and you are not my daughter. If you tell me how you did it, I'll let you go."

This man was an idiot. Lithia thought the best way to explain it was to ask questions, until his answers led him to the truth. This was how Dione usually convinced her of something.

"I'll answer your questions, but I hope you can answer a few of mine first. It will help me answer." *Don't be yourself, be diplomatic. Smile.*

He raised an eyebrow. "All right."

"How did you come to this planet?" Lithia said.

"I was born here," he replied.

"I mean, how did your parents come here?"

"They were created by the Farmer, then brought here. He created this paradise."

"Why were they created somewhere else?"

"Because the Farmer needs special tools that we don't have here to create human life."

For a few moments Lithia wondered in horror if somehow the Farmer had actually created humans, but then she remembered that Miranda had been recruited, and guessed that all the other colonists had, too.

"How did he create you?"

"I don't know. Do you remember your creation?" Michael asked.

"No," Lithia said.

"Neither did my parents."

Lithia suppressed a snort. She had kept it together this far. She decided not to press the how.

"Why?"

"The Farmer made us strong because we are his seeds. He created the forests and gardens of Kepos for us before he ever knew us," he said. "I assume you are getting close to your point."

These people thought they were the chosen ones. That was going to be a tough belief to challenge.

"Are your tests often wrong?" Lithia asked.

"Until today, they have been correct."

"Then what is the likelihood that they are wrong now?" Lithia said.

"The results are impossible, so you must have done something to tamper with the test." This track wasn't going to get far.

"I was locked up."

"We have never seen a demon like you before, one that could take on human appearance."

"You think I'm...?" They thought she was a demon. The idea scared her. *Shit. Would they actually kill me?*

Benjamin interrupted her thoughts. "Then explain to us how you have Miranda's DNA. We tested you because of your resemblance to Miranda and my niece."

These people were absolutely not ready for the truth, but she was ready to tell it anyway. "Miranda was my grandmother. She had another child before Clara. A son. My father. She left her family to come here."

Michael stared at her a moment, then laughed. "Miranda Min was the Farmer's wife. Her only life was here."

"Test my DNA again. He taught you those tests, right? They cannot be faked."

"He gave clear warnings. *Only demons fall from the sky.* You are not to be trusted."

"We have no records of the demons being shapeshifters," Benjamin said. "Do you think the Architect could have taken Miranda's DNA before she..."

"No," his brother said firmly.

"What if the Farmer himself created her?" Benjamin posited. "Perhaps he is planning his return?"

Michael stood and peered down at Lithia. She glared back in a mixture of fear and anger.

"She is no harbinger. Have her taken back to her cell."

"Don't you want to know where I got the Flyer?" Lithia asked.

Her captor stiffened. "The Ficarans will stoop however low they must, and working with demons is not below them."

She slowly shook her head. "I didn't get it from them. How can you be certain I didn't get it from the Farmer? What did he really tell you about his return?"

Lithia didn't expect them to believe her, but all she had to do was sow a little doubt and coax as much information as possible from them.

"The Farmer promised he would return with others, people who would make our gene pool even stronger. He left me with specific instructions about what to do if any demons should find us in his absence. Benjamin will run more tests tomorrow. We will discover whatever it is you're hiding." The man's voice was cold as the void.

***

Lithia found herself back in her secure room. For once, it was the truth, and not her truth-bending, that had gotten her into trouble. She didn't think they would accept her story, and she was afraid of how far they would go to hear her tell the lie.

She had known from the moment she saw Cora, but it was just now sinking in. All those years ago, Miranda, her grandmother, had left Grandpa Min, hopped on a colonizer, and found a new home. The only problem was that her colonizer didn't stay at its registered location. It dropped off a few people, then continued on, leaving no hint of a flight plan. Based on its supplies, speed, and other factors, Lithia had come up with an unfortunately large range, but this planet was on the outskirts of even that. She had hoped to use the Alliance data to narrow it down, but clearly that hadn't worked. She had ruled this planet out, only to find it hiding the biggest shame of her family: Miranda Min's legacy.

She had no idea what horrors tomorrow would hold, but she doubted it would be all harmless blood tests. She wished she could call Dione. She'd know what to say. She'd have an idea for how to get out of this. Lithia didn't think she'd be able to sleep, but Dione told her once that the brain worked out problems while you were sleeping, so when she was stuck on something, she took a day, got a good night's sleep, and came back to the problem in the morning. Lithia just hoped one night was enough for her brain to work this mess out.

29. DIONE

"Almost there," Brian said. He paused and looked around for something in the waning light. Just a few minutes later, he was on his knees brushing some sticks and leaves out of the way to reveal a secret door. He ushered her down into a small underground room that looked abandoned. It contained a humble table and a couple of cots, but not much else.

"It's a smuggler's den," he said.

"Are you a smuggler, then?"

"Only when the occasion calls for it. We'll rest here and get an early start tomorrow morning."

In the corner, he found a glowglobe. Dione watched in fascination as he opened the top, dropped in the remains of his dinner, and gave it a shake. The effect was almost immediate. A dim glow emanated from the sphere, which he hung on a hook from the ceiling.

"What do you smuggle? Food?"

"Mostly, though the Matching is coming up soon. Around this time, there are usually a few people looking for a way out."

"They can't just leave?"

"I'm sure some do and manage to live in the forest, or build a home far away, but the trackers often find the runaways. We offer them protection in exchange for hard work."

"Seems fair."

Dione was exhausted, but her curiosity led her to pull the journal out of her bag. Brian began to tinker with some small electronic he'd pulled from his own.

The diary picked up with the same vitriol against the Architect. But as the entries progressed, the author seemed to change her mind. Dione earmarked a few as she read, then came back to them.

I thought she poisoned me when she gave me that injection. But now I understand what she did. She was just giving me another chance to hold him. My son. I didn't believe it at first because I could only see him. But now I remember everything in 3D. Like the warmth of his tiny body against my skin. She won't tell me his name. She says she doesn't know and maybe that's true. How could I forget my own son? A part of me doubts these memories, like she planted them, but it's not just my mind. My body remembers him, too, and aches to hold him one more time, like it knows a part of it is missing now.

There were other memories she wrote down, but she kept coming back to the one of her son.

Things are clearer now, but she says it will only last like this for a couple of weeks. Then everything will go back to being hazy, until it's lost completely. I don't know why I let him do this to me. To all of us. To take our memories. Can it really be a new life, if you don't have an old one?

I see her plan now. I'm more than leverage to get what she wants from the Farmer. She thinks I'm her best chance to set things straight, because everyone will believe me. I don't know if this is true or not. She had me write these memories down, this truth down, in my own hand, so that I would read the words and change everything. She's going to lock the Flyers and give me the key. But I'll only have the key if I still have the journal, or at least that's what she said. It's just her way of making sure that there is balance. She thinks that I can heal the divide. The refugees have taken over the Field Temple, but she doesn't want the people divided. She talks about how things will be when he's gone, and I think she plans to kill him. Truthfully, I don't think her plan will work. She's put her faith in the wrong people. Or the wrong person.

Dione paused, considering what she just read. *She thinks that I can heal the divide.* Brian had mentioned a divide earlier. Was he talking about this?

"Brian," she looked up, "can you tell me more about the Great Divide that you mentioned last night?"

Brian nodded and set his project down on the table. He pulled an empty meal bar wrapper out of his pocket. "This is the Field Temple. And this rock," he said, grabbing a large pebble from the ground, "is the Vale Temple. Before the Ficarans existed and occupied the Field Temple, everyone moved freely between the two buildings and the Forest Temple. But no one was actually free. Your life—where you lived, who you married—was decided for you by the Farmer. He taught everyone a lot of important things, don't get me wrong, like best farming practices and what to forage. Breeding stronger musical responses in animals. The Aratians like to remember it as a utopia, but people who were 'genetic liabilities' were treated differently. The more dangerous recessive genes that you had, the less of a person you were."

"Dangerous? Like they increased the odds of disease?" Dione asked.

"Yes."

"How did they do such detailed genetic tests?"

"The Farmer taught his closest followers how to use the equipment and how to do the tests, but that knowledge is carefully guarded."

Dione didn't understand how they could know so much about genetics, yet think that the Farmer was a god. It was clear to her that he was just a man who longed for power. He had somehow managed to intertwine science and ignorance. Somewhere in their education he trained them to believe that science was magic. And as much wonder as the things she discovered evoked, to call them magic was an insult to the centuries of work done by persistent men and women.

Brian continued. "Eventually the Architect showed up. No one was sure where she came from, but she could see how upset people were. She's the one who told them that the Farmer wasn't a god. They could leave. They were free. She helped them organize and rebel. They took the weapons and the Flyers, and they took over the Field Temple. There they founded the Ficaran settlement.

"They tried to make her a god but she didn't want that. Supposedly the last thing that she said before she locked the Flyers was that they weren't machines of war and to use the weapons for protection only. She warned us not to believe the Farmer's lies and to trust what we could verify.'"

No matter what the journal's author said, Dione liked this Architect, assuming Brian's story was true.

"So she locked the Flyers after your people used them to escape?"

"Yes, she was worried we would go back to attack the Aratians. Then the Farmer's wife went missing and turned up dead a few weeks later. She had killed herself. The Farmer was furious, and everyone thought there would be war, but the Farmer left abruptly and never returned. When it became clear that he wasn't coming back, his most trusted advisor, David Bram, stepped in to govern until his return. Supposedly the Farmer had been planning to leave for a while, and the trouble with the rebels forced him to move up his plans.

"Bram legitimized his role by marrying his eldest son, Michael, to Clara, the Farmer's daughter. Somehow the Aratians weren't suspicious at all that Clara and Michael were a perfect genetic pair."

Well, for a story called "The Great Divide," she shouldn't be surprised that it didn't have a happy ending. "Why do you want a Flyer, if the Architect thought they were so dangerous?"

"I'm not going to use it to fight."

"For what then?" Dione believed him, but she still thought she should know what he planned to do with it.

Brian looked down and picked up the device he had been taking apart and proceeded to put it back together.

"We've already made a deal. You don't have to tell me."

Brian sighed. "It's not exactly a secret. Most people try to talk me out of it when I tell them, so I just stopped telling people."

"I won't try to talk you out of it," Dione said. Her experience with Lithia meant she was used to getting ignored when telling people not to do stupid things.

"My father is missing. He sailed to the southern island a few years ago and hasn't come back. He knew the Farmer was a liar, and that he didn't create us. He thought that maybe we came here from somewhere else, but he never found any evidence. Then he came up with this theory that all the evidence was on the southern island. But the currents make that a one-way trip."

"Is that why you asked us if we'd met any Ficarans?"

"Yes. I want the Flyer to go find my father. Maybe when we get there, you can show me around, since you're more familiar with the area than me." He glanced up from his tinkering.

Dione panicked. Lithia was not here to smooth things over and fill in the awkward silence that hung in the room.

"Sure, um... I guess I can do that. It's just—"

Brian burst out laughing. "You really are a terrible liar. It's a good thing you have Lithia with you."

"I don't know what you mean," Dione said.

"Come on, you've been a give-away this whole time. One day, I'll teach you how to lie. It can come in handy."

Dione could feel herself giving up. "So you're not mad we lied to you?"

"Everyone lies. You didn't know me, and you're clearly not from around here. Will you tell me the truth now? Where are you from? My father will be upset if he finds out I never asked."

Dione didn't feel like she had a choice. She needed an ally, and without Lithia here, she didn't quite know what to do. The truth wasn't always easy, but usually, it was the best option. Brian didn't even seem mad, just confused. What would happen if she told the truth? Would he believe her? At this point, she really couldn't refuse.

And so, Dione told him the truth. She told him about their ship, and the Ven attack. She told him that the Vens sounded a lot like the demons that fell from the sky. She told him that her friend Bel really was in trouble, and that Zane was still up there with her, waiting for them to bring back the medicine. She even told him about what she had found on the space station: the terraforming, the research bases, and how there were still things she didn't know.

For a few long, agonizing minutes, Brian said nothing. When he had finished processing, he looked up and said, "I believe you."

"You do?"

"I mean, my father... I don't think he suspected that we came from another planet. He always thought we were brought here from the other side of the world, or the southern island. That's why he went there. The Farmer forbid it, and even the Architect warned us not to go there. He thought that's where the big secret, some hidden civilization, was. Do you know what's there? Could you see it from… space?"

"We didn't even know there were people here. Something must have interfered with the scans we did. We didn't see anything, but that doesn't mean it's not there."

"You didn't know we were here?"

"Not a clue." It sounded like an apology.

"That explains why you crashed."

"That was all Lithia," Dione said, smiling. "Don't blame me." Her smile quickly faded. Lithia was still a captive. Or worse. She felt the tears coming, so she turned away from Brian and returned to her cot. She didn't need him to see her cry. "I'm sorry, I just…"

Then Brian did something unexpected. He moved over to sit next to her and just held her. The second his arms wrapped around her, she started sobbing. It was like an invitation to let everything out. All of the worry, the despair, and the guilt.

"My father always said crying was as natural as eating. When you are hungry, you eat and the hunger goes away. When you are upset, you cry, and then you feel some relief until the next time you are overwhelmed."

After another minute, Dione wiped her face on her sleeve and felt her anguish subsiding. Instead of telling her everything would be okay, he had let her cry. All of the anxiety from the crash and the pursuit and Lithia's abduction needed an outlet, and there it was. Everything was not okay, but she was doing all she could to change that, starting with getting some rest.

"I think I'm ready for bed now. Thanks, Brian, and I really mean that."

"Do you want me to stay?"

"What? Where are you going?"

"No, I mean, never mind," he said. In the fading light of the glowglobe, she thought she saw him smiling. He reached out and put a hand on her cheek. He leaned in and kissed her on the lips. He was gentle, slowly moving his hand back to brush her hair out of the way. She put one hand on his chest as she kissed him back, feeling his heart beat under the hard muscles there. After just a few moments, he pulled away. "Good night, Dione." Even in the dim light of the glowglobe, she could see him smiling that gorgeous smile.

"Night," she said. She heard Brian settling into one of the other cots, and she suddenly felt wide awake. What did his kiss mean? Was it simply out of pity for a crying girl? After a few moments of consideration, she realized what he had been asking. She had totally just blown it. He must think that she was an idiot. And probably a bad kisser, now, and she would never get another chance.

Her pulse was racing. After one kiss. Brian could probably hear her heart pounding from the other side of the room. She listened for his characteristic snores, but heard nothing. Could he be lying awake in his cot right now, too? She strained to hear him breathing, but her exhaustion closed off her senses too soon.

30. ZANE

Zane almost couldn't believe it when he woke up and went to the command center, only to find that the spider had worked. It was like power coming on after a storm. He didn't realize how much data had been trapped on the surface, but here it all was. Comms were back, but other signals escaped, too. He would have to sift through those later. The planet had also been blocking access to certain station databases, but now they were open. He downloaded everything to the *Calypso*. Eventually, whoever was down there would recover, but it would take a while with their outdated systems. For now, he had the upper hand.

The first order of business was finding Dione and Lithia. He was now receiving location information from their manumeds. They weren't designed to be trackers, but he was able to get their location from the *Calypso*. All their manumed traffic, including location, went through the ship. That was the easy part. He was alarmed that they were not together, but he decided to try Lithia first.

"Lithia? Lithia, are you there?" he said.

There was a long pause, and it filled him with uncertainty. She had to be alive.

"Hello?" A young female voice answered, but it was not Lithia. Zane did not recognize the voice. Someone on the planet had gotten a hold of her manumed.

"Who is this?"

"I'm Cora Bram. How are you doing this? The Farmer took all of the communication devices. Is he coming back? Has he sent you?" The voice had gone from confused to ecstatic in seconds.

Zane had not expected this. He was about to answer when a call from Dione popped up. He immediately answered, ending the other call. Maybe Lithia had lost her manumed, and she was with Dione.

"Zane, thank god. How is Bel doing?" she said, relief and concern both apparent in her voice.

"She's not doing well. The medical bed is helping her breathe. Where are you? Where is Lithia? Is she with you? I called her, but someone else answered. There are people that live on this planet."

"I know. And I'm with one of them right now, but some of them took Lithia."

"Why? What happened?"

Dione caught him up on the basics, explaining how the trackers took Lithia and that she and Brian were on their way to get another shuttle. Zane pulled up a map of the area in order to follow along. Lithia was now at the Vale Temple, which he assumed was the Vale Base on his map. On the other side of the forest was the Field Base. Dione was close.

"So you think that one shuttle will be enough to infiltrate the Aratian town? From the info I have up here, it looks like the terraformers called it the Vale Base. It's down in a valley, protected by forest, hills, and sheer cliffs. It won't be easy."

"We don't have a choice. They have the meds and Lithia."

"Well, someone named Cora Bram has her manumed, so maybe you can get her help."

"Cora Bram?" Dione said. "Brian, isn't that... Evy's cousin? Maybe she really is helping Evy. You have any ideas?"

Zane still didn't understand all this business about Ficarans and Aratians, but he trusted that Brian was a good guy. Or at least good enough.

"I don't know," Brian's voice came through. "Cora is Evy's cousin, and the daughter of the Aratian Regnator. She could have a lot of pull with her father and help free Lithia."

Zane's manumed buzzed. He had gotten a text message from... Lithia? No, Cora. Cora had figured the device out fast.

Who are you? Are you the harbinger? -Cora

"I just got a text from Lithia's manumed asking if I'm the harbinger. What does that mean?"

Brian answered. "The harbinger is supposed to herald the return of the Farmer. If she thinks you're the harbinger, you might be able to use that. After all, you do have communication devices, and the Farmer collected all the old communicators before the Great Divide. She might think that the Farmer gave them to you."

"And then she'll trust us?" Zane said.

"I don't know, but it's worth a shot," Brian said. "You might be able to convince her to give Lithia the manumed." Brian gave Zane a crash course in Aratian and Ficaran mythology. Zane hoped it would be enough.

Then Dione spoke. "I know we just got in touch again, but I'm going to have to leave my manumed soon. Brian says I shouldn't take it into the Ficaran settlement. I'll be out of contact for a few hours at least, until we secure the shuttle."

"Take me off speaker," Zane said.

There was a moment's pause, and then Dione's voice came through, closer, more intimate.

"What's up?"

"Are you sure you trust this guy? Why can't you take your manumed?"

"The Ficarans are really into… forced sharing. He doesn't want me to take anything that might be perceived as valuable."

Forced sharing. There was some of that on space freighters, too, if you were in the lower classes. The news made Zane even more wary, but if the Ficarans had the Flyers, there wasn't much of a choice. "All right. Check back in when you get the chance. Hopefully, I'll have good news."

Zane ended the call and read Cora's second message: *Hello? - Cora*

Zane smiled a little. Cora kept signing her messages like they were proper letters. Zane responded: *I am the harbinger. We need to speak privately. Are you alone?*

Cora replied: *Yes. -Cora*

Zane called her. "Cora?" he said, not knowing quite what to expect.

"I'm here," she said, way too loudly. He winced.

"You don't need to shout. I can hear you if you speak normally."

"Oh, sorry," she said at a more tolerable volume. "Is the Farmer coming back?"

"Not yet. That's why he sent us."

"Us?"

"Yes, Lithia is working with me," he said, mustering all the authority he could.

"Oh, then I can tell my father and uncle. They will release her."

"No!" he blurted out. Then, more calmly, "No, I do not trust them. I trust you. Will you give her this communication device? I need to speak with her."

If he could get in touch with Lithia, maybe she could do the rest of the convincing. She was much better at this sort of thing than he was.

"Is she... is she really my cousin? The DNA tests say she is."

Zane tempered his reaction. Lithia had gotten him remote access to the Alliance databases so he could pull certain private flight plans and unlisted planets, like this one. He knew she was looking for her grandmother, but he didn't realize she had found her. In fact, he doubted Lithia had known, or she never would have come here with the Vens on their trail.

"You should ask her that question."

"She's currently in the detention center, but I can offer to bring her morning meal," Cora replied.

"Thank you, Cora."

"Can I know your name?" she asked.

"My name is Zane."

"Thank you, Zane," she said and disconnected.

Relief flooded through him when he received a call from Lithia shortly after.

"Zane, what kind of crazy are you cooking up there? You got the manumeds to work again!"

"Are you all right?"

"Yeah, Cora left it with me and said she'd come back in a few hours. She called you the harbinger?"

"She thinks that I'm working under the Farmer's orders and so are you."

"You know about the Farmer?"

"Dione caught me up," he said. "She's okay. She and Brian are working on a plan to come get you, but it will be a lot easier if you're—"

"Not my usual tempestuous self?"

"—not in prison."

"I'm not leaving this place without the meds for Bel. How is she feeling?"

"She's in bad shape. Sleeping a lot, needs help breathing." Zane's voice caught in his throat with that last word.

"Shit."

"You'll have to convince Cora to get you the meds, then you'll hide out in the woods. After that Dione and Brian will come and get you. They're getting a shuttle right now. Just hang on to your manumed so they can find you."

"Dione's gonna fly the shuttle? I'm better off walking."

"Let's hope that everything goes smoothly, or you might have to. Dione will check back in once she has the shuttle. She's out of contact right now."

***

Exhausted, Zane went back to the med bay and lay on one of the beds next to Bel. She was sleeping. Zane could see the green glow under her skin. Once confined to her leg and one side of her body, it was now spreading to the other side. As he looked at her gaunt face, he asked himself the question he had avoided before. Would it be too late for the anti-parasitics? Had so much damage been done that it was irreversible? He closed his eyes, fighting against his worry for a bit of rest.

He hadn't been asleep long when an alarm went off. Its urgency shook any sleepiness from his mind, and he sprinted back to the command center. He silenced the alarm before he fully realized what it meant. A ship was approaching!

The sensors on the station had a much greater range than those on the *Calypso*, but they didn't have a ready profile for this ship. It must be a newer class of vessel, or a custom pirate ship, neither of which was in the station database. He could copy and transfer some of the profiles from the *Calypso* to the station, and that might allow him to identify the ship. It didn't take long, but in that time, the ship didn't move.

When the station identified the ship, he went cold. Venatorian. Marauder class, just like the one that had attacked them. The coincidence was too great. The Ven ship had found them because they had taken too long to destroy the tracer, but there hadn't been a choice. Once they jumped, without the matrix, they were stranded. They had intended to jump to an uninhabited planet where they could make repairs without dooming anyone else in case they failed, but they'd screwed that up, too. This planet supported around two thousand people, and the Vens were here to kill them all. Even a ship of fifty Vens like the Marauder could have a devastating impact on a small colony. So why wasn't it moving?

Maybe the jump had knocked out their stabilizers again. Maybe they were making repairs. Zane saw no signs of instability though. He would keep an eye on the ship and set up a link to his manumed so that if it moved, he would know immediately. He sent a message to both Dione and Lithia. They had to hurry. Maybe, just maybe, they could find a way to stop this ship.

31. DIONE

Dione felt naked without her manumed and machete. Brian had also left the stolen pistol in the small storage chest in the smuggler's den.

"No one knows about this one. These things will be safe here."

"Are you sure we can't we keep them?" she asked, watching as he slid the storage chest back against the wall. "Your own people won't take your things, right?"

Brian made an equivocating gesture. "Like I said, the concept of personal property gets shaky when resources are scarce and war is looming on the horizon."

He also stowed Lithia's pack, which he had stuffed with rations from the Forest Temple hideout. He handed her one, and ate three himself.

"Why aren't you taking those back? Don't your people need the food?"

"Everyone gets a share, but they don't get equal shares. These will go where they're needed."

Dione had never lived in want, let alone need. She tried not to, but she couldn't help pitying Brian and the Ficarans.

They left while it was still dark, and they reached the open plain in time for Dione to watch the sunrise gild the grass and trees. Soon, she saw it.

It was similar to the Forest Base, but it was smaller and surrounded by a wall. A patrol on the wall spotted them, and Brian waved in greeting. The man beckoned to him to continue on.

Its small appearance was just that, an appearance. Brian led her around the other side, and the building that appeared over the wall was just the tip of the iceberg. The structure had been built into the hill, and several floors were exposed to the other side of the plain.

Brian met the guard at the gate, said a few words, and they were both admitted.

"Victoria?" Brian asked.

"At the morning meal," the guard said.

"Thanks."

Brian led Dione straight inside the station where the entrance hall had been converted into a mess hall. Dishes and utensils clashed, and the low hum of conversation and laughter echoed through the room. The food was simple: porridge, fruit, and bread. A few diners even had eggs. As they walked among the tables, Dione noticed that some people actually had very little food on their plates. She supposed this was what necessity looked like.

They approached the table at the very back, and Brian muttered to her, "That's Victoria. Follow my lead."

The woman's posture and stern expression easily identified her as the leader. Her long, brown hair was in a no-nonsense ponytail, and when Victoria looked up, Dione couldn't see any warmth in her gray eyes. It worried her. Brian had already told her to keep all the stuff about space stations and aliens to herself, and she trusted his judgment.

"Brian," Victoria said. "We were expecting you two days ago. Have a seat. And who is this?"

"This is Dione. She was in the Flyer that went down in the forest. I assume you saw it."

"I did. And how did she get a Flyer?"

"Apparently they have a few still working on the southern island."

"The southern island?" Victoria said, looking at Dione with interest now. "We all thought the talk of a city down there was nothing but a myth. What brings you up here?"

Dione told the truth. "My friend is very sick, and we heard the meds she needs are up here."

"We?"

"I came with my friend, Lithia, who was captured by the Aratians."

"You crashed. Didn't you know about the Icon?"

"No, we don't use the Flyers unless we have to," Dione said. That sounded believable, right? Why was Victoria so suspicious? Dione didn't like this woman very much.

"Surely you have more experienced pilots. Why send someone so young?" Victoria asked.

Great. The leader of the Ficarans didn't believe that she had crashed. Victoria probably thought she was a spy, here to sabotage all their Flyers. She had a point, though. Why would a proper city send a couple of teens? She would let Victoria be clever and right, and maybe once she felt like she had been smart enough to see through her, she wouldn't ask questions that led to answers including space stations and aliens.

Dione did her best to look nervous, which wasn't hard under the scrutiny of Victoria, and began her confession. "No one sent us. We took the Flyer without permission. We heard about the medicines in your temples, and we decided to come find out. We didn't know about the Icon, or whatever it was that hit us."

A smug smile spread across Victoria's face. She enjoyed being right. "And you think you can unlock our Flyers?"

"Yes." The pit nearly dropped out of Dione's stomach. When they had met Brian, she always figured Lithia would be the one to unlock the Flyers, but now that task rested squarely on her shoulders.

"I suppose you want something in return."

"I want use of one of the Flyers. After we get Lithia and the meds, Brian will come with me to the southern island. After that, he'll bring the Flyer back to you."

Her piercing gaze shifted to Brian. "Interesting how you get exactly what you want out of this deal."

"That's the beauty of compromise," he said. "What do you say?"

Victoria thought for a moment. "Well, I've got nothing to lose if you fail to start them. But I mean all of them. We'll need them for what's coming."

Dione still wasn't certain why Victoria needed all of the Flyers so badly, but she didn't care. She was ecstatic. All she had to do was start a few Flyers, and she and Brian would be off to get Lithia.

"I've got some business this morning, but around midday, meet me in the shuttle bay. Brian, I'd like to see you in my office for a few minutes about your original mission."

"Jackson's tractor repair? Yes, ma'am," he said, grabbing his pack.

"Give her half a serving," Victoria said to one of the men sitting at the table as she rose.

Brian left, and Dione was sitting at a table of curious strangers. One of them was especially large, and he seemed to have twice as much food as everyone else at the table. His down-turned eyebrows gave him a look of permanent irritation. Dione avoided eye contact.

When the other man came back with a piece of greasy bread and a few slices of fruit, she thanked him. She knew what a meal meant to these people, and felt guilty that they were sharing it with her. The meager portion wouldn't take long to finish, even if she ate slowly. Still, she would have to try, because once she was finished they might start asking her questions she couldn't answer. Maybe that was Victoria's plan.

32. BRIAN

Victoria sat behind her desk. There were no elaborate decorations on her office walls, no ornaments. Everything in the room was functional and necessary. She lived the same austere life she expected of her people, and Brian had always respected that about her. She did not invite Brian to sit, and even though that bothered him, he stood without complaint. He needed her in as good a mood as possible.

"You're late. When Canto came back alone, I was worried," she said.

"That's why I sent him with the all-clear tag."

"But no real information," she countered.

"You must have realized I was caught in the storm."

"I figured, but I didn't count on you bringing back company."

"If Dione can start the Flyers, it will be worth it."

Victoria paused, smoothing down her ponytail. "You trust her?" she said.

Brian hesitated. "Not completely." He wanted to trust Dione, but he didn't. She didn't understand what life was like here, what was at stake. He would have to show her later. If she understood what things were like...

"Good." Victoria's curt reply brought him back to reality. "Don't be an idiot like your father. In fact, it would be better if you didn't fly off until after the attack. After we've taken over the Aratian food supply, I'll give you your own personal Flyer to keep. But we need every single Flyer if we want the assault to work."

Brian sounded confused. "The assault? You're going through with that plan?" The worse things got for them, the more eager Victoria was for war.

"If we get the key to the Flyers, then yes. It's long overdue."

"You know that's not what the Architect wanted," Brian said. He knew the Architect wasn't a god, but she had been sincere in her attempts to protect them all, and she had been the one to lock all the Flyers.

Victoria sounded bored. "The Architect did a great deal for us, but that doesn't mean she didn't make mistakes. She said herself that she was only human. I'm surprised to hear you defending her. I thought you hated her."

It was true, for the most part. He blamed the Architect and her enigmatic warnings about the southern island for his father's departure.

"She may have withheld some information, but I think she was right when she warned us about the Flyers. They're tools, not weapons."

"I'm not going to have this debate with you. I make the calls. I give the orders. You'll follow them if you want a Flyer afterward." Victoria's forehead wrinkled as she frowned at him. "I expect you to join us. You're more familiar with their territory than most."

Brian glanced up sharply, failing to conceal his surprise. He hated the Aratians, but this wasn't the way. Holding Evy hostage would have been one thing. Hostages don't have to get hurt. But an assault? That wouldn't go well for anyone. He didn't want to join the assault, but he couldn't refuse if he ever hoped to find his father. He bowed his head in a nod of assent and submission. He would figure something out later.

"Now, to business." Victoria motioned for him to have a seat. "Report on your appointment with Jackson."

"We made the arrangement for six, but when morning came, he didn't want to pay. Said he didn't have six, and offered me two, so I looked around and found them."

"How many were there?"

"Ten."

Victoria smiled. "Even better."

"I only took six."

Anger swept over Victoria's face faster than a wave breaking on the shore. "Explain."

"The deal was for six. I keep my word. That's why the Aratian farmers come to us."

"The message you sent is clear. Don't pay us, and you can get away with it."

Brian responded. "He didn't get away with it. I've got the full payment, right here."

"There's no reason to pay us in full. They can try to cheat us, and we'll still only take the original amount. There's no consequence for their treachery."

"I'm not a thief. We had a deal with him. I held up my end, and I made him hold up his."

"If something like this happens again, you take everything. Understood?" She paused for effect. "Or do you want me to cut your mother's rations because we don't have enough to go around?"

Brian struggled to control his tone. "You're barely feeding her enough as it is. She's so weak she couldn't contribute labor, even if she tried."

"She made a choice to stop working and take the ration cut when your father left. She knew what it would mean. And I cut her more slack than most because of your talents. Now, do we have an understanding?"

Brian enunciated so that every syllable of his reply dripped with hatred: "Yes, ma'am."

Maybe he should have taken all ten food packets. They certainly could use it. Still, he didn't want to sacrifice his reputation among the Aratian farmers because sometimes, he worked for them on the side to get a little extra food. With the cache they found in the Forest Temple, he wouldn't have to find extra work for a while. He would have enough to feed his mother and the others Victoria deemed unworthy.

He was waiting for her to dismiss him, but she still had something to say.

"This girl," Victoria said, "Dione, has she mentioned anything about the fabricator? Do her people have it on the southern island?"

"She hasn't mentioned it," Brian said. Victoria looked him in the eye, scrutinizing his expression. *She doesn't believe me.* "But I can ask."

"Good. That fabricator could solve a lot of our problems. Dismissed."

Brian left. *So that's her next move, searching for some mythical device that creates things out of nothing?* A lot of people thought the fabricator was there. His father had believed it. After all, if the southern island had been forbidden to them, there must be something important there. It didn't matter whether you thought the Farmer was a god or a man, because the Architect had forbidden them from going there as well. The two had very different motives, but the mystery of the southern island was a preoccupation of both Ficarans and Aratians alike.

If they found the fabricator, they would be able to manufacture new parts, which would ease some of the tensions with the Aratians. Brian thought the fabricator was a ridiculous myth. There were still some alive who had seen firsthand as the Farmer returned with supplies, supposedly from the fabricator, but no one had seen the device in person. Even his father believed there was a scientific explanation for what it could do. The Farmer hadn't told anyone where it was or how to get there. People swore they saw him heading south, but others claimed north, or east to the mountains, to the point where no one actually knew the truth anymore.

Dione wasn't from the southern island, but she still might have some insights into the fabricator. At least she could explain it to him. She was good at explaining things. Last night, when she had told him the truth about Kepos, it was like she could anticipate what he wanted to ask. Like something he had always wondered about. The fixed star in the sky was apparently a space station in a fixed orbit. She hinted at a much larger world. No, larger *universe*. There were still so many questions to ask, but Brian was afraid to know the answers.

Dione would not be happy to know Victoria's plans for the Flyers. It might even stop her from helping them. She didn't understand what life was like here. She didn't understand hunger or watching your loved ones die. She needed to understand.

On the other hand, Brian didn't like Victoria's plan either. She would start an all-out war between the two settlements, and a lot of people would die. If he could find the fabricator, there might be a way to resolve this peacefully. They would be able to replace the broken parts in Aratian machines in return for food shipments. If the fabricator was real, he could bring the embargo to an end, and prevent a war.

33. DIONE

The more Dione thought about her conversation with Victoria, the less confident she was in her decision to start the Flyers. Victoria was planning something, and it wasn't good. The man next to Dione was looking at her with curiosity, and she was on her last tiny bite of food. Pretty soon, they were going to start talking to her, or worse, asking questions. Would it be rude to pull out the journal and start reading? She had already read through it once, but if it saved her from questions about the southern island, or better yet, showed her how to unlock the Flyers, it might be worth it to be rude.

Brian returned just in time.

"Come on, I want to show you around," he said. He grabbed a slice of bread, then led her outside. It was early, but everyone outdoors was working. Some were repairing houses, others digging trenches. A few, she noticed, carried guns and bows and headed toward the main gate.

"Brian, I'm not sure how I feel about this deal. What is Victoria going to do with the Flyers?"

"Does it matter? You need a Flyer. This is the only way." He avoided both her question and eye contact. Victoria must have said something that got to him.

She put her foot down. "It does matter."

"Then you're prepared to let your friend die? For what?" Brian snapped at her.

Dione flinched away from him. She knew it was wrong. She knew she would be handing a powerful weapon over to one side of a conflict. They were on the verge of war. She hadn't really understood that until now. What right did she have to tip the balance of power toward one side? All actions had consequences.

"If I do help start the Flyers, what would happen to them? You think Victoria's going to just let you take one? Because I've known her for about five minutes and I can tell you what she's going to do. She's going to bypass any Aratian defenses there are and attack. Tell me, Brian, are all of the Aratians guilty? Can you risk innocents, like Evy?"

"You have no idea what you're talking about. You want to talk about innocents? Here, come with me."

He stormed off down a side street that crawled in between two buildings made of a mixture of natural wood and brick, plus pre-fab material that had come from a colonizer ship. They were poised at the end of a row of buildings, all nearly identical except for the designs painted on their doors. Each building looked large enough to house multiple families, like miniature apartment buildings. Dione walked quickly to keep up.

"See that house?" he asked, pointing to one with a tree painted in brown on the door. "They lost a daughter. Killed while trying to steal some food from Aratian fields."

He was walking slowly down the street now. He pointed to another house. "He lost his son, and then his wife killed herself."

Further down the row, he stopped in front of a house with deer painted on the front. "She lost her baby last week. Malnutrition." He turned to Dione. "You don't need to remind me about innocent people dying. So if you're still asking if I'm willing to risk a few Aratians, the answer is yes. Because no one has to die. They have more than enough food, and they won't trade it with us because their Artifacts keep breaking. They think it's our fault, but we just don't have the spare parts. The Aratians we smuggle out increase tensions, too, but we're not going to leave them there. And their Regnator is so stubborn that he won't even talk to Victoria about a treaty. She wasn't always like this, Dione. The last year has been hard. It's changed her."

Dione didn't know what to say. What hardship had she endured until recently? She had been too little when her mother died to really miss her. Her father had given her everything she needed. Her uncle had loved her. Professor Oberon had believed in her. She had never wanted for food or water or shelter or safety. She had to stop pretending that she was uninvolved in this conflict. Whether she meant to or not, she had joined with a Ficaran and offered him and his people help. It was too late to turn back. She wasn't sure if she actually trusted Brian or if she just wanted him to be worthy of her trust, but he was the only one on her side right now. If she wanted to survive, if she wanted to save Bel, she couldn't afford to screw that up.

"I'm sorry. It's hard for me to understand what it's been like for you here." Brian said nothing. He didn't understand her perspective either. A question popped into Dione's head.

"Do you think all lives have equal value?"

He looked at her, puzzled. "No, of course not." He paused. "Do you?"

"It's what my uncle taught me. That every life was valuable. I don't think my father agreed, but he never said anything."

"How can you possibly think that all lives are equal? It makes absolutely no sense. Should an old man, incapable of defending the settlement, receive food and medical treatment when our supplies are scarce? Every life may be valuable, but certainly not equal."

"What if you didn't have to ration supplies? What if everyone could access what they needed? Would all lives be equal then?"

Brian stared at her a moment, thinking. "I can't even imagine a world like that. If that's what life is like where you're from..." He sounded bitter. "What about murderers? What about people so stone-hearted that they can't even be called human?"

A pang of guilt wrenched her stomach. *Or brutal aliens who send their children to murder other children? Can you disregard those lives?* Dione didn't have the moral high ground, even though she knew that she made the right choice when she killed that Ven.

"I guess you're right. We all do what we have to in order to survive." Dione said the words, but she didn't feel them. Not yet. She had lived so far thinking she was a good person, but apparently, she had just never been challenged.

His shoulders relaxed and his frown receded. "Come on. I want to show you something else."

He led her up one of the wooden scout towers that lined the stone rampart. They were new. They looked out of place, made out of newer materials.

The two looked out over the plain surrounding the settlement. The Ficarans were easy targets. Dione wondered what kept the Aratians at bay.

"All of this used to be farmland. We were able to irrigate it with water from the river that runs along the ridge there. We knew we had to find a new source of materials for Artifacts, because demand was growing and the supply was dwindling. The Temple here has equipment that can refine ore mined from the ground, so we headed up into that mountain to the mine that the Architect had told us about. But we got greedy. It poisoned the water, which poisoned our crops, which poisoned us."

"It sounds like your people have had terrible luck."

"You can help change that. Victoria talks about making attacks, but really she just wants to feed her people. Deep down, she knows that intimidation, using the Flyers as leverage, will be enough to get bigger food shipments. Their embargo is practically a siege. We can only hunt and gather so much, but we're having to go deeper and deeper to find game, and you saw firsthand how dangerous the deep woods are. I don't think the Aratians will fight back."

"How do you keep them from attacking now?"

"We have most of the Artifact weapons. That pistol I took was probably worth a fortune among the Aratians, and here they're not for sale. They are stockpiled and issued only to guards on duty."

They headed back down the wall, and Brian led her to a shady area to rest. They had barely sat down when a beautiful young woman about Brian's age came striding over.

"Brian, when did you get back?" Her pale blue eyes stood out in contrast to her dark wavy hair. Beautiful didn't cut it. This girl was stunning.

"Melanie!" he said, jumping up and giving her a big hug. "Dione, this is Melanie, my best friend. Melanie, this is Dione."

Dione regained her confidence at his fast use of the term 'best friend.'

"Hi, Dione, nice to meet you," Melanie said.

"You, too."

Melanie turned back to Brian and raised an eyebrow. "So you finally ran out of hearts to break in our own settlement, and now you're smuggling in Aratian lovers." To Dione she said, "Has he tried to seduce you yet?"

Dione felt her cheeks grow hot as she remembered last night's kiss. Well, she had already figured out that Brian was a flirt. That would explain his interest in her last night. She did have a pulse, after all.

"Cut it out, Melanie," he said. He was smiling, but Dione thought she saw a hint of embarrassment there. "She's not Aratian. She was in the Flyer. You saw it fall, right?"

Melanie's expression changed from playful to interested in an instant. "Then where are you from? Where'd you get the Flyer?"

Dione turned to Brian. This was his friend, his settlement, his lead.

"You can trust her. Tell her the truth."

Dione told her about everything. Melanie's jaw dropped when she got to the part about the space station.

"That's not all. Now that Dione's here, Victoria wants her to start all the Flyers."

"As leverage?" Melanie said. "But Victoria is way too angry to just threaten the Aratians to get more food. She'll—"

"Start an all-out war, I know," Brian said, "and we can't risk it, not if those Venatorians could be on their way."

"So what's your plan?" Melanie asked. Brian smiled. He looked so relaxed, talking with her. A moment of silence fell over the trio.

Dione wanted to help them. She could give them the Flyers, but would that really help? That would just start a war. "Is this really the best way to solve the problem?" she asked Brian.

He frowned. The question seemed to catch him off-guard. "I don't want war, but we're suffering. We're dying. We don't have any leverage when it comes to trade. We don't have any more supplies or parts that the Aratians need, and we have nothing they want, except for the guns. And Victoria will use those before she trades them away," he said. "Unless…"

"Unless what?"

"There are rumors of a machine that creates things. A fabricator. Apparently the Farmer would periodically take a Flyer and come back with fresh supplies."

Dione lit up. "Of course. Every colonizer would have been equipped with a fabricator."

"It's real?" Brian said. "I always thought it was a ridiculous story as a kid. How can a machine create something out of nothing?"

"It doesn't use nothing. It requires raw materials, but it can render almost any design into a 3D facsimile."

"What?"

"If you tell it what to make in a lot of detail, it uses raw materials to create that object."

"Then there's another way," Melanie said, smiling at Brian.

"What?" Dione said.

"We steal one," he said, turning to her. "I don't want war either. When Victoria talked to me this morning, I learned that if she gets the Flyers, she's going to make a preemptive strike. If we can find the fabricator, we can open up trade again."

A weight lifted from Dione. This had been her hope all along, but she didn't dare bring it up after he talked about the Ficarans who had died.

"Melanie, I have a few other things to tell you, and a favor to ask. Come on," he said. "Dione, I'll be right back."

So for the next ten minutes, he had some sort of secret conversation with Melanie. Or he was making out with her. Probably both. The best thing Dione could do for now was to ignore her attraction to Brian, and work on starting the Flyer. She kept looking through the journal, though by this point, she had read the whole thing. It was repetitive and confusing in places. The author started out angry at the Architect, then the entries became incoherent for awhile, jumping from memory to memory. Toward the end, things got clearer again. By that point, the author trusted the Architect, who had clearly given her the key to the Flyers to use at the right moment, but she never explicitly said what the key was. Soon, Brian returned alone.

"Melanie had to get back to work, but she says, well, it's not in my best interest to repeat it, so I won't. Have you figured out the key?" he asked.

"I'm not sure. There's this one passage that I keep coming back to, though she mentions a few times that the journal holds the key," Dione said. "I'm hoping that once I see the Flyers, something will click. It's the last entry."

The Architect, no, she asked me to call her Samantha. She doesn't like how they call her Architect. She sings me the lullaby every night, even though I won't remember it later. She tells me it doesn't matter, because she's hidden it in the pages for me. I'm supposed to give it to the Aratians when the time is right, after no one believes the Farmer anymore. Jameson. She tells me I should use his name, too. I ask myself how I could love such a monster, and as much as I make excuses, I know why. I'm a monster, too. Why else would I abandon my husband and son?

Really, she expects too much of me. I can't live with the memories of what I've done, but when they start to slip away, how can I go back to being that blind woman? This journal won't save me. It won't save us. What do you do when you hate who you are and hate who you'll become?

"It sounds like the lullaby is the key," he said.

"Yeah, but it doesn't say what lullaby it is, or what part of it contains the key."

Brian didn't have any ideas, but Dione gave him the book to puzzle over while she thought. The last line. The writing was darker, as if the author had traced back over it again with her pen. What would she do? No, what would the author do? The journal progressed from hatred toward the Architect to self-hatred, and these very last words seemed like just that, final words. Had the author committed suicide? Dione had suspected this before, but she needed to say it out loud.

"I think this journal belonged to the Farmer's wife. In the earlier entries she makes it sound like the Architect, Samantha, is trying to use her to get to the Farmer, Jameson, and this last entry, well, look at the final line." She showed Brian the page with the last entry. "Didn't she commit suicide?"

"She did. Maybe you're right." Brian looked up from the journal. "Does it help you unlock the Flyers?"

"Probably not."

"I'm sure once you're in the Flyer, you'll know what to do," he said, though Dione thought he looked a little nervous.

The key had something to do with the lullaby. Or maybe there was some sort of alphanumeric code hidden at intervals in the pages. Maybe if Dione had spent more time with Lithia playing at detective holos, she would be able to figure it out. When Victoria summoned them, they were out of time and out of ideas.

34. LITHIA

Lithia waited impatiently for Cora to return, just as Zane had instructed. When she entered the prison, she addressed the guard on duty.

"My father requested that I come and show Lithia around. She's the one in cell four," Cora said.

"Yes, the only captive right now. Do you have a release from the Regnator?" The guard seemed a little nervous.

"No, but I could go and get one. He's probably not in his meeting yet, but if he is, I'm sure he won't mind an interruption from me," she said.

"No!" the guard protested. "Don't bother him. Restraints?"

"No, thank you," she said. "My guard is waiting for us just outside."

A few minutes later, they left the detention center together.

Lithia spoke first. "Where's your guard?"

"Not here. I slipped away."

Lithia was impressed. "Now you know why I'm here. Did Zane tell you about my mission?"

Cora shook her head. "Only that I'm supposed to help you."

"I need the medicine that treats the demon sickness, the one where your cuts glow green. Do you know where it is?" Lithia couldn't believe she had actually just called it "demon sickness" with a straight face.

"It's probably in storage with all the other rare medicines. I can check the catalog once we're down there. But we need to be fast. My father really is in a meeting, and you need to be gone before he realizes it."

Lithia was surprised how quickly she had agreed to help them. The Farmer must really carry a lot of weight around here.

No one stopped them, or even really paid much attention to them. Cora led her to the base entrance, and she was easily allowed to pass. No one suspected she wasn't doing so at her father's wishes. Lithia couldn't fathom that level of trust. She had never bothered building it. When someone pushed her, she couldn't help pushing back. She was practiced at ignoring the little voice in her head that told her to back down.

Cora began explaining what the different floors of the building were for. The top floors were living quarters for her family, the middle levels were for research and government business, and the basement levels were for storage, among other things. The roof functioned as a landing pad, but there were no Flyers there.

Cora led her into the basement, cheerful and calm. She looked up the location for the anti-parasitic, and they easily found its case. Cora looked inside to find it missing, and Lithia watched her cool disintegrate.

"It should be here," Cora said.

"Maybe it got mislabeled, or someone put it away in the wrong place."

"No, it hasn't been moved in a long time."

"Why would someone move it?"

"They wouldn't. Unless…" She trailed off. "If someone checked it out to study it or use it… I didn't bother checking requisitions."

Cora passed the catalog, and scrolled through the requisitions log. "Moira has it. She's running tests in her lab."

"So, we go and get it," Lithia said. "Where's the lab?"

"It's upstairs, but you don't understand. Moira hates me. She'll never let me into her lab."

"Hates you? I can't believe that anyone hates you." Lithia had seen nothing but respect and deference shown to this girl.

If asking nicely wouldn't work, she had another idea. "Is there any way to get my stun rifle, the one I came here with?"

Cora looked alarmed. "Your weapon? Why would you need that here?"

"It doesn't do any permanent damage. Just knocks you out for a while."

"Oh," Cora said, looking relieved. "No, I don't know where it is. The techs are probably checking it out. Plus, carrying around a weapon would make it a lot harder to hide in plain sight."

She had a point. It was amazing that no one had stopped them yet as it was, but would they really question Cora? As much as she wanted to look around for her rifle, they didn't have time to waste.

Cora led them upstairs, and a few turns later, they were at the entrance of a small work room. Tucked away at the back of the hall, it was rather remote compared to the other labs.

"In there," she said.

Lithia barged in without knocking. There was a short-haired blonde woman in the corner reviewing notes on a computer. She turned at the sound of the door and frowned at them.

"You can't be in here. Who's this?" she said.

"I'm getting the tour. What is it that you work on here?" Lithia said.

"A lot of things," Moira said. She turned to Cora. "And how did my miserable little lab become a stop on your tour?"

"You know how valuable my father considers your work," Cora said.

"Some of it, certainly. That's the only reason I've still got a lab. He doesn't much care for my work with plants," she said. "Says he has no use for study into phytoremediation."

"Phytoremediation?" Lithia said. "That sounds familiar." Dione had talked about it a few times.

"Healing the land through plants. The Ficarans destroyed their farmland with heavy metals, and I've been working on a way to remove the contamination with plants. It's long-term, but I seem to be the only one to see the cliff up ahead. We need the Ficarans, which is something no one around here likes to admit."

"But they're the enemy," Lithia said.

"They don't have to be, but Regnator Bram won't let go. He's not interested in trading knowledge for peace." She turned to Cora. "When we go to war, and it's a when, not an if, you're gonna see that boy you've been pining after beaten and bloody. I don't want that. Not for anyone. Now your father's got it in mind to send this medicine to me and tell me to make more like demons are on the way." She pointed to a vial on the cluttered table. It didn't look like Moira had spent any time on it yet. That was it. That was what they needed. Just one dose.

"So here I am, wasting my time, when the real threat is our own stubbornness."

"Cora's here to listen to what you have to say," Lithia said, positioning the confused girl in front of Moira.

"You want to learn, child? I'll give you the general principles. Maybe you can talk some sense into your father."

Moira explained the research she had been doing, though in basic terms. She sounded like Dione trying to explain her latest obsession.

"Phytoremediation uses certain plants that are tolerant of heavy metals to clean up the soil. The plants pull in the poison along with other nutrients they need, and the poison doesn't kill them. Once they've absorbed the poison, you remove the plant, taking the poison with it. The soil is cleaner. It takes years and multiple applications, but it's amazing what these plants are capable of."

When Moira turned to produce a few diagrams, Lithia struck. She stole the small bottle of medicine, and put it in her pocket, now surprisingly grateful for the billowy parachute pants.

At the next pause in Moira's lesson, Lithia broke in. "Thank you, but we've got to continue on. Cora, maybe you can come back sometime?" Lithia thought she could stand to learn a little more from Moira, who seemed to have some human decency when it came to the Ficarans.

"And who are you, anyway? Why are you getting a tour? You look an awful lot like Miranda."

Lithia had no good answers. There were no long-lost cousins in this world, at least none that wouldn't cause immediate suspicion.

"Just a friend who's never seen the Temple. I offered to show her around," Cora said. Apparently she wasn't supposed to talk about the whole cousins thing. Or maybe Moira would have started asking questions.

"Hmmm."

That explanation was good enough. Moira was reading something in her notes, even as she listened to Cora, and Lithia knew that look. She had seen it in Dione's eyes a million times. Moira was eager to get back to work.

The two left the lab, and after easily walking back to the entrance, they emerged into the sunlight. The city was beautiful. Small houses made of brick and stone and concrete formed neat rows, each one unique yet a complement to the one next to it.

The buildings were new, yet permanent. Cora led her to an open-air market selling fresh produce and crafts. It was full of people, and the perfect place to hide in plain sight. On their way, Cora innocently bought a few pale lavender fruits and a painted wooden pendant necklace. She gave the necklace to Lithia, as well as a piece of fruit.

"What is this?" Lithia asked, rubbing the small bumps on the fruit's textured surface with her thumb.

"A polla. It's my favorite. Try it."

Lithia waited for Cora to dig in for a clue on how to eat it. The apparent answer was skin on, leave nothing. The fruit was sweet with just enough tang, and the only downside was the sticky juice that Lithia wiped on her pants.

They were out. She should update Zane on their progress. She couldn't believe they had succeeded. She looked down to her manumed and read the message waiting for her there: *The Vens found us. Holding position at the moment.*

Her entire body went cold. The crowds moved around her, but she tried not to look at their faces. These were the people who would die when the Vens landed. And she had led them here. When she got the data from Zane, the list of all the planets outside the Bubble where her grandmother could have landed, she had never had much hope about this one.

Could the Icon save this planet? It had struck them down after all, but they were just in a shuttle. The Ven ship was much larger and had better defenses. It really wasn't much of a weapon at all, and Lithia puzzled over why it had even been left there. Maybe it was broken.

"Lithia, what is it?"

She wasn't ready to tell Cora. Not until she had a plan.

"I need to tell Zane what's going on. Is there somewhere less crowded we can go?"

Lithia couldn't help but laugh when Cora brought her to a tree house, just inside the border of the woods. The few children playing in it scattered when they saw them coming.

Lithia put some distance in between herself and Cora. "Zane," she said in a low voice. "Got your message. Where's Dione?"

"I haven't heard from her yet, and I'm a little worried. She should have checked in by now."

"Give it a little more time."

"I don't know how much time we have. Lithia, the Vens are just sitting there, like they're waiting for something."

"Like what?"

"I don't know, but it can't be good."

"We can't let them come here. We just can't."

"I know," Zane said, "and I've got an idea."

35. DIONE

Dione's stomach was in knots. If the journal contained the answer, she hadn't found it, and now she was out of time. She had to deliver on her promise. If she failed, she couldn't save Lithia and Bel. Maybe everything would make sense once she saw the shuttles.

Victoria was already at the hangar. She was flanked by two men, one of whom Dione recognized as the especially burly man from breakfast.

The hangar had also been built into the hill, and the doors were open. Victoria proudly walked her through the two rows of shuttles. Dione counted there were about ten in total, but there were two different designs. At the front of the row was the simple carrier design, just like the one Lithia had flown, or rather crashed, a few days ago. At the end of the row were some slightly larger shuttles, probably designed for cargo transport. They looked as if they had been built by different manufacturers, but Dione wasn't certain. Lithia would know these things. She would ask her in a few hours once they rescued her.

"Here it is," Victoria said. She opened the doors, and inside everything looked fine, at least Dione thought so. Lithia was the pilot and would be much better suited to this, but she was on her own. She would figure it out, but for now, she had to stall.

Dione needed some time to think. Once Victoria left, she would be able to think out loud, maybe bounce a few ideas off of Brian. Most importantly, she'd be able to relax. Victoria made her feel nervous and prevented her from thinking.

"I'll need to conduct a visual assessment," Dione said. Lithia had said something like that when they crashed, right?

Victoria followed her. Every movement that Dione made, Victoria was her shadow. Dione thought everything looked all right and went into the shuttle. She took the pilot's seat. There was power, which was a reassuring sign, but none of her commands were accepted. She was indeed locked out. The issue was, she didn't see any place to input a code. That must mean this was a spoken code, and as such, could be anything.

She thought about just reading the diary out loud, hoping that the right combination of words was in there, but Victoria was there, staring at her.

"Go ahead," Victoria said. "You claimed to know how to start it."

"It's not the starting it that's the issue. It's the controlling it. I can unlock it, but I'll need some time."

"That wasn't the agreement. You said you knew the key." Victoria could see straight through her delay tactic.

"Do you even know why the Architect locked them all in the first place? She didn't trust you. This isn't going to be easy to do." The longer she sat there, the worse she felt. She couldn't just hand over a bunch of weapons to Victoria. She would have to find a way to start and take just this one shuttle. The relief she had felt when she knew Brian was on the same page was immeasurable. His cooperation would make this whole thing easier. She knew that offering the Ficarans the key to unlocking all the Flyers, if she ever figured it out, would lead to war. That's what happened when one animal had an advantageous adaptation.

It made her think of invasive species. Normally, predator and prey would co-exist in a balance. Invasive species could disrupt this balance. Often, an invasive species would come in and decimate an existing native species because it had no natural predators, but sometimes it wasn't that simple. The Cornula boar was introduced on a Rim colony as a food source. However, the boars routinely lost the tips of their horns, which were hollow and perfectly-sized for the hermit crabs of the jungle floor. The only problem was that the birds' beaks had evolved to break the crabs' old shells. They couldn't get through the new horn ones. They were too tough. The birds that couldn't find another food source died.

Humans liked to pretend they weren't animals, but if she gave this harried leader a weapon, even if it wasn't her intent, she would use it. In this scenario, Dione was the Cornula boar, and she didn't like it.

Starting and taking just one shuttle was the only solution. In order for that to work, Victoria couldn't learn how to start the shuttles. Brian would still get it when she was finished with it, and he could control the use of the Flyers. Dione trusted him a lot more than she trusted Victoria.

The Ficaran leader looked angry, but swift footsteps echoing outside the shuttle caused her to turn. A man stood outside the shuttle, breathing heavily and fidgeting with his hands.

"Victoria," he began. Dione relaxed her shoulders once Victoria shifted her gaze.

"What is it, Nick?" she asked, as if she had been interrupted while reading a very good book.

"There's a dispute about the rations again," he said, squeezing out the words in between gasps.

"So settle it. That's your job, right?"

"I've tried, but they are requesting your judgment."

"Send them away with nothing, then."

Dione was watching the exchange with interest, no longer fiddling with the panel. She watched Nick open his mouth and close it twice before finally getting the words out.

"It's Melanie."

Victoria stiffened next to her, clenching her hands at her sides.

"Melanie?" Dione whispered.

"She's our best tech. Can fix almost anything. Gotta keep her happy," Brian whispered back. He was smiling, and Dione suspected he had something to do with this distraction.

Victoria turned to the burly man. "Colm, stay here and watch them." She pointed a finger at Dione. "You'd better have this thing up and running by the time I get back."

Victoria didn't wait for a reply before leaving, trailed by Nick.

Colm, the large, muscular man from breakfast, stayed close, watching, but not with the same interest. In fact, he seemed more interested in glaring at Brian than watching her. She figured now would be her only chance to look at the journal. She pulled it from her bag, and flipped to one of the more enigmatic passages.

She had barely reread the first sentence when Colm was on top of her, swatting the book from her hands.

"Get to work, now."

Brian stood up and looked like he was about to take a swing at the muscular mass in front of him. Luckily, Brian was too smart for that. He knew he would not win in a physical altercation. Despite that, he was not shaking like she was. Dione hated getting yelled at.

She glanced down to the journal, which had landed open and face down, causing the pages on either side to fan out. Her heart pounded in her chest when she realized that the answer had been hidden in plain sight.

"This journal is the key. Hang on," she said.

Colm backed up a step when she reached for the book.

"What is it? Did you figure it out?" Brian had already grabbed it off the floor and handed it to her.

"Look at this," she said. Brian leaned in close, while Colm gave them space. Dione fanned the gilded edges of the journal, and revealed an image. No, not an image. Measures of music. Dione adjusted the edges until the book was fully fanned, revealing an entire song. This was it. This was the key. It had to be.

"The lullaby," she said, so quietly only Brian could hear. "I've heard this one before."

Dione didn't know why lullabies were so dreary, but she started singing. She wasn't going to win awards for her musical talent, but her voice was smooth and pleasant as it followed the tune.

Oh the waters are rising,
Uprising, my dear.
And there's no compromising
This time, no, my dear.

She paused after the first verse, waiting to see if anything would happen, but the Flyer's controls were still not responding.

"I don't understand. This had to be it," Dione said, deflated.

"Let me see the journal," Brian said.

Before she could, Colm approached. "Give it to me," he said. "This is a waste of time. I'm taking you back up to Victoria."

"Stop, Colm, just give her another chance," Brian said, stepping in between Colm and Dione.

Dione knew what was about to happen, but she was powerless to stop it. Colm punched Brian in the gut, hard. Brian doubled over, gasping. Despite being strong and fit, Brian was no match for Colm, who probably received five times the average Ficaran's rations to get that size.

"It's the wrong key," Brian wheezed. "Just change it."

Change it to what? How could it be wrong? Before she could ask, Brian got back to his feet, but Colm was already stalking past him toward Dione.

"How's your daughter, by the way?" Brian said. Dione watched Colm's eyes go wide before they narrowed. Dione immediately deciphered the meaning behind that comment, but she couldn't figure out what Brian meant by the wrong key.

How could something so well hidden be the wrong key? That had to be the code. This had to be it. Maybe she needed to sing the whole song. She fanned out the pages again to look at the lyrics for each verse. There were three.

Oh the waters are rising,
Uprising, my dear.
And there's no compromising
This time, no, my dear.

For the rain drops are falling,
Befalling us, dear
And no shelter is stalling
This flood, no, my dear

Still there's no time for drowning,

Or frowning, my dear.
It's a new king their crowning
Bow down now, my dear.

Still nothing. And with her song over, she could better hear Brian groaning.

"Colm, stop." Dione was surprised to hear Victoria's voice. "Don't kill the boy. He has his uses, but starting Flyers just isn't one of them."

Dione knelt by Brian. His forearms were already bruising from blocking as many blows as he could, but she could see his right cheekbone swelling as well. He clutched his abdomen in pain, but still managed to moan something to Dione. "Change the key. Be..."

He was making even less sense. How could she change the key? Be what? She couldn't change the lock, so what use would a different key be? If you've got the wrong key to a door, you can't just change the key. You have to find the right one. And what did he want her to be? Careful?

The echo of footsteps crashed through the hangar for the second time.

"What is it now, Nick?"

"The Aratians are attacking. There's an inbound Flyer."

"Colm, organize the men and women." He left immediately, but Dione's relief was short-lived. Victoria had pulled a small hand gun on her. The hairs on Dione's arms stood on end when she heard the cocking of the gun.

"Start this Flyer now, or I'll kill you."

36. ZANE

Zane was getting worried. He'd checked on Bel, and at first, she hadn't responded. If it weren't for the monitors and the gentle rise and fall of her chest, Zane would have thought she was dead. After a few minutes, she opened her eyes long enough to look confused before going back to sleep. There was nothing he could do until Dione and Lithia returned, so he channeled his energy into figuring out what to do about the Vens.

Zane knew it was a long shot, but based on what he knew about this station, it was certainly possible. His parents had never been stationed on those state-of-the-art ships that actually did have self-destruct mechanisms, but he knew they existed. This station, well, it certainly had been home to terraforming pioneers. Geniuses.

What Zane didn't know was where to start. If there were any self-destruct capabilities, they would be very well hidden. So, the first thing to do, of course, was run a search for "explosives."

There were a lot of results. Apparently there were records of a few small explosions on the station due to some experiments gone wrong. Then there was the explosion of an experiment gone right. Too right. Some sort of reaction between... plants? Weird. Dione would be interested.

None of these things would work for blowing up the station, but he hadn't expected "explosives" to reveal a self-destruct program. He had just hoped that he would find an alternative that didn't involve digging around in code for hours.

Self-destruct programs were not searchable. They often had completely boring and innocuous names, and they required multi-pronged initiation. He didn't know if he could find it, start it, or if it even existed.

Zane began to slog through code, line by line, looking at the station's automated protocols, waiting for something to jump out at him. *This is what desperation feels like.* He had about a zero percent chance of success, but he didn't know what else to do.

After an hour or so, he stopped. This wasn't working. There had to be a way to figure out if a self-destruct protocol even existed. Time to take a step back and think through things.

Why install one?

Because you don't want your technology to get into enemy hands.

What's the easiest way to stop an enemy corp from getting your tech?

Blow it up.

No, it's not. That takes time, money, permits, additional risk of a malfunction. Look at the hardware around you. It's top of the line for a century ago, sure, but none of it is truly mind-blowing. Today only the most innovative hardware is equipped with self-destruct programs. What was the real value of this station?

The scientists.

You're a corporation, people are irrelevant.

Their research. The data. The genetic blueprints for all the new species and terraforming techniques.

Bingo. So how do you prevent that type of theft?

Data wipe.

Well, that was not the conclusion Zane was hoping to reach, but that tended to happen when searching for the truth. Sure enough, Zane found evidence that a data wipe procedure had been initiated over fifty years ago. What was unexpected was that all the data had been restored. Apparently it had been downloaded not only by the people initiating the data wipe, but a second time by someone in the Forest Base. After the wipe, everything had been restored, and no one had come back to check. And so, everything, all the research, records, and absence protocols that kept up the station, was still there.

That's when he noticed that new records had been added after the data wipe. After whoever was in charge metaphorically torched the mainframe, someone stuck around. Someone added a tiny little protected corner for some audio and digital logs, new research, and who knows what else. They were added to a personal file that had existed before the wipe.

Zane read the name aloud. "Myer, Samantha." He downloaded this data to his manumed. He wanted to know more about this Samantha. If she was around after the data wipe, she might have had something to do with the Farmer and whatever else was happening on the planet.

He skimmed through the titles of the entries. Some of them were just dates, but others had titles. It didn't take long before one audio log caught his eye, "Just a farmer." He pressed play.

I got assigned to Jameson's team, and I couldn't be more excited. Up to this point, I've spent most of my time modifying species, rather than engineering them. What if colonists could control their livestock with a measure of music? What if hunters could summon their prey with a whistle? What would happen if another predator learned these musical cues? But working with Jameson will be something new. I've spent the past few hours familiarizing myself with his research, and it's incredible.

Let me put it this way. In the early stages of terraforming, a rocky sphere is painted in broad strokes, like a primer. Then it's seeded with life in primary and secondary colors. Finally, they bring in the artists to paint the details that really bring the planet to life. I am an artist. But Jameson? He's Peter Paul Rubens. He's Vincent Van Gogh. And he knows it, even if he tries to downplay it with stories of his humble origins. He claims he's 'just a farmer,' but he's so much more.

This woman, Samantha, had been one of the original researchers on this station. And this Jameson guy, could he be the Farmer? Or was that just a coincidence?

He didn't think these entries would help him find a solution to the Ven problem, so it surprised him when he found an entry from much later, years later, after the station had been abandoned, titled, "Venatorian beacon."

Jameson's going to shut down the distress beacon on the Venatorian scout ship. The Icon, the weapon he installed in the Mountain Base, didn't work. His AI was too slow, not smart enough to pick up the threat in time to completely destroy it. Two Venatorians survived the crash. I found the bodies. All of them. So many dead colonists. And there were only two! How could two Venatorians kill more than twenty men? Even those loyal to him, brainwashed into thinking he's some god, didn't deserve the deaths they got. Blood everywhere, and I bet Jameson only weeps for their precious DNA.

I need to put a stop to this. In my desire to be left alone to my research and find a non-violent solution, I've let him get away with too much. Without him around, maybe these people can find peace. But I'll need to figure out a way to improve that AI. No Venatorian, no pirate, no despot, can ever find this place again.

This was the last entry. As curious as Zane was to find out what had happened in between, he already knew bits and pieces. He was fairly certain that Jameson was the Farmer and Samantha was the Architect. They were the only ones who had been here after the evacuation. Why they had both stayed and where all the colonists came from was still a mystery, but the answers were within reach. Unfortunately, there was nothing in that entry that would help him blow up the Vens. However, he did have one new, useful piece of information that Dione and Lithia might be able to use.

The Mountain Base definitely had an AI.

37. LITHIA

Lithia and Cora had been sitting in the tree house for over an hour.

Lithia kept messaging Zane, but he'd stopped replying. Something about working on his plan to get rid of the Vens.

Every time she thought about them, her anxiety grew. Why were they just waiting? Why not attack? What would happen to the people here? Was it her fault?

She knew the answer to that last one. Yes. And here she was, just sitting in a tree house, waiting for Dione to come rescue her and for Zane to save them all. If she had been short enough to stand beneath the low, rough ceiling beams, she would have been pacing.

"Are you sure they won't look for us here?" she asked.

"My father had a meeting until early afternoon, so they probably still don't know you're missing," Cora said.

"But pretty soon they'll start looking for me."

"I guess." Cora looked bored, and from the sound of her stomach growling, she was hungry. Cora was not accustomed to discomfort, and this time alone was allowing the doubt to creep in.

Lithia didn't completely trust her. She was so... pious. Lithia never trusted people who were absolutely convinced of their beliefs. It had never made sense. It was something she had learned from Dione, when they were younger. *Never close your mind to a new perspective.* Dione had probably read it in a book before programming it into a flowery font and adding it to the rotation of inspirational quotes that cycled through her wall display.

"We can't stay here much longer then," Lithia said.

"What does Zane say?" Cora asked. Cora didn't know what a Ven actually was or that they were here, portending death like a black cloud promises rain. They were demons out of her father's stories, ready to be vanquished, not living, breathing murderers.

Lithia checked her manumed again. Zane had still not replied. That was it. "We're taking the Flyer, the one I came down in. Do you know where it is?"

"Right where you left it. I overheard my father and uncle talking about posting a guard."

"It's guarded, then?"

"Yes. A few techs have been working on it. They were talking about doing a test flight tomorrow."

Hope flickered inside Lithia. If they were planning a test flight, they had probably made some repairs. She still had their crash coordinates, the ones Dione had figured out, in her manumed.

"All right, let's go. It's this way," she said, pointing off into the woods.

"With no machi?"

"What's a machi?"

"It's a machi, you know, we use them to get around."

"I've only seen maximutes."

"Machi have long noses, like this," Cora said, extending her arm in front of her face, "and strong legs. They have short fur, usually brown or black, and they're very affectionate."

"Are they fast?"

"Not as fast as maximutes, but they are much easier to command. Maximutes require too much precision with the pitches and sequences you use. I can ride one, of course, but you'd never be able to."

As much as Lithia wanted to accept that challenge, she didn't like the idea of Cora going back to the town, where someone was probably looking for them already.

"We're walking. It'll take a couple of hours, so we'd better get started."

Cora kept complaining, but much to Lithia's satisfaction, she did so while following her. Lithia didn't really think that wandering off into the woods again was the best idea, but she wouldn't sit around and do nothing. No one ever played the damsel in distress in the holos. That role was utterly boring.

***

Just a couple of hours later, Lithia was soaked with sweat and tired of Cora. Lithia had shushed her almost immediately after they headed out, worried that they would be discovered, so Cora had taken to whimpering in discomfort at regular intervals. She had almost given them away to a passerby in a green cloak, but he seemed in too much of a hurry to wonder about a few strange noises.

Still, something had been nagging at her the whole trip. She felt like they were being followed, but every time she turned around, there was no one. After a while, she shook the feeling off. If someone had been following them, they never would have gotten this far.

She finally caught sight of the shuttle in the distance, large and sleek despite its dents. Outside stood two guards, wearing the same type of harem pants she wore to dinner, except theirs were dark brown. Their shirts were the same color and had a more masculine cut. Each held some kind of sword.

"What's he holding? Is it made of wood?" Lithia asked.

"Yes, it's a *pila* blade. Sharp and lightweight."

"So no guns?"

"There's no need."

A man she presumed to be a tech was examining her shuttle. He had no uniform, and wore simple shorts and a tight tank top. His outfit reminded her a lot of Brian's, well worn and not nearly as baggy as Aratian harem pants. He was limping as he moved along the hull. She noticed that her own ankle was not sore at all, even after their hike.

A few boxes of supplies had been brought to the crash site, and that's where she saw it. Lying on top of one of the crates was her stun rifle.

Minutes ticked by. Two guards, one tech outside. Probably more inside the shuttle. Her only chance was to get the stun rifle, but the crates were right in front of the guards. Why were there guards, anyway?

That's when she figured it out. The tech wasn't limping. His feet were chained together. Of course. The Ficarans were the tech-savvy ones, so they liked to keep a few handy for big projects like this. This was good news. The techs probably wouldn't try to kill her.

"You need to distract them so I can get the stun rifle," Lithia said. "Right now, both guards are staring straight at it, and it's clearly visible from the shuttle."

"What do I say?" Cora asked. "Are you sure this is what the Farmer wants us to do?"

"Ask them about their work and themselves. People love complaining about one and talking about the other. Just make sure you get them away from the shuttle and the crate." Lithia looked at Cora saw the worry in her eyes, and for a moment, Lithia felt a little sympathy for her. Or maybe she just needed something. Either way, she offered Cora a little encouragement.

"Cora, by helping me, you will save lives. A very important life. I know this is difficult for you."

The girl smiled and hugged her. Lithia was not a hugger, but she did her best.

Cora walked up toward the shuttle, but stopped at a distance before calling out her greeting. Good. The guards would move closer, away from their posts.

Lithia doubled back and approached again from a different angle, closer to the crate. Her back was touching the side of the shuttle that faced away from the center of the clearing. When she peeked out, the two guards had their backs to her and the tech was on the opposite side of the shuttle, completely out of sight.

She was about to dart forward and grab the rifle, but another guard dressed in brown emerged from the shuttle.

"What the—" For a moment, she thought she was busted, but he'd apparently noticed the Regnator's daughter and stopped himself.

He took a few steps in Cora's direction. Lithia crept forward, but the man began to turn. She was too far to get to the rifle in time, and too far from her hiding place. The only option was to go inside the shuttle.

She ducked inside and saw a tall man and dark-haired woman staring at her. The man was holding a metal wall panel that the woman had just removed, judging by the tools in her hands. They didn't scream for help, which she assumed was a good thing.

"Are you Ficarans?" Lithia whispered. They nodded. "If I can get to that stun rifle there, I can stop all the guards. When the coast is clear, I'll—"

The man suddenly looked behind her and rushed forward, using the panel like a shield. She turned and realized that the shuttle guard had been about to return to his post. If the man's feet had been unshackled, he probably would have knocked the guard over. Instead, he knocked the guard off balance. The woman charged in to help. The second guard was running back to help, and the last was protecting Cora. He took a horn from his belt and sounded the alarm at the same time that the third tech joined the fray.

Lithia sprinted for the rifle, but the second guard saw her. She was ahead of him, and managed to grab it first, only to feel an arm closing around her throat from behind. She tried elbowing her assailant in the ribs, but couldn't land a blow.

The edges of her vision were beginning to blur when she heard a strange clicking sound. Sweet oxygen came rushing back into her lungs. Maybe Cora had managed to help after all.

Instead, she saw Evy, holding some sort of electrified cattle prod. *Unbelievable.*

"Evy, where did you come from?" Lithia said.

"I followed you."

Lithia smiled. This kid was going places. "Thanks for the help, but it's time to go."

"Nadia, look out!" said the other tech, but it was too late. Cora's guard had decided it was time to intervene and jabbed his blade at the dark-haired woman. She turned at the last moment, but not soon enough. Blood poured from a gash on her abdomen, a dark splotch on her shirt radiating outward from underneath her hands.

Lithia shot Cora's guard, and he collapsed with a loud thump, his red, wet blade slipping from his grasp. The shuttle guard looked at her, eyes wide, and the third tech punched him. Lithia fired again, but her hands were shaking and both her shots missed. They were enough to send the guard under cover. Lithia took a deep breath and tried to steady herself as she waited for the man to peek out from his hiding place. Moments later, when he did, she hit him. The final guard was unconscious.

Evy looked worried. "Are they dead?"

"No, they're just sleeping," Lithia replied.

The male tech was on the ground with Nadia, pressing on her wound. His hands were covered in blood. It looked bad, but then again, it always did. That's something she'd learned from shadowing her mother and father at the hospital. When it came to bleeding, it always looked worse.

Cora approached, face pale. Evy looked just as frightened. They definitely weren't used to this. Honestly, Lithia wasn't used to this either. "There might be something on the Flyer that can help," she said. A horn sounded in the distance. *Shit. Not a lot of time.* "Move her on board."

"What the hell is going on?" the tech asked.

"Jeremy, settle down," said the tall man who was still applying pressure to Nadia's side. Nadia was conscious, but weak.

"I'm going to take us all to the Ficaran settlement," Lithia said.

"We can't escape by foot, and the Flyer isn't fixed."

"We'll see about that." Lithia hoped they had made enough repairs. "Your friend is hurt and we need to move her onto the shuttle."

The tech looked at her for a minute, trying to decide if he should listen to this teenager, but Lithia exuded confidence like a tracking squirrel exuded its disgusting stench. Jeremy took the clean *pila* blade from the ground and cut their leg restraints. Nadia moaned when they moved her.

Lithia pried open a floor compartment and pulled out a first aid kit. This stuff was old. It might not work, but it wouldn't hurt to try. She tossed some clean bandages and a small brown tube at Jeremy. The other man's hands were back on Nadia's side.

"It's a coagulant. Topical, but it's the best we've got. When you're done, clean your hands. There are a few wipes still in the kit."

"Who are you?" Jeremy asked.

"It's a long story," Lithia replied.

She went straight to the navigation console. Time for a systems check. If this thing couldn't actually fly, they were screwed. Lithia was alarmed to see that they had already done a systems check. Error messages littered the screen.

"My god, this thing is red for days," she said, swiping through the readout. After a few minutes, Lithia made her diagnosis: "Huh. Let's try this anyway."

"So it's fixed?" asked Cora.

"Ish."

"Is it safe?"

"The major systems are fine. External cameras are down, stabilizers are, well, not completely shot. Altitude would be a problem, but we'll have to stay low to avoid the Icon anyway. If we get hit… your dad's men wouldn't shoot you out of the sky, right?"

"Of course not!" Cora said. "Maybe we should just tell him that you are working for the Farmer. He believes. I'm sure I could convince him."

Mother of the void. This girl. "The Farmer doesn't want us to tell anyone. I know it's all a little strange, but trust him. He honored you by choosing you to help me. If you aren't up to the task, I'll find someone else."

"No, I'll help. I'm sorry." As she apologized, she seemed to be looking upward rather than at Lithia. "I just… the Matching is in a few days."

"You'll be back by then."

At that moment, Cora remembered Evy, who had buckled herself into the copilot seat. She was so little that she was impossible to see from behind. The harness was too big, yet somehow Evy looked like a natural.

"What are you doing here?" Cora said.

"Evy, I can't take you with me. It's too dangerous," Lithia said. Evy pretended like she couldn't hear.

"I don't want you to get hurt," Lithia said.

Cora strapped herself into a passenger seat. "Evy, you can't go. We can't both go. Our parents will panic. The Farmer chose me for this mission. You have to stay."

The debate never got settled because Lithia heard another horn and distant shouting.

"All right, time to go. Looks like your parents will freak out together." The thought gave her some pleasure, tinged with guilt. Benjamin and Michael deserved to feel a little pain. The techs in the back looked concerned as the door closed.

"This won't work. It can't fly. We just tried." It was the tech who was trying to tend to Nadia's wound.

"You just didn't ask it nicely enough," Lithia said. She had sweet-talked a few systems into thinking they were in better shape than they really were. It wasn't a long flight. And they weren't leaving the atmosphere or anything. It would be fine. "Buckle in. Use the straps to secure Nadia. This is not going to be a smooth ride."

Lithia prepared for take off. *Here goes nothing.* Even inside the shuttle, the noise was extreme. The shuttle was rattling violently, but she continued their ascent. There was no way out but up. Once she hit the lowest possible cruising altitude, she urged them forward, slowly, afraid to go too fast or too slow. No one spoke, and Lithia was glad. If flying this rickety shuttle didn't demand her full attention, she was sure she'd be losing it right now. Her hands were still shaking. *Focus on the controls. Steady. All right. Need directions.*

***

Once they were under way, Lithia called Zane. After he got over his initial surprise and irritation that she had taken some initiative and done something about their predicament, Lithia was able to extract some useful information from him.

"Zane, where am I headed?"

"I sent you the coordinates."

"Didn't get them."

"Now?"

"Nope."

"Okay, can you input them manually?"

"Yeah, it's not like I'm busy flying a machine held together by metaphorical duct tape."

"Is that sarcasm?"

"Zane, I need the coordinates. Where are we going?"

"I can help," Evy said. She was in the copilot chair.

"Who was that?" Zane asked.

"Evy. Cora's cousin. Don't ask."

"This looks like some of the stuff in the temple. I can use it."

Worth a try. "Zane, read out the coordinates. Evy will put them in."

He did, and Evy entered them. A destination popped up on her interface, even though the AutoNav wasn't quite sure how to get there. It had been one of the damaged systems. One of her main reasons for choosing this particular Post-16 trip, aside from hanging out with Dione, was the chance to log some pilot hours, and this would certainly be a test of her skills.

The AutoNav helped some, but the shuttle was still difficult to control. The techs had been trying to solve a different problem. They were trying to get the shuttle into good shape, probably taking their time. All she needed was a getaway vehicle. They had made enough repairs to get this thing in the air, but it was probably a one-way trip. There was no time to relax, think, plan. She hoped Zane knew what came next.

Evy stared quietly out the front viewport. Cora was holding on so tight her knuckles were white. The ride was a bit bumpy, but at least it was brief.

They were about twenty minutes out when Zane got on the comms.

"Lithia, you need to hurry up."

"Why, is Bel okay? Are the Vens moving in?"

"No change. The medical bed gave her something to make her rest. It's Dione. I really should have heard from her by now."

"Do you think something happened?"

"I don't know, but I just got the most recent satellite images, and their hangar is open, if you can land there."

Lithia laughed. "Much like my cat, once this thing lands, it's not getting up again. We're gonna have to hover to pick her up. I guess we head to the hangar and hope she's in there."

They needed a plan. She wanted to talk to the two conscious techs in the back, but they were having their own hushed conversation. They were also too far away to overhear.

"Cora, Evy, what do you know about the Ficaran leader?"

Cora replied first. "Her name is Victoria. She's not very nice and doesn't want to trade with us. She wants all of our farming Artifacts to be destroyed just for spite."

"Yeah," Evy said, having nothing to add, but still wanting to contribute.

"What do you think she'll do to us if we're captured?"

"Captured? I thought you were working for the Farmer and his harbinger! They would never allow us to be captured."

Lithia rolled her eyes. She really ought to reassure Cora, but she couldn't help herself. "Don't presume to know his plan. Adversity is often a tool that gods use to test their followers." The lies only got easier. She glanced at Evy, who gave her a puzzled look.

Lithia did feel a twinge of guilt when she heard a big sniff come from Cora behind her as if she were trying to contain her tears.

"Cora, I will do everything I can to protect you. I am grateful to you for helping me." It was a promise she couldn't necessarily keep. "My friend is very sick, and she still may not make it." Lithia paused here, taking a breath for composure. "Without your help, she would have no chance."

This seemed to calm Cora down. Evy continued to stare at her thoughtfully.

Why was she so cruel to Cora? This girl had risked everything to help her, and she couldn't even muster up a little compassion. It was bad enough she and Zane had manipulated Cora, using her faith. But every time she saw Cora, she saw her grandmother's betrayal and remembered her grandfather's pain. *It's not Cora's fault.*

She couldn't wait until they got off this planet and never looked back. Zane was figuring out how to lure the Vens away, or destroy them, or something. Getting up to Zane was still a problem, but once she got Dione, they'd be able to head off and make some repairs.

Lithia had been stupid to even look for her grandmother. Miranda deserved to be forgotten. For a long time, Lithia hadn't known the truth. Her grandpa always talked about Miranda as if she had died tragically young, but a few months ago, she had found the letter. From that point on, every time her grandpa talked about Miranda, Lithia hated her a little bit more.

Grandpa had been reading and fell asleep in his tattered old chair, like always, but when Lithia removed his tablet from his lap and covered him with a blanket, she glanced at what he'd been reading. She should have stopped when she realized it was a personal letter, not one of his fantasy stories. Miranda wrote to him from the colonizer. It was the worst apology in history. Instead of taking responsibility for her actions, Miranda blamed everyone and everything else.

She even blamed Grandpa Min, and after all these years, and he still felt the wound. He was still reading that letter.

After that, Lithia had made up her mind to find Miranda, to ask her why she had done it. She would show Miranda that she had grown up to be an incredible person without her. That her father ran the biggest hospital on one of the core planets. That her grandfather still laughed and flipped pancakes way too high in the air and told her stories of the expansion. She wanted Miranda to know that they hadn't needed her.

And now she knew that all of that would have meant nothing. Miranda had a family here. She had loved them, nurtured them, and never abandoned them. She was dead, and all of the gloating in the world couldn't make her realize what she had left behind. So Lithia was going to save Bel, blow up the Vens, leave this planet, and erase it from her memory, just like it was erased from the public archives.

Some violent turbulence brought Lithia's wandering mind back to the task at hand. She watched their approach on her Nav panel, but it was a little off. This was why, instead of approaching cautiously and getting an update from Zane, they arrived to the panic-inducing pings of gunfire.

Super. She turned to the techs in the back. "Anything you can do to help out?"

"Not until we land," Jeremy said.

"That might be a problem." Lithia had no intention of landing.

38. DIONE

Dione knew it was bad because she couldn't remember the digits of pi to recite to herself. She didn't like time pressure assignments, especially ones that involved a gun in her face. What was worse, she could hear weapons firing outside. Where had the Aratians even gotten a shuttle? Brian said they didn't have any.

"I'm trying. I just need a few more minutes," she said.

"Time's up," Victoria snapped. "Either you have it or you don't. Now give me the key."

"I can't."

"Just give her a—" Brian began. Before he could finish, Victoria smacked him across his temple with the butt of her pistol. He hit the floor, out cold. Dione flinched.

"The Aratians are attacking, in a Flyer of their own. You gave them the key, and now you'll give it to me, or I kill him first, then you." Dione could hear gunfire coming from outside.

"He's one of your own people!"

"Hardly. I've seen the way you and this traitor look at each other. He only cares about his personal mission." Dione's face felt suddenly hot, and she didn't look at Brian. "You two were planning to take this Flyer. That's why he sent Melanie to make a fuss about her rations." Dione cast a furtive glance at Brian, but he just lay there. "Oh, he didn't tell you? Maybe I was wrong about the way he feels. Either way, the life of one foolish boy is insignificant in the larger picture. My men are poised to take these Flyers up and out. What's the key?" Victoria's finger curled around the trigger. "Now."

What's the key? That phrase awakened a memory inside of her, but her mind was iced over with fear. She could feel the answer just out of reach.

Suddenly, she had it.

Dione opened her mouth, but before she could respond to Victoria, a smoking heap of metal skidded through the rows landing just thirty meters away. Smoke billowed up from underneath it, and bullets had dented the hull. The shuttle emitted a high-pitched whine and bang before suddenly powering down. It would not be getting back off the ground, but it might distract them all just long enough for her to escape.

The shuttle door opened, and every Ficaran raised their weapon, uncertain about what they would find. From the wreckage, a Ficaran emerged, carrying an injured woman. She could tell by the clothes, even though they were both covered in blood. A few people rushed to help.

One Ficaran stayed behind in the shuttle. Then Lithia appeared, holding the stun rifle. Dione could hardly believe it. Lithia was here! The soldiers who had accompanied Victoria to the hangar looked confused. Dione could read the questions on their faces. Should they kill her? She knew the secret of the Flyers, too.

"What happened to Nadia?" one soldier asked.

"An Aratian wounded her in our escape. This girl helped us escape the Aratians. Please, Victoria, do not hurt her. We owe her," said the remaining tech.

"She's probably got a weapon aimed at you. We'll detain her, then you will have the opportunity to speak freely. Unless she makes this too difficult."

Dione was impressed with how quickly Lithia reacted. She returned to cover, and by the time Victoria figured out what was going on, it was too late. She scrambled out of the way as the energy pulse from the stun rifle narrowly missed her. The guards returned fire, but their weapons were lethal. Lithia fired off a few shots, but she didn't seem to hit anyone. She stayed close to the smoking craft. How did she look so comfortable in all this? Dione was impressed. Fortunately, with a Ficaran still on the shuttle, Victoria's guards took time aiming each shot.

Pretty soon, though, they would surround Lithia, and Victoria didn't seem very concerned about keeping her alive. Dione refocused. She had to get this shuttle into the air. She fanned the journal pages once more, and directed her attention to the musical notes. She needed the *key*, and that meant she had to sing the song, but in the correct musical key. She'd had music lessons, and she could tell what note she needed to start on, a B, but she didn't have perfect pitch. She didn't know what a B sounded like, and there wasn't enough time to guess. She needed her manumed. It would have a tuner.

Victoria wasn't paying much attention to her, now that she was under fire. Somehow even a woman like her could underestimate a girl. There was no time to think her way around the problem. She would have to tackle it head on.

Dione pounced. Victoria stumbled, but recovered her footing. She did, however, lose her grip on the gun. Dione scrambled for it, but she saw that she would not make it in time. Victoria was just about to grab it when she jumped back. An energy pulse from

Lithia's stun rifle had narrowly missed her shoulder. Dione lunged for the weapon and pointed it at Victoria.

In her biggest voice, Dione shouted, "Everybody stop or she dies!"

The already cocked gun trembled in her hands. Victoria nodded to her own soldiers, who lowered their weapons.

Before Dione could speak, Lithia stood up.

"Thanks all, but that's our ride. Come on," Lithia called into the shuttle.

A young woman and a wide-eyed girl emerged from the wreck unscathed. Lithia could crash as well as she flew.

The three girls headed to Dione's shuttle. Who were they? And why had Lithia brought a child with her? Wait, was that Evy? The other girl looked a lot like Lithia.

In Dione's moment of distraction, Victoria twisted out of her sights and caught her by the wrist. The pistol fell to the floor and Victoria shoved her in the opposite direction. As Dione tried to right herself, Victoria grabbed the pistol and aimed it once again at her.

She was going to die. After everything.

In that same heartbeat, Lithia knocked Victoria out with one shot. The woman went limp, and shots began ringing against the hull of the shuttle. In another moment, all three girls were on board, and Dione closed the back of the shuttle. The weapons fire stopped.

"Please tell me you can start this thing," Lithia said.

"Yeah, give me your manumed."

Dione found a tuner app and played a B. She sang the lullaby one more time, all the verses, just to be sure. Beneath them, the engines powered up and the shuttle hummed to life. The controls would now respond to commands.

"Nice, Di," Lithia said, settling into the pilot's chair. "Let's get out of here."

With Victoria on board, no one took a shot at them as Lithia guided them from the hangar. The Ficarans hadn't thought to lock them in until it was too late. They passed through the hangar doors with plenty of room to spare. They were out of the danger zone, but Brian was in bad shape, and Victoria would wake up eventually. Evy and the other girl were staring at her. Dione put a hand on Lithia's shoulder.

"Thanks for coming to get us," she said with a serious sincerity she rarely used with her best friend.

"Well, I wasn't about to let you stand me up," Lithia said.

"Hi, Evy," Dione said, giving Evy a warm smile. She turned to the unfamiliar girl who was still pale and shaking. She extended a hand. "I'm Dione." It was amazing how much like Lithia the girl looked.

"This is my cousin Cora," Evy said. Cora nodded at Dione, but left her hand unshaken.

"Will you two tie up Victoria?" She would check their work later. That seemed to help Cora, who focused on the task.

Meanwhile, Dione checked on Brian. He was waking up, but he looked terrible. She gently touched the bruise by his eye, and he groaned as he straightened himself against the bulkhead.

"Anything broken?" she asked.

"Maybe a rib or two," he said, "but I'm probably fine. Colm's a real jerk though."

"You did antagonize him," Dione said.

"I just inquired after his daughter." Brian played innocent. "Nothing wrong with that."

"You'll have to tell me that story sometime." Dione laughed, and Lithia joined their conversation.

"Any thoughts on where to go? I don't want to take this baggage all the way with us," Lithia said, nodding toward the still-unconscious Victoria.

"We could leave her at the coast," Brian said. "We have some shelters there, and it's a manageable trip to get back."

"Then maybe we should leave her somewhere else a little less manageable," Lithia said.

"We don't want to hurt her," Dione said.

Lithia laughed bitterly. "She had a gun pointed at you a few minutes ago. I sure as hell want to hurt her."

"It's... complicated," Dione said. Lithia hadn't seen what it was like for the Ficarans.

"You say that like I care. She was going to shoot you."

"Probably not fatally. She still needed something from me."

"Whatever, we'll figure it out once we land. Brian, can you give me some directions?" Lithia said.

"Directly south from the settlement," he replied.

"How far?"

"Stop when you see water." Brian grinned at Lithia. She looked at him for a second, then laughed. The tension that had been building relaxed.

Dione helped Brian into the copilot seat so that he could monitor the external cameras and tell her where to set down when the time came. She was probably imagining it, but she thought he had leaned on her just a bit more than he needed to, and his hand had lingered on her shoulder just a little too long. Victoria had been right about her feelings for Brian, so maybe she was right about how Brian felt. Even though she had a million other problems, she couldn't stop thinking about the night in the smuggler's den, parsing his words and actions until she wasn't even certain what had really happened.

Dione shook off the distraction and went to check the ropes. She was struck by how peaceful Victoria looked. Minutes ago, this woman had been willing to kill Brian, and Dione didn't doubt that she meant it. The thing that bothered Dione the most was that she understood Victoria, mostly thanks to her conversations with Brian. She couldn't fault her for being a good leader, for her willingness to sacrifice one person in order to save her people.

Dione couldn't help doing the opposite. She would give up everyone else to protect those she loved, at least when there was a chance. A wave of sadness washed over her as she remembered Professor Oberon. Whether it was loyalty or folly, she didn't know, but there was a part of her that admired Victoria. How close had she been to helping Victoria and dooming an entire city full of people she had never met? Full of people who were loved and would be missed, like Evy and Cora.

"Is she secure?" Lithia called back to her.

"Yes," Dione replied. For the first time since the Ven attack, she felt truly hopeful. They had a shuttle again, and they knew where the Icon was, thanks to Zane.

Zane. She had never checked in.

"Lithia, can I borrow your manumed? I want to call Zane."

"I already told him we made it. Just wait until we land. I want to talk to you first."

What was she afraid that Zane would tell her? Had Bel...

"Is it Bel? Is she?" Dione couldn't say the word.

"No, she's alive, but not responsive. Don't worry, I've got the meds. Once we drop off Victoria, we'll head to the Icon. Zane has its location."

Despite the good news, Dione's hope was waning. If it wasn't Bel, what was wrong? A dark fear crept into her thoughts as she cycled through what it could be, and settled on the most likely reason. She hoped she was wrong.

39. DIONE

Lithia set them down near the coast just before the grass faded into sand. Once the shuttle door opened, they could hear the ocean. The salty air quickly permeated the shuttle.

The first thing Dione did once they landed was hug Lithia. She pulled her in tight, and Lithia, who didn't really like hugs, squeezed back. For all Lithia's jokes, she must have been worried.

"I'm glad you're not dead," she said.

"Ditto. Thanks for coming through back there. Where did you get that shuttle?"

"Don't tell me you didn't recognize Nate!"

"Nate?" Dione said. Then she remembered. "Shuttle N-8. No way."

"That mess I was flying is the same one we came down in. The Aratians patched him up with the forced help of Ficaran techs, but it was like using a fig leaf to cover up—"

"No need to add imagery. I get it." Dione grinned. Lithia was back. Relief flooded through her. Her best friend was back.

"We need to talk, Di," Lithia said.

Brian could take a hint. "I'll keep an eye on things here," he said.

"Me, too," Evy said, taking up position next to Brian. Cora, who looked a little sick, stayed seated. Maybe all this flying didn't agree with her.

They stepped from the shuttle and walked down to the beach. They were close enough to see and hear the ocean, but no evidence of the southern island was visible. "How's your ankle? You seem better."

"The Aratians have some magic tea that patched me up. It's barely sore." The breeze caught Lithia's straight black hair and sent it billowing behind her. Dione's hair, now short, blew in her face. Even physics was playing favorites.

"What's wrong?" Dione said, once they were out of earshot.

"There's a Ven ship here, the one that attacked us, but it's holding position."

Dione shivered as the wind picked up. She knew it. The minute Lithia wouldn't tell her on the shuttle, she knew.

"Why isn't it moving?" Dione said.

"Zane thinks it may still be damaged and that it's making repairs." Lithia looked up at the sky as if she was trying to see what was going on up there.

Dione closed her eyes, but she couldn't think. She kept imaging green monsters tearing through the Ficaran square. "What do we do?"

"We go destroy the Icon, or find its off switch or whatever, then go cure Bel. Zane's been working on a plan to take care of the Vens."

"What is it?"

"I don't know, but I'm just as curious as you."

They called him to find out.

"Zane, we made it," Dione said. "Lithia's got the meds, and we've got a working shuttle."

"Good, I've got the coordinates for the Mountain Base where the Icon is. Sending them now." Lithia's manumed buzzed.

"What's your plan for the Vens? Lithia told me they're here."

"I'm trying to figure out if there's a way to make the space station explode."

Dione and Lithia exchanged a look.

"And how's that going?" Lithia asked.

"Not good. There are no explosives on the station, and I've found no evidence of a self-destruct protocol. It was a long shot to begin with," he said.

"No giant red button, huh?" Lithia said.

"What? No, that's ridiculous."

Dione could hear the confusion in his voice. He wasn't very good at picking up on sarcasm.

"She's kidding. Keep trying. We'll head to the Mountain and disable the Icon." Dione was worried.

"We could always try to program the Icon to only shoot Vens," Lithia said.

"I already considered that," replied Zane. "If it can't even destroy a shuttle, what chance does it have against a Ven ship? Besides, I found something up here to suggest that the weapon's AI doesn't allow the weapon to operate at peak efficiency."

"AI? What else do you know?" Dione asked. This was news to her.

"Not much, just that the Farmer installed the AI, but it wasn't able to stop a Ven scout ship that came here decades ago," he said. Dione and Lithia had both heard all about the "demons that fell from the sky." That scout ship must have been it.

"How do you know all this?" Dione said.

"I think I found the Architect's audio logs. Apparently she was a researcher here named Samantha. She ended up working against the Farmer, who she called Jameson. He was a terraformer, too, but he left during the evacuation, according to the records."

"Maybe he came back later," Lithia said.

"And brought the AI with him," Dione said.

"Possibly. Maybe you could bypass the AI and directly control the weapon," he said.

"And you think we'll be able to control it with more precision and accuracy than an AI?" Dione asked.

"I don't see a lot of other options."

"Point taken," she said.

"Hurry," Zane said, ending the call.

A sense of dread was creeping up, but Dione pushed it back. Time to regroup. And confess.

"I told Brian everything."

"Including your major crush on him?" Lithia said. She was smiling, but Dione thought she detected a hint of irritation in her voice. Was Lithia mad that she had told him, or mad that she had gotten to spend some time alone with him?

"Stop it. No, I don't." Dione rolled her eyes and tried not to think about their kiss. No need to tell Lithia just yet. "I mean, he knows about Bel, the Vens, and the space station."

"How'd he take it?"

"I don't think he gets the scope of just how big the universe is, but that's not really easy to grasp. For anyone. He knew we were holding something back, and I think having a dad who didn't believe in any of their myths or superstitions primed him to understand."

"I didn't tell Cora anything. She thinks Zane and I have called her on some mission from the Farmer. They have a myth that the Farmer will return with more colonists, and that there will be a harbinger of his arrival. That's us. She's not gonna last, though. We need to get her home ASAP."

"And Evy?"

"Evy hasn't said anything, but she's not exactly a model Aratian child. By her parents' standards anyway." Lithia paused. "Di, there's something else I need to tell you. The reason I had these coordinates, the reason I used your dad's access—"

"You don't have to tell me," Dione said. She wasn't sure how deeply she felt it, but it was true. Lithia didn't have to tell her anything. The argument of two days ago seemed ridiculous now, given everything that had happened.

"You need to know. It's because I was looking for my grandma."

"What?" Dione said. That was not the answer she'd been looking for.

"Not Nana. Grandpa Min's wife. My dad's mom."

"I thought she died," Dione said. "The way he always talked about her..."

"She might as well have. She left him and broke his heart, and I wanted to find her. So I got Zane to help me find all the potential coordinates from colonizers at that time, even the unlikely ones, like this planet. But she came here. She had a life here, a family, before she died." Lithia paused. "Di, Cora is my cousin."

Dione didn't know what to say. "Are you going to tell her?"

"She already knows. Her father, the Aratian overlord, or whatever, thinks I'm making it up. They think I somehow faked my DNA, which they can test, by the way, and altered my appearance. Zane told her to trust me, though, and it's worked out so far. Apparently because we have communicators, we must have gotten them from the Farmer."

The genetic lock in the Forest Temple made sense now, but it should have been keyed to the scientists, not the colonists. No one could get into those rooms, according to Brian. She had an idea about why it was keyed to Lithia, but she had to double-check first, before she said anything.

"Once we get out of here we can find a way to come back. Maybe we can renegotiate this planet into the Bubble, or—"

"No. I don't know what I was thinking. I want nothing to do with these crazy people."

Dione didn't respond. Lithia might change her mind later, but if Dione pressed her now, she would only become more resistant to the idea. Time to change the subject.

"We have to tell Brian the Vens are here. He deserves to know," Dione said.

"What about Victoria?"

"She wouldn't believe us anyway. I'll talk to Brian. You can tell Cora and Evy where we're going."

***

Brian headed toward Dione. He was straight out of the vids, his dark hair unbound like a mane in the wind, his eyes fixed on her. She wanted him to kiss her again, and for a moment, she thought he would, but he stopped short, leaving a gap between them. She could always kiss him first.

"I heard you wanted me?" he asked. Dione blushed. He was doing this on purpose. She could tell by the smile on his lips. He didn't expect her to do anything. Her heart was racing. She would blame all of this on the adrenaline from their escape, even though she knew that it wasn't the reason. She would be sad to leave him.

"Yeah, we're leaving Victoria here, like you said, but I wanted to make sure it's safe. We don't want to hurt her."

"My people are probably already on their way. They think you're all Aratians and that I'm a traitor."

"I know." Dione looked down. "I'm sorry. I never wanted that to happen."

She felt him take a step closer, and when she looked up, she was staring straight into his brown eyes. Her instinct was to look away, but this was probably the last moment they would have alone. She wanted to remember his face.

"You know I made this choice, right?" he said. "And I don't regret it."

Dione didn't think. She kissed him, and felt his arms wrap around her waist, filling her with warmth. When they broke apart, Dione's heart was beating fast. Brian smiled at her.

"What will happen to you?" She was worried about him.

"I don't know. I'm just hoping I can cash in a favor or two from you before you leave."

"Anything I can do to help, I will." Dione looked back to the shuttle. Lithia was still inside with everyone. She didn't imagine that was very fun.

"Are you sure Victoria will be safe if we leave her here? We'll leave food and water, of course, but no weapons."

Brian paused before answering. "The coast and plains here are pretty tame, especially if she waits to be found. But Victoria isn't likely to stay put."

"Would she take it as a show of good faith?"

"Victoria holds a grudge better than anyone I know," he said, "but she'll at least be confused. She doesn't understand that you're not really her enemy."

"I don't think leaving her here could make things worse," Dione said. "We're heading to the Mountain Base. Apparently the Icon is controlled by an AI."

"A what?"

"Artificial intelligence. A machine that's programmed to think like a human."

"That's terrifying," Brian said.

She opened her mouth as if she were about to speak, but then closed it again.

"What is it?" he asked, eyes intent. "What don't you want to tell me?"

There was no avoiding it. She had to tell him. "The Vens, the so-called demons, are here."

Brian frowned. "They followed you?"

"Probably. But we're working on a plan to stop them."

He looked down, frowning, but he didn't say anything. Over his shoulder, she could see Lithia waving to her.

"Lithia's calling us over. Let's go," she said. She was responsible for leading death to his planet. How could you forgive that?

The two met Lithia at the shuttle entrance. She pressed her fingertips against her temples.

"Victoria's stirring," she said to Brian.

Brian knelt by Victoria, who was propped against the bulkhead. A bruise was beginning to darken her forehead.

She looked confused when she opened her eyes, but only for a few seconds. Then she straightened and glared at Brian.

"Listen to me, please," Brian said. "Dione and Lithia never wanted this to happen. They are just trying to save their friend."

"You can't be that naïve," Victoria said. "They're Aratian spies. They even showed up with Aratian nobility. I don't care what they're trying to do. I'm trying to save our people. Even your father would be ashamed of you, and he was the most selfish man I knew."

"You think I'm working against you?" Brian came back swinging. "I'm doing what you're too afraid to do. To trust them. These two could have offered us so much more than a Flyer, but you refused to look beyond your plan. What if they could clean up the runoff from the mine or help us fix the broken Artifacts that we can't? The only reason Dione hesitated to help us is because she knew what you planned to do. She knew you would use the Flyers to attack. Was she wrong?"

Victoria glared at him. "You have no idea what their Regnator Michael is capable of. If you did, you'd take that Flyer to the Aratian settlement yourself."

Evy took a step closer. "What did the Regnator do?" Dione could see the girl blinking back tears. Somehow Evy was always observing, always listening.

"He's a murderer." Victoria wasn't yelling, but her voice was low with controlled anger.

"That's a lie!" Cora yelled.

"I don't know what else to call starving children."

"Stop it!" Cora said. "Evy, don't listen to her. She's a liar."

"They're starving?" Evy asked.

Lithia moved to intervene, but Dione held her back.

"Yes, the Aratians have refused to trade with us. Our fields are poisoned, and your people have more than enough," Victoria said, looking straight at Evy. "So our children are starving alongside the adults."

"But you won't fix the plows anymore. And you won't trade us parts and equipment that we need for our research. That's what my father says," Evy said.

"We don't have the parts. We barely have enough equipment for ourselves. The supplies the Farmer left are almost gone, and we have to learn how to make do without them." Victoria almost seemed to have a soft spot for Evy.

"But you kidnap our people," Evy continued. "I know it. My friend's sister was taken."

"We don't kidnap anyone. Some people come to us begging to leave. They want to be free. Many wish to avoid the Matching."

Cora couldn't contain it any longer. "That's absurd. The Matching is an honor, but you don't understand that. All you understand is your greed."

Dione thought Victoria would be angry at that, but instead she looked deeply sad, more human than she had ever looked before.

Victoria's voice was steady. "The Matching is barbaric. I wish I were lying, child, but I have the scars to prove it."

Child? The word was jarring. *Isn't that what the Aratian man had called Lithia at the shuttle crash site? Had Victoria been an Aratian refugee herself?* Brian did not look surprised.

"You were Aratian," Dione said, completing her thoughts out loud.

"Yes, I was," she replied.

"That's impossible. My father would have told me," Cora said.

Evy said nothing. She just stared at Victoria. Dione could see her thinking, probably trying to make sense of this new information.

Victoria frowned. "You look about sixteen. For some, the only way to learn a painful lesson is to survive it. We accept anyone who needs refuge from the Aratians and the Matching." Cora seethed, her arms folded across her chest. Victoria looked at Evy and softened her tone. "There's time yet for you."

Dione could hardly believe that this side of Victoria existed. An hour ago she had pointed a gun at Dione's head. She still wanted to use the shuttles to raid the Aratian settlement. Dione saw for the first time that above anything else, Victoria had a purpose which drove her every action, and she never doubted that purpose.

"She's a liar. You work with the Farmer and the harbinger. Tell her," Cora said.

Victoria raised an eyebrow, but said nothing.

"We need to go," Dione said. She opened her own pack and dropped some food and a water bottle in front of Victoria. "That bottle removes contaminants from the water that you put in it, making it safe to drink. Even your river water. Just give it about a minute to work. This indicator on the side here will turn green when it's safe." Victoria glanced toward the ocean, and Dione answered her unspoken question. "Don't use it on salt water. It doesn't work very well."

"And you expect me to believe you?" Victoria said.

"At this point, I don't really care. I'm doing everything in my power to help you out. Use it or don't, but try to stay alive. I don't want them saying we kidnapped you and left you for dead."

With that, they untied her and left for the Mountain Base.

Cora was frowning as the took off. "Why didn't you tell her she was a liar? You work for the Farmer, and he taught us the Matching was necessary for the colony's survival. The very fact that they've rejected Aratian ways endangers us all. Our strength is our diversity."

Lithia opened her mouth to answer, but Dione cut her off. This question didn't need to be answered with a lie. "Because sometimes people are too caught up in their own reality to hear the truth. You have to wait until they are ready to listen, or they won't hear you."

Cora thought about her answer, but she didn't seem completely satisfied. She didn't say anything else.

After that, the ride was uncomfortably quiet.

40. DIONE

Dione had to convince Brian to eat something, which was alarming, considering he was always hungry. The food seemed to help, though he still looked terrible.

"You look awful," Lithia said.

"You really know how to make a guy feel special," Brian said. He winked at Dione, and then winced.

Dione watched the exchange, but she didn't feel jealous. Flirting was as natural as breathing to those two. Dione was so lost in her thoughts she almost missed the Mountain Base. Evy was the one who noticed.

"What's that?" Evy said.

If it weren't for the giant landing pad, Dione didn't think they would have found it. It was nothing more than a door built into the mountain side. Lithia brought them down gently near the entrance.

Cora was fidgeting. "I can't believe we're here. No Aratian has been here since the Farmer left."

"Do you ever call him grandpa? Or is he always the Farmer?" Lithia said.

"The Farmer. It's a sign of respect."

Dione hesitated in front of the door, so Lithia opened it and walked in.

The lights came on when they entered a small atrium. The place looked abandoned, but everything still looked functional. A layer of dust covered every surface. When they entered the main entrance hall, the room opened up with a higher ceiling than the hallways that branched away from this central area. There were a few desks, tables, and benches, and it reminded Dione a little bit of the Ficaran entrance hall where she'd eaten breakfast yesterday. The bases must have a common design, but that wasn't surprising.

"It looks like home, but kind of wrong," Evy said. She moved around to examine everything in sight, full of wonder. "Do you think the upper floors are the same, too? Like our bedrooms?"

Before anyone could stop her, Evy ran off, up the stairs. Cora followed after her. "Evy, wait!" she said.

"What the—" Lithia was looking at her manumed. "My manumed is connecting to something here. Weird."

An emotionless female voice came out of nowhere. At least that's what it seemed like until Dione noticed a small console on the wall.

"I am the Mountain Base Artificial Intelligence. Who are you? State your purpose for coming here."

"What?" Lithia said.

"Are you pirates?"

"No," Dione said.

"Why have you lowered the dampening field?"

"Our friend on the space station needed to be able to communicate with us. The dampening field prevented this."

"It prevented many things, and without it, the Venatorians have found this place."

She knew about the Vens! Clearly she didn't know about the tracer that had been attached to their ship. No need to make her angrier, though.

"We know about the Vens, too," Dione said. "We came here to help. We know about the weapon in this base, but it failed to destroy our shuttle and a Ven scout ship because..." This was awkward.

"Because the AI couldn't cut it," Lithia finished.

"And you think that AI was me?"

"Is there another AI?"

"Not anymore." Her voice was chilling. She sounded so much more real than the simple AIs allowed back home. "That may have been why the Venatorian scout ship got through years ago, but the reason your unauthorized shuttle survived is a completely different matter."

"Enlighten us," Lithia said.

"Your shuttle survived because the weapon did not have enough power. Decades ago, a Venatorian scout ship came here, and the Icon failed to destroy it completely because of the AI. Two Venatorians survived the crash and set up a distress beacon. Jameson thought he destroyed it, but later, a backup signal began transmitting."

"So you think the distress beacon alerted the Vens," Dione said. Maybe it wasn't the tracer after all. Having a backup signal definitely sounded like the Vens.

"Yes."

"Jameson's the Farmer, right?" Lithia asked.

"Yes, Jameson is the one who brought all these people here." This was news to Dione. The Farmer, Jameson, left and came back with these people. Why?

"So you know how my people came to this planet?" Brian asked.

"Yes, but now is not the time. My primary objective is to protect the colonists and they are all in danger."

"Zane, our friend on the station, was working on a plan to stop the Vens, but he's not having much luck. We need to go up there and help him. We also have medicine for our other friend Bel, who's very sick. We need you to let us go without shooting us down."

"I cannot let you leave. There's work to be done."

"What? We'll come back down, but Bel needs these meds or she'll die."

"Do you know why the Venatorian ship is currently stopped?" she asked.

"It's making repairs," Lithia said.

"It's waiting for reinforcements. Once they arrive, they will lead a full assault on the colony."

All of the hairs on Dione's arms and neck stood on end. More Vens?

"Can one of us go?" Lithia asked. "That way you know we'll come back."

"No, but your friends can come down here. I will allow them to land. I think Zane, the one you say shut down my dampening field, can help me."

"But he's working on a plan up there," Dione said. The AI didn't need to know that things weren't working out or that they planned to turn her off to work the Icon themselves.

"The Icon will work, and I can strike with much more precision than the previous AI."

"Then why not destroy our 'unauthorized' shuttle?" Lithia said.

"Because my energy cells have been depleted and damaged. They need repair. I cannot let you leave until the threat has been neutralized. The Icon and dampening field must be restored."

Lithia raised her voice. "I don't think you understand. Our friend will die without these meds."

"As I've said, you can bring her down here," the AI said.

Dione thought about it a moment. Lithia did not.

"Zane can't fly our ship, and I'm not leaving it up there on the station."

"It's not a long trip," Dione said.

"Have you ever landed a ship like the *Calypso* in atmosphere? A shuttle is like a car. With a little thought, you can figure it out. That jump-capable ship is ten times more complicated."

"But there's an autopilot," Dione said.

"Do you trust the autopilot to do all the work after that Ven attack? If something goes wrong, he's screwed."

"It's the only option. Plus, the repairs should be complete by now. Get on your manumed. We're calling Zane," Dione said.

"But—"

"Compromise, Lithia. It's the only option, and I'm not wasting anymore time arguing."

Zane answered immediately. "Please tell me you've disabled the weapon," he said.

"Not exactly. And just FYI, the AI can hear you. Think you can fly the *Calypso* down?" Dione said.

"Probably, but I thought it wasn't safe. Especially if the weapon's still functioning. Why can't you come back up here?" Zane said.

"The AI you mentioned is here, listening, and won't let us leave until we restore power to the weapon, the Icon. She knows about the Vens, and she thinks they're waiting for backup."

"That's actually probably a good plan. I'm no closer to figuring out how to blow up the space station. Bel is going to be hard to move, though."

"The AI here controls the weapon that hit us, but claims it was a different AI that failed to destroy a Ven scout ship that crashed here a while back and set up a distress signal. If we can fix the power issue, she'll be able to destroy the Vens for us," Dione said.

"Assuming we can trust her," Lithia added.

"There doesn't seem to be much of a choice. The scientist Samantha, the Architect, who stayed behind said she would try and fix the AI, so maybe it worked. I'm going to prep the ship. Bel doesn't have much time left, and maybe I can help with whatever's wrong with the weapon," Zane said.

"Do you have any training flying the *Calypso*?" Lithia said.

"I spent a lot of time watching you fly, Lithia, and I'm a fast learner. You should realize that by now. I know Dione thinks I'm an idiot, but you know better." The comment made Dione blush. She had been pretty unfair to him before they got into this mess. She would need to apologize later.

"Zane, I know I make flying that ship look like a breeze, but it's incredibly difficult, especially in atmosphere," Lithia said. "I'm going to walk you through it. Keep your channel open. I wish Oberon hadn't banned the holo interfaces for our manumeds. It would be so much easier if I could show you."

The AI rejoined the conversation. "He can come down safely, but you need to get started right away. My diagnostics show a problem with the energy cells. They're in sub-basement three."

Evy and Cora came back downstairs. Cora looked a little more relaxed than she had before, and possibly less annoyed. Maybe she was actually enjoying exploring this place with Evy.

"What's happening?" Cora asked.

"We have to make some repairs. I'm headed to the basement. Zane will be coming."

"Zane is coming here? The Farmer's harbinger?" She sounded a little too excited. Evy, on the other hand, rolled her eyes and ran off down a corridor that lit up as it detected her motion.

"Evy, come back! You'll get lost in this place," Cora said. She looked to Lithia for something, sympathy maybe, but Lithia just smiled. Cora ran after Evy.

Dione headed to the lift, but Lithia wasn't following.

"I can't lose signal. I need to be here to answer any of Zane's questions. Plus, Evy will eventually come back."

"I'll help," Brian said, moving to stand next to Dione.

"You sure you're up to it?" Dione asked. His bruises looked painful.

"Yeah, it looks worse than it is."

Dione and Brian headed down to the lower levels to better understand the energy problem. She was probably the worst one of the group to try to fix something like this. She understood biology far better than electronics, but there was no one else left to do it.

When they left the lift and went down the short hallway to the reactor room, she was expecting to see some large nuclear device that had been popular around the time this facility was built. After all, that sort of technology powered the space station. Or maybe solar energy, like she had seen at the Field Temple. What she found was completely unexpected. Before her stretched a row of microbial fuel cells. Not the small science fair projects, but the large industrial grade ones that had been developed to power entire towns.

"Whoa," Dione said. "Do you have these in your temple?"

"No," Brian replied, "we have mostly solar cells."

"I'm not surprised. These MFCs are extremely efficient and renewable, but they require a certain amount of maintenance. Maybe they were experimenting with them? I can't believe they're still functioning after all this time."

"It sounds like they're broken, though," Brian said.

"Without regular maintenance, they can be a bit temperamental. Especially these older models. But a lot of them are still working."

"They look newer than the rest of the equipment."

"Maybe the Farmer, or Jameson, I guess, brought them and installed them later."

The AI spoke through the intercom by the door, making Dione jump.

"At first, I had enough power for the weapon and the dampening field, but as power cells failed over time, I had to make choices."

Actually, your algorithms dictated your course of action based on available data, Dione thought, but she wasn't going to say it.

"The power going to the weapon was greatly reduced, making it ineffective."

"It didn't seem so ineffective to me."

"The size and defensive capability of a small transport shuttle should have made it an easy target to destroy. At full power, the weapon can destroy entire mid-tier ships."

Dione felt goose bumps run up her arms. That kind of fire power would have pulverized their shuttle, and not many colonies had them. No wonder the old AI had trouble controlling it. The research done here must have been well-funded to afford something that could take out mid-tier ships. Or the Farmer had deep pockets before his arrival.

"How many cells do you need to power the weapon?"

"Sixty percent would power the weapon and the other basic functions of this station. The reason it's so high is because I'll need to fire in swift succession. There will not be time to recharge once the Venatorians start their descent."

"Did Zane really blow this many power cells?"

"No, but his actions disrupted the dampening field, and there was not enough remaining power to reinitialize the field. My attempts to stop him only made things worse. The power cells were not designed with a dampening field in mind."

"What does that mean?" Brian said.

"Dampening fields require an insane amount of power to generate, though less to maintain. No one would use microbial fuel cells for that. These things are slow burn type of energy. Keeping them too hot for too long led to early degradation," Dione explained.

She thought she understood. In the AI's attempts to fend off Zane's attacks on the dampening field, she overloaded a lot of these power cells. Not only could she not reestablish her dampening field, but she didn't have enough power to protect the planet from things like the Vens. And the Vens had possibly found them because the dampening field was down now. Whether it was the tracer or distress signal, the Vens' appearance here was definitely their fault.

"They were failing even before Zane took out the dampening field. It was only a matter of time before the field died on its own," Dione said.

With a few directions from the AI, Dione called up the readout and grimaced as she looked over the diagnostic results. Barely twenty percent of the cells were operational, but most of them were salvageable.

"I think we can jump start the process in most of these and get you back up to eighty, maybe eighty-five percent operational."

"How long will that take?" the AI asked.

"I'm not sure. Some of them need some mechanical adjustments. Others need a fresh infusion of bacteria. It's easy enough to get—just find some mud or waste—but the quantity we'd need is the issue. With our limited manpower, probably a couple of weeks."

Even as she said it, she knew it was hopeless. They would never repair the weapon before the Vens came. It was funny. They had come here to disable the weapon, and now they were trying to fix it. Too bad the fix would be too late. Maybe there was another way to defeat the Vens.

"I want to check in with Lithia. Zane should have left by now." She headed to the lift, but the doors wouldn't open.

"Base, what's wrong?" she said.

"Before you return to Lithia, I want to ask you another question. You say you have a jump-capable ship. What powers your jump drive?"

"A charging matrix."

"Look at the power requirements for the weapon on the console. How long does it take your matrix to produce enough energy to power the weapon?"

Dione looked up the specs on her manumed and answered. The pit of her stomach dropped when she realized where this line of questioning was headed.

"Base, I know you want to use our matrix to power the weapon, but I don't know if the two pieces of technology are compatible, or if we'll ever be able to disconnect it."

"I understand that," was the AI's only reply.

This AI was serious. It wanted to take part of their ship and use it to power the weapon.

"If we incorporate our charging matrix here, we may never be able to reinstall it in our ship. We could be stuck here." She was thinking out loud. "There has to be something else."

"Would this weapon really be able to destroy the Vens?" Brian said. "Based on your description, they pose a threat to everyone, even you. Unless you're planning on leaving the Vens behind for us to deal with."

It wasn't quite an accusation, but it stung nevertheless. Dione knew what the answer was supposed to be. Yes, we'll try this out. But in that moment, the reality of their situation was sinking in. Before, she had been thinking only of escape, of return home. It had seemed so close. But now, she again found herself worried about survival, and not just that of herself and her friends, but of the people of this world. Their arrival had brought this enemy down on them one way or another, and they had a responsibility to fix it.

"It's not that simple," she said. When she turned to Brian, the dark look in his eyes surprised her, and he wouldn't meet her gaze.

"If these Vens are as bad as you say, how many do you think will die?" he asked so casually he might have been asking for tomorrow's weather forecast.

"And you think Victoria or the Aratians will welcome us with open arms? Where will we go?" The minute the words spilled out of her mouth and into the heavy silence, she regretted them. They were selfish. They were the product of the same kind of thinking that had gotten them into this mess.

"Does it really matter?" The tense anger in his shoulders had relaxed a bit, and he bowed his head in what looked like despair.

Dione wasn't just thinking of herself, though. She thought about her uncle. He would mourn her. Her father might miss her, but he wouldn't cry. She had never seen him cry, even after her mom died. He had gone about his life and meetings like the world hadn't collapsed beneath them.

Dammit. Why couldn't she do both, save them and leave? She tried to weigh the pros and cons of each scenario. If they stayed, there was a chance that no one died, even if that meant she lived in a prison cell. They would be around to alert the colonists and help them with tactics, assuming anyone listened to what they had to say after everything.

If they left, the Vens would murder many or maybe even all of the settlers, while she and her friends escaped, leaving behind the planet they had doomed. The answer was obvious. Multiple choice was easy. Just eliminate all the wrong answers, and then choose the best one.

This decision—doing the "right" thing—gave her no rush of satisfaction. This was not like giving up her Saturday mornings to tutor, or organizing a supply drive for Ankari refugees. This was her life. Her dreams. Her ambitions. But he didn't really understand all of this, at least, he didn't grasp the scale of her world.

"Brian, you're right, and on some level I know that. But there's a part of me that wants to pack up and go home, and bring you with me. I know there shouldn't be a question, but there is. I'm human." Brian's jaw unclenched, just a little. She hadn't completely lost him.

"So you'll do it?" he said.

"It's the right thing to do. But... it's so hard. It's so hard to give up what I'm giving up, and I can't promise that Zane and Lithia will go along with it." With that, she stepped into the lift, followed by Brian, and went to break the news to Lithia.

41. LITHIA

"No," Lithia said. She was past shouting. The quiet anger was always worse. It hurt more because she was aware enough of her anger that she was trying to contain it.

She had been waiting outside on the landing pad. The warmth of the afternoon was just beginning to wane, but it was still bright out.

"We have no choice," Dione said. "It's the only chance we have to save these people."

"There's always a choice. There's gotta be something other than taking out our charging matrix. Why don't we take that AI offline and fly up to meet Zane, try his plan?"

"You heard him. His plan was a bust."

"What if we can't put the matrix back? Even if we jump to the max of our current charge, and go the rest of the way on engines, we'd run out of water and air long before reaching the nearest colony. The *Calypso* was not built for that, and we've cannibalized her emergency beacon. We'll be stuck here."

"If we don't, these people will die."

"They're not our people. Just because you want to jump Brian doesn't mean we all want to stay here."

All the colonists here were just stupid people who decided to live outside the Bubble. They had brought this on themselves, and Lithia wasn't going to suffer for their bad choices.

"What would Bel say?" Dione asked. Lithia didn't want to hear it. Of course, Bel would want to save these people. But Bel wasn't awake to give her vote.

"She's unconscious now because of you. You dragged a live Ven onto our ship, and it nearly killed her. She can't say anything," Lithia said. She was crossing the line into truly hurtful comments, but she didn't care. She just wanted to be left alone. "And Oberon, the only one who might know how to get us out of this mess, is dead, because you left him to die on that ship."

Dione raised her voice. "And who brought us here to this planet? If anyone doomed these people, it's you, and now you won't help them because it's an inconvenience!"

"It's more than an inconvenience! I won't get trapped here. I don't trust that AI in there. I won't abandon my family to live out some ridiculous life here on Kepos like my grandmother. I won't. Find another way."

"Is that what this is about? You don't want to be like your grandma? 'Cause I've got bad news. Looks like selfishness is an inherited trait. You lied to me—used me—to find this place, and now you'll let the Vens kill them all. Because that's what's going to happen, and I know there's a part of you that understands that. This isn't you. There is no other way."

Zane called over the manumed and interrupted their shouting match. "Lithia, I'm heading down now."

"Fine," Lithia said, her anger flowing through the cracks in her voice like a leaky dam.

"Is everything okay?" he asked.

"Zane, we won't be able to fix the station's power cells in time," Dione said. "We're going to have to use our charging matrix to power the station's weapon to protect these people from the Vens."

"And then we reintegrate the matrix back into the *Calypso*?" he asked.

"I hope so," Dione replied.

Zane was silent for several long moments. Finally, he replied, "It's what Bel would want, too." *Unbelievable.* Zane couldn't possibly be on board with this.

"And if we can't take back the matrix?" Lithia said. "We're going to be stuck forever, Zane. This AI is holding us hostage. They shouldn't be able to do that. No one will look for us out here. Are you ready to die on this planet with the idiots who live here?" Lithia could feel herself losing this battle.

"Has Bel ever told you her story?" he said.

"No."

"When she's better, you should ask her what it was like to survive a Ven colony assault. If we can stop that, it's worth it."

"Lithia, I—" Dione began.

Lithia cut her off. "I need to focus on helping Zane. Why don't you go back inside and figure something out?"

Lithia felt her resistance buckling, but she wanted Dione to leave her alone. She hated being around people when she was angry. She always ended up saying things she regretted. Dione knew her well enough to leave.

***

"All right, take her out and let me know when you're approaching atmosphere."

Lithia heard the station door open again, and tensed her shoulders. If Dione was back, she didn't think she could take it. She didn't turn, and instead kept her eyes on the horizon. The sun was sinking lower in the sky. Cora appeared in her peripheral vision. She didn't want to deal with her right now, but she didn't have much choice.

"Is it true we're not going back to the temple tonight?"

"Yes," Lithia replied.

"I don't know why the Farmer sent us out here. I'm not sure why you released the Ficaran leader, but we still have this Flyer. What is his plan?" Cora said.

The girl was clearly homesick and scared. Somehow Lithia doubted she had ever wandered off into the woods and helped some strangers evade Aratian trackers like Evy.

"What do you think he wants from you?" Lithia asked, unsure of what to say.

"I think I'm supposed to save my people from the Ficarans. We've separated them from their leader. Now is the time to act. Did you know she gave orders to kill any Aratian on sight, just because we won't trade with her? And it's her fault, too. The Ficarans have pretended to fix stuff for years, but they only ruin the Artifacts so they break permanently."

"Not everything can be fixed forever. Sometimes things just break."

"Not the Farmer's magic. The only thing that could stop that is sabotage."

Lithia sighed. She couldn't condemn her ignorance and take advantage of it at the same time. When the Aratians had captured Lithia, she was ready to say anything to escape. Dione had needed her help then, and Bel still needed her now. But talking with Dione had forced her to question herself. She hated that. She hated how

Dione had such an easy time making the right choice. Dione genuinely cared about these people and their conflict. Lithia was just trying to get to the next checkpoint.

Lithia thought up some lie about how the Farmer had sent them to stop the demons that were on their way, but she kept it to herself. Maybe it was time to start telling the truth. And facing the truth. Of course they would save all these people if they could, but that wouldn't stop her from hating every minute of it. It was a struggle not to hate Cora.

"Cora, this is bigger than the Ficarans. Tell me what you know of the demons that fell from the sky."

"A long time ago, before the Great Divide, all of us were one group," Cora began to recite the familiar story. "All of us were Aratians. Everyone lived in or around the Vale Temple. We visited the Forest Temple and the Field Temple, but no one lived out there. Both Temples had their own specialties. The Field Temple allowed us to mine resources and repair Artifacts. The Forest Temple had ways to control the animals. The Field Temple has now been overrun by Ficaran scum who looted the Forest Temple, but not before we got most of the supplies. We've managed to control our livestock by careful breeding, but the days of hunting with harmonicas are gone."

Hunting with harmonicas? Lithia opened her mouth to ask, but again decided to simply listen.

"Anyway, before the Divide, something appeared in the sky, like a Flyer, but bigger. And it was too high up. Everyone knew that Flyers couldn't go that high because they'd be struck down by the Farmer's Icon, and sure enough, a bolt of lightning destroyed it. After that, the Farmer took a Flyer from the Field Temple to the mountain alone. When he came back the next day, he assembled his men and told them that demons had fallen from the sky. He took thirty men with him, telling everyone that the demons would be dealt with, and a week later, only he and a few men returned, bloody and broken. But the demons were dead. Everyone was safe. Until the Architect showed up and ruined everything."

"What happened to the Farmer after that?"

"Things were fine until the Great Divide, but shortly afterward, the Farmer disappeared. He had been planning a trip for a while, but after everything that happened, he needed to move up his plans. We needed more colonists to protect us from genetic diseases."

He probably planned on bringing more than just people, but Lithia didn't say anything. Both sides acknowledged the Farmer was gone, but the Aratians believed the Farmer was coming back. What had really happened to him?

It didn't really matter. She kept thinking about Grandpa Min, and what he would think of Cora and all of the people here. He would want to help these people. He would welcome Miranda's other granddaughter with open arms. While Cora was talking, Evy had joined them. *Good. She should hear this, too.*

"Cora, I need to tell you the truth, and it may sound a bit strange. We really are cousins. My grandmother abandoned my family and started a new life here. I wasn't born here."

Lithia paused to gauge her reaction. Her eyebrows furrowed, creasing her forehead. *No screaming yet.*

"The Farmer didn't create everyone, but he did bring everyone here. The demons that came here were actually aliens. From another planet. I'm from another planet, too. The aliens, we call them Venatorians, or Vens, attacked us, and we ended up here. But the Vens found us, and now they're coming. The Vens are the threat you need to be concerned about, not the Ficarans."

It was an oversimplified explanation, but she was tired and it was the best she could do.

"So we are not on a mission from the Farmer?" Cora clarified.

That was not the most important take away, but of course Cora would only hear that the Farmer was a liar.

"Technically, no," Lithia said, "but our friend really is sick, and your home is in danger."

"You lied to me. You led them here." Cora was blinking back tears.

"We didn't mean to," Lithia said.

"The Icon will protect us," Evy said.

"The Icon needs to be repaired, and we'll be able to do that once Zane brings our ship down."

"I thought... you look so much like me, and you had the communicator. You had to be sent by the Farmer. I trusted you." A look of disgust crossed Cora's face. "I have to warn my father. He'll know what to do."

"We're going to destroy the Ven ships before they land."

"What if some of them survive, like last time? We need to prepare." A tone of urgency entered the girl's voice. "Take me back home."

"I can't. Not yet."

"Please," Cora said, tears welling up in her eyes, "I just want to go home."

This was not going well, but what had she expected? She had lied to Cora, made her betray her father, and now alien monsters were coming. She hadn't really had a choice. Without playing into Cora's beliefs, she would still be locked in an Aratian cell and Dione would be at the Ficarans' mercy. There had been no place for the truth in all of this, and now had been a terrible time to start.

"In the morning, I'll take you home myself. But for now, I have to guide Zane in, and we have to repair the Icon. It's the only hope for all of us."

She hated admitting it, and she wasn't thrilled that the brainwashed girl in front of her was family. She wished it were Evy who shared her DNA. Still, she was certain of one thing. She would find a way off this planet if it meant building a damn charging matrix herself. After they stopped the Vens from attacking, of course.

Cora did not look satisfied with that answer, but there was not much she could do. Zane was calling.

"It's Zane. I need to walk him through this."

Cora stormed back into the station, but Evy stayed to watch for a few minutes before following her cousin. This girl had true curiosity, and her father hadn't yet ruined her ability to question everything around her. She hoped more Aratians were like Evy, because she would be here for a while. Moira had seemed decent, too. As much as she didn't want to accept it, she knew that giving up their charging matrix was unavoidable.

The call to Zane was open, but it was the AI's voice coming over the line. She apparently had access to the manumeds now. Great.

"Another Venatorian ship has arrived," the AI said.

"How much time until they come to the planet?" Lithia said.

"They are holding position."

Lithia sighed in relief until she heard Zane's response. He had heard the AI's declaration as well.

"They're waiting for more ships. How big is this one?" Zane asked.

"Invader class."

Lithia cursed. That meant over two hundred Vens, and they were still holding position. How many more were on the way?

42. ZANE

Zane hit the turbulence just like Lithia said he would, and he struggled to maintain control. Lithia really did make flying look easier than it was, but he could handle it. Maybe Dione would have a little faith in him after this. He looked to Bel, whom he had strapped into the copilot seat, immobilizing her as best he could. He had carried her to the *Calypso* because she wouldn't wake up, but Zane wasn't going to think about what that meant. The medical bed had given her something to help her rest, but he didn't know if this was normal. She gave no sign that she felt the turbulence, and why would she? She was unconscious. He had found some sort of mobile breathing device, but it was nothing like the medical bed she had been in.

"Don't descend too quickly," Lithia advised over the comm. "You want to go gradually, even though your instincts will tell you to go down fast and get out of the turbulence. That puts way too much stress on the ship."

"Got it," he said. She was right about instincts. He wanted to press on toward the surface and avoid the unpleasant rattling. The stabilizers at last adjusted to their new load, and the ride smoothed out.

"Don't get comfy. There are a few more bumps along the way, and you've got to watch your own inputs, because the controls are going to feel like glue."

What did that even mean? Zane wasn't sure, but as he tried to maneuver toward the landing site, he got it. In space, a little thrust went a long way. In atmosphere, well, it was like running through water. It would be easy to overcompensate.

Extreme caution and admittedly good guidance from Lithia did get him to the landing site. Now only the hard part was left. Actually landing.

"Bring her down gently," Lithia said, "then let her go at the last second. She'll detect the ground and adjust."

"What? Let go?"

"No, don't —"

Immediately, the ship plummeted and Zane's stomach was in his throat. He pulled back to slow his descent, and it worked.

"Your angle's off. Readjust, now!"

Zane could see what was wrong. The moments of free fall had rotated the ship slightly, which meant he would not land properly. Not good. He could either fix his orientation or his speed, but not both, because he was still coming in too fast. Way too fast.

"I need to slow down first," he said.

"No, the rotation's more important! It's the difference between landing really hard on your feet or hard on your face."

Zane obeyed, righted the ship, then braced himself.

With a mighty thud and awful scraping, Zane landed the *Calypso*. He hoped it sounded worse than it was, because the hairs on his arms were standing on end. As soon as he was sure they'd stopped moving, he freed Bel from her restraints and carried her. Sweat soaked her forehead and she was burning up. Without the medical bed regulating her fever, he had no idea what her status was, beyond the general and alarming "very bad."

Lithia helped carry Bel inside, and they set her on the table closest to the door. There was no time to lose.

Lithia rifled through her pack. "Where is it?" she said. "Oh, hell no."

"What's wrong? Where are the anti-parasitics?" Zane asked.

"Cora. I told her the Vens were coming. She must have taken the meds," Lithia said, growing pale. He had never seen Lithia so overwhelmed.

"Where is she?" Zane asked, the panic in his voice mounting. They didn't have the meds, and Bel's fever was already dangerously high.

"I don't see Evy either," she said. "They're probably with Dione. Come on."

Zane followed her into the lift, looking back to where he left Bel's motionless body. Soon, the doors opened again, revealing another hallway. A giant, red double door labeled *Danger: Trained Personnel Only* made their destination easy to find. Inside they found Dione and a young man he presumed to be Brian disconnecting some extremely large power cells from the main energy distribution center. Despite their lukewarm relationship, Zane was glad to see Dione.

Lithia spoke first, leaving no time for pleasantries. "Where's Cora?"

"She's not with you?" Brian asked.

"No, and the anti-parasitics are missing from my bag. Did you take them?"

"Of course not. Where's Bel?" Dione said. Zane could detect the frustration in her voice. She and Lithia must be fighting again.

"Upstairs. We need those meds," Zane said. A girl burst through the doors. She was out of breath, so Zane couldn't understand her. By her age, Zane figured this was Evy.

"Evy, where is Cora?" Lithia asked.

"She said she was going to leave," Evy said.

"I told her I would take you both home in the morning. Do you know where she might be hiding? I know you both have been exploring this place."

Evy looked hesitant, but finally spoke. "We found something. It looked like a giant tractor. I've seen them before, but ours don't work anymore."

"Base, are there any vehicles here?" Zane said.

"Yes, I can send directions to the garage to your manumeds," she replied. Not every room had an audio interface with the station computer, and the manumeds made communication easy. Before Zane could suggest it, Lithia was already removing her manumed and handing it to Brian.

"Here, this way we can stay in touch," she said. He realized that Dione had probably never gotten a chance to retrieve her own manumed.

"Come on," Zane said. "Bel's running out of time."

They followed the AI's map and found themselves outside the garage. When they entered, Zane heard the mechanical whir of the external garage door opening. Early evening light filtered in, illuminating an all-terrain vehicle idling with its doors open overhead, like the wings of a bird in flight. Then he saw her, hunched over a control panel. With the noise, he thought they could sneak in, but Lithia charged straight for her.

When Cora turned, it became clear she had taken more than the meds. She held Lithia's stun rifle, and at such close range, had no trouble hitting her target. Lithia stopped as if she had run into an invisible wall and dropped to the ground with a loud thump.

Zane immediately raised his hands. "Please, Cora, hold on."

"Zane?" she asked. "I recognize your voice."

"Yes, remember, the harbinger?"

Cora scoffed. "That was all a lie. Lithia told me everything. And now that you've brought the demons here with you, I need to get this medicine back home where Moira can replicate it."

"I wasn't lying about my friend. She's upstairs, right now, you can see her. I only need one dose. The rest is yours. I'll fly you home tonight, since Lithia is… indisposed."

"Like I could trust anything you say. You tricked me into betraying my own father! I won't let you do any more damage."

She raised the rifle, but he managed to duck behind one of the vehicles before she got her shot off. He thought he saw movement out of the corner of his eye, but he was too afraid to take his attention from Cora. Maybe some wild animal had gotten into the garage. He had seen the kind of monsters they'd created on the space station computers. He didn't know how many had been truly viable and able to reproduce, but there had been a few that were utterly terrifying.

He peeked around the vehicle and was met with another shot. Cora was making her way toward the open ATV. Could she even drive it?

"What about Evy?" he called. "She's with Dione and Brian. Are you really going to leave her?"

"She said she wants to stay, and I've had enough of trying to get that girl to do anything she doesn't want to do," Cora replied. "You won't hurt her."

It was almost a question, but Zane couldn't bring himself to threaten Evy, even if he didn't mean it.

"Of course not. Cora, those ATVs are hard to maneuver, especially out here. How will you even find your way back? I promise you I will fly you home tonight after we give Bel one dose of the anti-parasitics."

"The Base AI will give me instructions on where to go and how to drive."

"This wasn't the deal, Base," he said.

"I will explain later," the AI replied through his manumed.

"She can't take those meds!" he yelled.

When Cora climbed in the ATV, Zane charged forward. She lifted the rifle to shoot, but he grabbed the barrel in time to redirect it. He pulled hard on the weapon, almost pulling her out with it, but suddenly she let go. Zane flew back and hit the floor. His vision blurred for a moment with pain, and by the time he scrambled to his feet, it was too late. Cora was gone. This couldn't be happening. After everything, he wouldn't let things end like this.

"Base, send me the same information you sent her." He would tell Dione where to find Lithia once he was on his way. There was no time for any distractions.

"Wait!"

Zane turned to find the owner of the voice. Evy. She had followed him.

"There's no time. She has the meds that will save my friend," he said. His voice sounded strange. He was yelling. He hadn't meant to raise his voice.

"No, I've got them." Evy held up a small vial full of a clear liquid. It looked so boring and inconsequential that he could hardly believe that this was it, that this drug could save the girl he loved. Sometimes context was the only difference between ordinary and a miracle. Evy handed him the vial.

"How?" Zane asked, his voice catching in his throat. He had always known it, but that moment was the first time he had ever admitted it to himself. He loved Belen. Now he could save her.

"When you were arguing. Is Lithia—"

"She'll be fine. I'll come back for her soon, but Bel needs this now. Base, close the garage door." He didn't want anything coming in and attacking Lithia while she was out cold. Evy looked worried, so he said, "Will you stay here and keep an eye on her?"

Zane didn't wait to hear her reply. He took the stairs, which were closer than the lift, two at a time. In no time, he grabbed an auto-injector from the *Calypso*. He came back inside and injected Bel with a dose of the anti-parasitics. He stared at her for a long time.

"Base, do you have a medical facility?"

"No, there is a small infirmary, but any serious ailments and injuries were handled on the station."

"Do you know anything about the Venatorians?"

"My information is limited and probably out of date. Vens found this planet, and two survived their crash. They were killed by the colonists, before the civil war."

There was so much to ask this AI, yet she spoke to him from his manumed. That was odd. He should have been able to communicate with her throughout the base, unless everyone who had worked here had manumeds, or something similar.

"Why isn't there a central interaction system for communication?" He would have expected more hardware around to facilitate the AI's monitoring and interaction with the Base and the people in it. Maybe she would tell him.

"This facility was not originally equipped with an AI."

"I know, but why didn't Jameson incorporate those systems when he installed the first AI?"

"I see you discovered the logs on the station. The original AI lacked the communication abilities I have. There was no need to install an interaction system because it could not use one. I was installed after he was already gone."

If Jameson integrated the AI in order to monitor the sensors and weapons in case someone showed up, it wouldn't have needed to communicate orally. But where did this AI come from?

"Why did you help Cora leave? Why didn't you warn us?"

"My primary objective is to keep the colonists safe. The anti-parasitics can be replicated at the Vale Base."

"And we're not technically colonists?"

"No. Cora convinced me that returning her and the medicine to her people would keep them safe."

"So you just protect the Aratians?"

"No, I protect both groups."

"Why is that? Wouldn't Jameson want you only to help the Aratians?"

"I do not do what Jameson wanted. My objective is to protect the colonists."

"Who installed you here?"

The AI paused. "The Architect."

"Samantha Myers."

"Dr. Samantha Myers was known as the Architect, yes."

Zane had guessed as much, but it was nice to have it confirmed.

"That explains why Jameson didn't install the interaction system then. Why didn't she? How did a biologist create a new AI?"

"It was more of an enhancement. She had to make use of what she had on hand." Well, that was delightfully vague. Something didn't feel right about this AI. Before he could ask more questions, he heard the lift reach their floor. Dione and the same guy from the power supply room, covered in sweat, came down the hallway.

"I gave Bel the meds. We just need to wait and see." Dione hugged him, which caught him more off guard than anything else.

"I'm sorry," she said, "for being such a jerk before."

"It's okay," he said. The muscular guy stepped forward, his long hair a stark contrast to Zane's close-cut shave. "You must be Brian."

Brian nodded and sized him up. "And you must be Zane. I've heard a lot about you. Think you can fix the Icon?"

"I'll do my best," he said. Brian smiled, but he seemed no less tense. Zane couldn't blame him.

Dione looked around. "Where's Lithia? Where are Cora and Evy?"

"Crap," he said, jumping up. "Cora hit Lithia with the stun rifle before escaping. She's still in the garage. Evy's watching her."

"Cora escaped?" Brian said. "We've got to stop her."

"I don't think we can. Plus, we've got bigger problems to worry about."

"So you know about the second ship?" Dione asked. Apparently the AI had told them, too.

"Yeah, I heard, but now I'm more worried about what the final count will be."

The AI spoke calmly. "The final count is three. They have begun their approach. Based on the specifications of this charging matrix, the installation must be completed in two hours in order to leave sufficient time to charge and prime the Icon."

43. DIONE

The AI was insistent. "The schedule is already tight. There is no time to waste."

Dione felt the panic welling up, but she pushed it down.

"Understood. Brian, will you go get Lithia? I need Zane's help removing the charging matrix, since he's the one that rigged it to work in the first place."

Evy came running into the room. "Did you forget?"

"No, Brian was just about to come help. Here, Evy, take this and keep an eye on Bel. Let Brian know if there's any change," Zane said, handing her his manumed. "Thank you. Without your help, Bel would be dead."

Evy smiled at that and nodded, glad to have helped. Dione wished she had been that impressive when she was ten. Evy had this way of watching so quietly, you didn't know she was there.

Once they were safely on board the *Calypso*, Zane spoke. "Something's up with that AI. I don't know what, but we need to be careful."

"What are you talking about?"

Zane explained about Cora's escape and the AI's mysterious origin.

"That makes sense, though, that she would help Cora if her mission is to protect the colonists," Dione said.

"I know you haven't spent a lot of time around AIs, but the ships I grew up on had them. They have limitations built in, like they cannot lie."

"She didn't lie, not exactly," Dione said.

"She's deceptive. Her programming shouldn't allow her to do that. Something about her seems… off. I can't explain it. It's just this feeling, like when you know something is wrong, even when you can't say why."

"Like hoverflies."

"What?" he said.

"Bel was telling me about them. They're flies that have bee-like markings for protection, to scare off predators."

"Why else would they look like bees?"

"More nefarious motives, like infiltrating a hive. We just need to figure out what the AI really wants."

"The Base is too free for an average AI," he said.

"What does that mean?" Dione asked.

"She's not bound by the usual programming constraints put in place that prevent things like deception and the sophisticated decision making we've seen, like connecting to my manumed the second I walked in the door. She didn't ask permission."

"She did the same to Lithia," she said. "Before she even spoke to us."

"She may be harmless, but keep your guard up. Based on some logs I found on the station, I think that the Architect did something to the Base AI, but she didn't really have the right background to make something this complex."

"All right, I trust you."

Dione watched his shoulders relax a little. She hadn't known he spent so much time on ships. AIs were strictly regulated on core planets, so she rarely encountered them, and when she did, they were little more than glorified assistants. On freighters and colonies, they were often essential, though there were still restrictions. The penalties for untethered AIs were extreme, but people's own fears and superstitions kept these infractions to a minimum. Zane was picking up on something, and she wouldn't take his warning for granted. Plus, the AI gave her the creeps.

She realized that neither she nor Zane had a manumed, so she couldn't check the countdown. He had probably done so on purpose so that they could speak freely about the AI. She had no problem accessing them to communicate, and there was nothing to stop her from listening in, except for their removal.

"Can we do this in two hours?" Dione asked.

"We don't have much choice," Zane said. It wasn't all that reassuring, but it wasn't his job to make her feel better. She had almost relaxed for a moment in the comfort and familiarity of her own ship.

Removing the charging matrix was easier than she thought it would be, probably because it wasn't fully integrated in the first place. The moment they reentered the Base, the AI met them with the countdown.

"One hour and thirty-one minutes remaining for installation. Two hours and forty seven minutes until the Venatorian convoy arrives."

Dione didn't respond. That was more than enough time to plug in a new battery. She was going to check on Bel and Lithia.

Brian sat there with Evy. Bel was still unconscious, and now Lithia was lying on the floor next to her, though she just looked like she was sleeping.

"I think she feels a little cooler," Zane said. Dione hoped he was right. "I'm staying here. I want to see if the infirmary has any useful equipment that can help us monitor her. I'll come help in a bit."

"You think I can do this on my own?" Dione asked.

"It should be straightforward. The AI will direct you," Zane said.

"I'll help," Brian said. Dione was grateful, and not just because she wanted to spend more time with him. He was much more familiar with the local technology, and if Zane was right, he might be able to get more information out of the AI, since he was a true colonist.

***

"Why isn't it working?" Brian said.

"I don't know," Dione said. "Let's walk through it, out loud."

"That's what my father always used to do when he was working on a problem." Brian smiled, but she heard the sadness in his voice.

"We've tested the matrix, and it's fine. Power output is good," she said.

"And the capacitors are all working, storing energy. They worked with the microbial fuel cell we tested," he said.

"So it has to be a connection issue," Dione said. "I know we tested the connections already, but we must have missed something."

"The matrix is being very stubborn," Brian said.

"Either that or this base is," she said. "I don't know what else to try. Any ideas?" Brian shook his head. The AI had already led them through the trials that ruled out all other issues.

"Zane," Dione said over the manumed, "we could really use some help." Zane was using Lithia's manumed, and she had taken his back from Evy. Bel's was still broken after the Ven attack, and hers was locked away back in the smuggler's den.

"Have you tried turning it off, then back on?" he replied.

"Go ahead, make jokes. It's your life, too."

"I'm serious. Disconnect it, then reconnect it. Half the time it works. I'm on my way."

Zane was there in a couple of minutes. He redid all of her tests. The AI reminded her they only had thirty-nine minutes left. As irritating as it was, she was surprised to find out how much time had gone by. Dione stepped back, unable to help. She wished that her passion for biology translated into more technical skills.

"It looks like the hardware is fine. Did you test any of the software?"

"Batteries have software?"

"Calling the matrix a battery is like calling the *Mona Lisa* a picture. While true, it doesn't do the complexity of it justice."

"So what do we do?"

"I don't know. All of that stuff is well protected under intellectual property law. I've never gotten a good look at it. I don't think I can figure this out in time."

"But you got it to work on the *Calypso*."

"It probably recognized its own ship ID, or something. You're trying to hook it up to some really old tech. Most of the stuff in here is a century old. The matrix probably has some sort of anti-theft response."

"I think I can help," Brian said.

"How's that?" Zane said.

"We have two different kinds of Artifacts here, and if you want to use them together, you have to trick them into working together. This sounds similar."

Zane nodded, thinking. "Probably the tech left behind by the scientists and the tech brought by the colonists."

"Try it," Dione said, thinking back to the different types of shuttles she saw in the Ficaran hangar bay. Maybe this was the answer!

Brian opened the panel on the top. "This is a lot more complicated than what I usually deal with," he said.

"A physical bypass?" Zane asked. "I don't know if that will even work."

"That's the only way I've been able to get things to work together, in some cases."

"I guess it's worth a shot."

"Twenty-three minutes remaining for installation." The AI sounded... worried. Was that possible?

Dione felt a chill go down her spine. She couldn't take any more of it. "I need a minute," she said.

The boys were too engrossed in what they were doing even to hear her. She walked down the hall, looking in windows, testing doors, feeling useless. She knew it was fruitless, but she thought maybe she would find something else down here that would help her. That would make sense of everything.

Mostly, they were supply closets. She had reached the last door on the hall, but before she could open it, the AI said, "You need to go back to Zane. He needs your assistance."

"Okay." Dione got on her manumed. "I'm on my way back, Zane. Give me a minute."

"Huh?"

"The AI told me you need my help."

"No, we've got it covered for now."

The hairs on Dione's arms stood on end. That was an explicit lie, not a deception.

"Why did you lie, Base?" Dione asked.

"I didn't. I simply thought that Zane and Brian could use a hand. I was mistaken."

No, this didn't add up. Why send her to Zane? What was the AI planning?

Dione looked up at the door in front of her. What was behind it?

She opened it, and immediately regretted it. The smell was not as strong as she thought it would be, considering the decomposed body in the room. She let the door close, but not before she had seen enough. A corpse, some cables, a console.

"Zane, you need to see this. I'm at the end of the hall."

"I'm a little busy at the moment," he said. "Let Brian do it."

"We can't trust this AI, and now I have proof," Dione said.

That did the trick. Zane appeared moments later at a jog. She opened the door, and followed Zane in. In her brief glance, she hadn't really examined the scene closely. She had let her shock get the better of her, but then again, this wasn't jumping at a mouse. There was a freaking dead body down here. Cables and wires were connected to it, running from body to the console.

"The AI tried to lie to me to stop me from finding this place."

Zane, who had been examining the cables, stopped what he was doing. "Who programmed you?" he said.

"That information is irrelevant," she replied.

"No, it's not. You call the Farmer by his real name. You say that you're not the original AI he installed. I know that Dr. Samantha Myers was going to try to fix you, but now I think she failed. I think that Jameson got some discount on a crazy AI, that you let the Ven scout ship survive, and that you plan to kill us all. That's why you want us to fix the weapon, so you can control all these colonists."

The AI laughed. It was terrifying, because it sounded fully human, rather than the monotone female preset she had been communicating in.

"That is ridiculous. The connection is almost complete. We can discuss this later." All pretense was gone from the voice. What had before been a mostly monotone female voice now expressed a whole range of emotion that Dione had only heard hints of.

"No, explain. Now," Zane said.

"My name is Samantha. Call me Sam."

"Impossible," Zane said.

Dione wasn't completely sure what was going on, but if her guess was correct, this was horrifying.

"That was my body. The AI here was insufficient. Jameson's AI was a piece of crap, but by the time he realized it, there was nothing he could do. By the time *I* realized it, this was my only option."

"There's no way. You'd go crazy," Zane said.

"I'm sure I would have already, if I didn't spend so much time asleep. I didn't kill the crappy AI. It's still here. I only handle the important stuff."

Dione looked confused. "What do you mean she'd go crazy? Has this been done before?"

"It has been done, but not very often," he said. "The necessary equipment is expensive. You have to have a computer system already capable of supporting an AI, and that's the easy part. People do it because they think they'll be immortal, but the mind wasn't meant to live in a computer system. Your neural pathways degrade. You lose yourself piece by piece, and you are aware it's happening until you're so far gone you aren't really you anymore. It's a fate worse than death which is why no one chooses it." Zane looked at the body, still hooked up. "I'm sorry, Sam, but the degradation has probably already begun. How long have you been here?"

"Like I said, I spend a lot of time sleeping. It significantly slows the degradation rate, but you're right. Eventually I will degrade past usefulness, but that won't be for a while, if I play my cards right. However, I wasn't expecting outsiders like you to show up here. This changes things."

Brian interrupted over her manumed. "Zane, Dione, there's less than ten minutes left on the countdown. I need your help. Please."

"Come on," Dione said.

"We're not done talking about this," Zane said, "and I don't trust you."

"Good," Samantha replied, "but you should read my logs. Assuming you power the Icon before it's too late."

"Dione, if this really is Samantha, she's the Architect. It would explain why she wants to help the colonists."

Either the Architect was alive as an AI in this base, or the base had killed her when she tried to fix the existing AI. This was absolutely unbelievable, and they had no choice but to work with her, even though it was impossible to trust her.

***

When they reached Brian, he was just sitting there, staring at the matrix. Dione would fill him in later.

"I've done everything I can. I have no idea how to bypass it. Your matrix will not cooperate with the base. It's too sophisticated," Brian said.

"Then we're screwed," Zane said.

"Is there anything on our ship it will cooperate with?" Dione asked.

"The jump drive," Zane replied, "but that won't fit down here."

"Are you sure?" Dione asked.

"It weighs hundreds of kilos, and I don't think it can actually be removed from the ship," Zane said.

So we are screwed. There had to be some part of the ship that would recognize the charging matrix. What was portable?

"Is there a way to just take part of the jump drive?" Dione asked.

"No, Dione, it doesn't work like that. The matrix—"

Dione stopped listening and started thinking again, ignoring Zane. Time to change her perspective. What could be removed from the ship that was part of the ship? Certain equipment. Like what? Dione closed her eyes and imagined herself on the ship, running through each section, looking around for something useful. She filed away possibilities, and when her mental avatar reached the cargo bay, she found what she needed.

"Holy crap, the emergency beacon!" Dione said. "We can use it as an intermediary."

"Trick it into thinking it's powering the beacon, but really, it's charging the weapon," Zane said. His eyes lit up. "I'll be back."

Zane ran out, leaving her there with Brian.

"What was going on out there?" he said.

Full disclosure. She would tell him everything. "We found something. A body. It belonged to a Dr. Samantha Myers. She merged her consciousness with the station AI somehow. Right, Sam?"

"Samantha? The Architect?"

"That's right," Sam said. It still gave Dione chills to hear her fluid voice, stripped of its mechanical stiffness. Brian looked surprised, too.

Brian surged to his feet. "Why did you leave? Why didn't you tell us how we got here? What do you know about my father?"

"Brian, these are all good questions, but I don't have all the answers. I don't know where your father is, and as for the first two questions, it's complicated. I can explain later."

"You sound different," Brian said.

"This is my real voice. Before, I was pretending, trying to sound more like a machine than a human."

"So you're human?"

"I don't think so, not really. Not anymore."

"Why would you do this? You left us with so many questions."

Before Sam could respond, Zane reentered the room. He was panting, but he looked a little hopeful.

Sam, in her new, unnerving voice, said, "Time's up. There is no longer sufficient time to charge the Icon and destroy the three approaching Venatorian ships."

"There has to be something," Dione said.

"There is not enough time."

Samantha was matter-of-fact about it all, but Dione was still in denial. Brian looked unnaturally pale. Zane was ignoring her, working away to install the beacon as an intermediary.

"What does this mean?" Brian said. In the jungle, he had been confident and commanding. Now he was lost, and looking to her.

"Just help me," Zane said. He had not brought the entire beacon, just a part of it.

"The rate of energy flow from your matrix is insufficient to give the weapon enough power to destroy the ships."

"Then we increase the rate," Dione said.

"It's not set up for that. It's the same reason this thing would take a week to charge our jump drive," Zane said. "If we can trick it into thinking it's charging the beacon, we can get it to start powering the weapon."

"I thought tricking it didn't work," Dione said.

"That's when we were trying to get it to work with really old tech. It will recognize the beacon, and begin charging, but we'll divert that energy into the weapon. Before we essentially couldn't get it to charge at all."

It reminded Dione of cowbirds. They laid their own eggs in the nests of other birds and let the other mother birds take care their own eggs. The host mothers channeled precious resources to alien eggs, none the wiser, just like the matrix was channeling energy to the Icon, a foreign system.

Dione glanced over at Brian, who hadn't been paying attention to them. He was leaning against the wall, hands over his eyes like he had a headache. Before she could pour out a flood of apologies and reassurances, Sam spoke.

"It's working," she said. "The weapon is beginning to receive power."

"But it's too late," Brian said.

"We'll figure something out," Dione said.

Brian looked up. He was looking at her expectantly. He believed her. "What's your plan?"

Dione didn't have one. *Yet.*

She went to the readouts for the weapon. She didn't understand them completely, but she got the gist. She wanted to understand every last detail, but she could get Sam to fill in the blanks.

"Sam, how does the weapon work? You need to hit a certain power threshold, right?"

"Yes, it works in charges."

"So, how long until you have enough power for one shot, not three? Will it be before the Vens arrive?"

"Yes," Sam said. "But even one Ven Invader will pose a deadly threat to the colonists."

"But it's not an all-or-nothing scenario," Dione said. "Taking out one ship will give them a chance." She was surprised that Sam was pushing back at all. "It can't hurt to have fewer Vens in the equation." Was this evidence of her neural pathways degrading, that she couldn't see the middle ground in this scenario?

"Dione's right, Sam. We have to give it a try," Brian said. "You've spent so much time trying to protect us that you don't think we can protect ourselves. Destroy one of the Invader class ships, and leave the other Vens to us."

44. BRIAN

"How many Vens will that leave?" Brian asked Dione.

"About fifty on the Marauder, and nearly two hundred on the other Invader."

"So just two hundred fifty Vens?" Brian said. "That doesn't sound so bad."

He smiled, but Dione looked terrified, and Zane looked utterly defeated. He knew the stories about the demons, and he still had hope. Dione and Zane didn't understand his people. They would find a way. They had been fending off the Aratians for years, and they would fend off the Vens as well.

"I know you don't think we can win, but I have hope. We have weapons. We're not complacent farmers. We're hunters. We're warriors. We have a better chance than you give us credit for."

Dione perked up, but Zane still looked doubtful. They would see.

"Samantha, is there anything else we can do here?" Brian asked.

"No. There are no modifications left to be made," Sam said.

"Then we have some time. I think I deserve the truth," Brian said. He wanted Sam to explain herself. His father had filled him with so many questions, he barely knew where to start. "How did we get here?"

"There's no short answer to your question. I was part of an elite group of terraforming researchers working in the space station and on the planet. Our goal was to introduce new species and optimize the environment for colonial life. Our discoveries here would shape how other worlds were made habitable. The project had been going on for decades before I arrived, but I was excited to be here. I had been studying ways to embed musical keys in DNA. Jameson had already been around a few years and had built up a reputation. I eventually got assigned to his team. At first, I was in awe of him. He could somehow find the perfect balance for a new creature. But as time went on the power went to his head. His creations took a dark turn."

"And your supervisors allowed that?" Dione said.

"As long as he completed his assigned projects, no one cared what he did in his spare time," Sam said. "I had barely been here five years when the call for evacuation came. The Venatorians had arrived in our corner of the galaxy, so the station and the planet Kepos were no longer safe."

"If everyone evacuated, how did you get back here?" Dione said.

"I never left. I had no family. I was only interested in discovery, and I figured that one day someone would find my research. If not, I would have satisfied my own curiosity at least."

"But you could have continued your research somewhere else. There are other terraforming programs," Dione said.

"None with the freedoms Kepos offered, believe me. The liberties we took at times… I am not proud to remember."

"So Jameson stayed, too?" Brian asked. "Did you work with him?"

"No, his arrival was a complete surprise. He left with the rest, but he had poured too much of himself into his work here, I think. He had engineered perfection and destruction, and by the end, he believed he was a god. Not an actual god, he wasn't delusional, but he saw himself more as creator than created."

"He came back," Brian said.

"Yes. Jameson was charming. I have no doubt that all the people he recruited thought they would be coming to paradise. He used his savings to buy a colonizer, filled it with willing travelers, and returned here, knowing it wasn't safe, but banking on his weapon to protect the colony."

"That's ridiculous. No one remembers coming here," Brian said. "How is it possible that hundreds of people forgot a journey through space?" He would never forget such an incredible experience.

"That's what the nanotech will do."

Dione gasped. "That's horrible. How is that even possible?"

"What do you mean?" he asked. "Why is nanotech so bad?" Dione's response worried him.

"Nanotech is never supposed to be used on humans. Even medically. People have tried to heal others using nanotech, but it's been deemed too dangerous," Dione said.

"I think it works better than people know. A few high-profile deaths early on, and some bought-and-paid-for studies forced the government to shut down research. That, and lobbyists who made money from people being sick." Dione looked shocked at Sam's words, but Brian wasn't surprised. He'd dealt with enough Aratians to know that for too many, power was more important than anything.

Sam continued. "Jameson used it on his crew, I'm sure of it. It's the only thing that could explain the memory loss. I had a little luck restoring memories, but the nanotech adapted quickly. I couldn't give people back who they were for more than a few weeks, so I stopped trying. Sometimes the memories were too painful."

"Miranda," Dione said. "I read her journal."

"Yes, Miranda Min. I thought if I could show her what Jameson had done, she would be able to convince others. When the memories started to fade again, I thought the journal would help her. That she would see her own handwriting, her own words, and believe them, but… it didn't work."

"She killed herself," Brian said. He knew the stories. The Ficarans always got blamed somehow.

"I don't think she remembered everything when she killed herself, but she could still feel it. She hated who she had been, and she didn't want to lose herself again."

"Is that why you never told us the truth?" Brian said. He was sitting with his head in his hands.

"I tried to help you all. I tried to find a way to permanently reverse the nanotech, but I couldn't. You called me a god, because I was like Jameson. I knew things. I hated it. I just wanted to be left to my research with no one to disrupt me, but eventually I got swept into the struggle. So many people were unhappy. Anytime you focus on eugenics like Jameson did, women stop being people. They become breeders. That I couldn't stand."

Brian couldn't stand it either. That's why he helped smuggle out Aratians around the Matching. The next one was in a few days, and they'd already smuggled out one couple. But that confession didn't make him any less angry. She could have stopped it all.

"So you let us live like brainwashed puppets?" Brian couldn't believe it. That someone who wanted to protect them, who saved them from Aratian rule, had let the Aratians continue unhindered.

She had the power to stop the Matching, but she had just left the remaining Aratians to their rituals.

"When reversing the nanotech didn't work, I realized there was nothing I could do. My attempts at explaining everything didn't go well. I sounded crazy, and I needed people to listen to me, to fight back against Jameson, so I took on the role of Architect. I convinced as many as I could to leave. I locked the Flyers, but I didn't stick around to rule."

"No, you abandoned us. We could have used your help."

"There was more at stake. I didn't abandon you, I killed the puppet master. Jameson came looking for me after Miranda died, and I didn't give him a chance to speak. I just shot him."

"You could have told us more. My father left looking for answers that you could have provided."

"Do you think he would have taken my word?"

"There was plenty of proof you could have given us," Brian said.

"You can hate me all you want, but there are other problems that require your attention. The Venatorians were able to find this place decades ago, and they've done it again, but this time, it's no scout ship. I won't be able to stop them all. You'll need to prepare everyone, Ficarans and Aratians alike," Sam said. Brian clenched his fists. Sam's tone made it clear she was done talking to him.

"I need some air," he said. He left Dione and Zane in the basement and went straight outside to the landing pad. He wanted to watch the Ven Invader explode. The Vens would have to be taken care of before he went to the southern island to find his father. And maybe even the fabricator. He would have to inform Victoria of all that he knew, and he wasn't sure she would believe him. She probably wouldn't kill him, though, and that was a start.

If Dione would come with him, and explain everything, Victoria could be persuaded. Dione had this amazing way of explaining things clearly, just like his father. Victoria would see the ships arrive. She would figure out what was coming, and realize that these people could help them.

45. DIONE

Upstairs, Bel was still unconscious, and Evy was asleep in a chair. Lithia was stirring, but still looked groggy. She would be upset that she slept through everything. No, not everything. More trouble was coming their way, of that Dione was certain.

After a few minutes, the somber mood began to suffocate her, so she followed Brian to the landing pad outside where he was sprawled out on his back, looking up at the now dark sky. There was no moon, but stars came into view. The mountains buzzed with the sounds of life. Bugs, mostly, and a few noises that reminded her of frogs, though on this planet, who knew what was out there. The air was fresh, but held no fragrance, unlike the green, humid scent of the forest.

"I'm here for the show," Brian said. "She'll get one of them. My people will get the rest."

The first ship was streaking low across the sky. Dione watched it disappear into the distance.

"What's in that direction?"

"The Field Temple."

Brian's home. She wanted to pour out how sorry she was and explain how she would fix it, but she couldn't. It was all she could do not to cry. She should be researching every article in her manumed with information about Venatorian colonial assaults, looking for patterns, weaknesses, anything, but her arms and legs wouldn't move. Then Brian wrapped her hand in his own, warming his fingers against her leg. Every part of her was cold and numb, except for the electric warmth that spread from Brian's hand.

He was confident that the colonists could resist the Vens, and she wanted to believe him.

She heard the door open and crossed her arms. Soon Zane and Lithia joined them. They were carrying Bel. Evy followed, rubbing her eyes. Lithia sat down and cradled Bel's head in her lap.

"We wanted to watch Sam shoot them down," Lithia said. "We thought Bel would want to see, too."

The humid night air was warm and saturated with unspoken words. She wondered what would have happened to this planet if the Vens had killed them all and taken their ship, or if the professor had been the one to plant the explosive on their ship. According to Samantha, there was a Ven distress beacon in the forest somewhere, and only her dampening field had protected them this long. How many years of protection would the colonists have had if they hadn't come along?

None of it mattered. This wasn't some experiment she could redesign and retry, controlling for more variables, improving her accuracy. The results were here, and just because she didn't like them didn't mean she could deny them. She would have to work with what she had.

The next Ven vessel, the Invader class by the sound of it, rumbled in, flying in the same direction as the last.

Dione broke the silence. "Maybe, if we—"

But Lithia cut her off.

"Bel? Can you hear me?" she asked.

"Zane?" Bel said.

Zane was there in a heartbeat, hand on her forehead. "I'm here. She feels cooler."

Dione sat up too quickly, and dizziness washed over her along with relief. Bel was alive, at least. She was going to be okay. If she was awake, it meant the anti-parasitics were working. Bel would know what to do.

"We're all here," Zane said.

"Where?" Bel said.

"On the planet," he said.

"Home?"

"Not yet," he said, tucking a piece of hair behind her ear.

Above them all, a loud explosion boomed out across the mountains, and fire and pieces of debris burned up as they rained down, like fireworks. Destruction had never been so beautiful, but that's because it was more than just destruction. She visualized a horde of Vens, then removed half. This was very good news. It was hope. It was hundreds of Vens that she didn't have to worry about.

Dione smiled. It was a good omen. Bel was alive. One of the Ven ships had been destroyed. There were only a few hundred more to go, and they could be killed. She had already killed one. In order to kill the rest, they would have to come up with other methods of destruction. She would make this right, not because she was now tied to the fate of these colonists, but because it was the right thing to do. How she had ever hesitated in the first place, she didn't know.

"What was that?" Bel said, trying to prop herself up.

They all exchanged looks, sharing the same unspoken question: *Do we tell her yet?* Dione knew the answer. People were always more powerful with all the information. Bel needed to know. If the Vens had failed to kill her twice now, she could handle some bad news.

"Remember the space station? We're all down on the planet it orbits. The Vens found us. It might have been the tracer, but there's also a distress signal emanating from an old Ven ship that crashed in the forest. Two ships headed toward one of the settlements here. And we can't leave because we used our charging matrix to power the weapon that just destroyed the third Ven ship."

Bel closed her eyes, and at first, Dione thought she was unconscious again. But soon, she reopened them and spoke, her voice a little stronger.

"How many Vens?"

"Estimated under three hundred."

"How many colonists?"

Brian was the one who answered. "Nearly two thousand all together."

"We've got a chance. Destroying that third ship may just make this a battle, not a massacre."

Dione felt one of the weights lift from her shoulders. All of the trials of the last few days seemed worth it now that Bel was awake. But now, there was someone else she needed to talk to.

"Lithia, I have something for you. Come on."

To her surprise, Lithia followed her back inside the base without snark or comment.

Dione pulled a book from her bag. "The journal I found in that apartment in the Forest Base? I think it belonged to your grandmother. Miranda was the Farmer's wife." She offered it to Lithia. "It's why you could open the DNA lock in the Forest Temple."

Lithia didn't seem surprised. "I don't want it," she replied.

She was so stubborn. Dione opened it to a page she had earmarked and began reading:

I don't remember what it felt like to be the Miranda Min who left her family. Each new memory feels like I'm seeing a recording. I hate her. She's a coward. I don't understand how she could leave her son. I know that she was afraid, but I can't feel that fear. I can't understand it. I keep searching the fragments of memory for the real reason. I keep waiting to remember my husband hitting me or abusing me, but there's nothing. I have no choice except to believe that I left because I was selfish. Because I didn't want to be a mother. Because I wanted to explore the galaxy. I thought that living a quiet life would be my regret, but I was wrong. I think of my son and Clara, and I wonder if they'll forgive me.

"See, even she can't believe what a horrible person she is," Lithia said. Dione thought her eyes looked a little glassy.

"You don't have to read it. But I still think you should have it."

Lithia took the journal from her outstretched hands. "Thanks." Lithia opened it to the end and glanced at the last entry, but Dione could tell she wasn't reading it.

"I also think you should know…" There was no easy way to say this. "She committed suicide, shortly after writing this journal." Dione watched Lithia's jaw clench, but she didn't say anything. Dione needed to change the subject.

"How are you feeling after… Cora?"

"Horrible actually, but not because I got shot. Because I somehow pissed off a very friendly person who was predisposed to like me. Enough to make her shoot me."

"Well, it certainly makes the family resemblance easier to detect."

Lithia gave her a faint smile. "I've got some wrongs to right with Cora. I don't think I ever really accepted the fact that she's my cousin. I feel like she's an impostor." Lithia hesitated a moment. "Hey, about lying to you about your dad's access code, I'm sorry. I should have just told you."

"No, it's okay. You were right. I don't know if I would have helped you. I don't know if the rule-follower inside of me could have let you."

"I know. I didn't want to put you in that situation," Lithia laughed. "Now that we're here, we'll make a rule-breaker out of you, yet."

"Don't get too crazy. Maybe a rule-bender."

They could have said more, but they didn't need to. Dione knew that they would fight again, that they would let each other down, but that was okay. The storms defined the calm, and she would take the next few hours of calm before plunging back into the storm.

The Vens were here. It still didn't seem real.

"So what do we do?" Lithia said.

"Get some rest, and in a few hours, we take inventory, gather all the information we can, and make a plan. You heard Bel. If there's going to be a battle, we're going to have to think outside the box to win," Dione said.

"Then I'm glad you're here," Lithia replied.

The two friends stepped back outside. Dione looked up at the burning debris falling to the ground. They could do this. They would find a way to stop the Vens.

Thank You

Thank you for reading! Every review helps me immensely, so if you'd take a minute to review my book on Amazon or Goodreads (or both!), I'd greatly appreciate it.

If you want to receive updates on new releases and deals about my books, sign up for my mailing list at **subscribe.ericarue.com**. I send out emails about once month.

If you want to read about some of the real-life inspiration for the biology in this book, check out the blog post "About the Science: The Kepos Problem" at **ericarue.com**.

Acknowledgments

First, I'd like to thank my mom **Jane.** She has always believed in me and helped me achieve my dreams. I'd also like to thank my husband **Jacob** for his eternal patience and support throughout this process. A huge thank you goes to my beta readers: **Maggie Burnside, TR Dillon, John Dwight, Jane Eickhoff, Adrianna Foster, Donna Royston, Bradford Karl Slocum, Martin Wilsey, and Jason Winn.** An extra thank you goes out to **Martin Wilsey** and **Tannhauser Press** for helping me navigate the world of indie publishing. I also owe a great deal to my writing group, The Hourlings. Thank you for the feedback and support, especially the previously unmentioned **Liz Hayes, Jeffrey C. Jacobs,** and **David Keener**, who are regulars at our meetings along with TR, John, Donna, and Marty. I'd also like thank **Jessica Hatch** of Hatch Editorial Services for the fantastic editing. And finally, thank you to **Emily** for all the book recommendations.

About the Author

Erica Rue is a reader and writer of science fiction and fantasy, especially YA. Her abandoned biology major and handful of astronomy classes have prepared her well for writing sci-fi. She enjoys learning new words and promptly forgetting them so that she can rediscover them. When she's not writing, she forgets to water her garden, completes every side quest she triggers, and boosts her dog's self-esteem.

Made in the USA
Middletown, DE
15 September 2022

10521991R00203